"I know what you're doing."

She tugged the lapels of her robe closer together at the neckline. "You're trying to ⟨⟩m me. It won't work."

"⟨⟩orked just fine earlier today."

⟨⟩s mouth dropped open, and she felt her ⟨⟩s burn. It took her a moment to recover. ⟨⟩on't happen again," she assured him.

⟨⟩ghed, unable to tell if he was serious or ⟨⟩. "I agreed to accompany you to find ⟨⟩ller. I'm not interested in starting a short-term affair with you, Jack Ramsey. It was insane, the way we behaved earlier."

"But you enjoyed yourself."

"So what? It's been a long time."

She wasn't about to tell him it had never been that way for her. Not ever.

Dear Reader,

We've got a terrific lineup of books to start off the New Year. I hope you'll enjoy each and every one. Start things off with our newest Intimate Moments Extra, Kathryn Jensen's *Time and Again*. This book is time travel with a twist—but you'll have to read it to see what I mean. One thing I can promise you: you won't regret the time you spend turning these pages.

Next up, Marie Ferrarella's cross-line miniseries, The Baby of the Month Club, comes to Intimate Moments with *Happy New Year—Baby!* Of course, this time we're talking *babies* of the month, because Nicole Logan is having twins—and it's up to Dennis Lincoln to prove that a family of four is better than a family of three. Sharon Sala's *When You Call My Name* brings back Wyatt Hatfield from her last book, *The Miracle Man*. This time, Wyatt's looking for a miracle of his own, both to save his life and heal his heart. Beverly Barton continues her miniseries, The Protectors, with *Guarding Jeannie*, Sam Dundee's story. Alexandra Sellers gives the ever-popular secret-baby plot line a whirl in *Roughneck*, and I know you'll want to come along for the ride. Finally, welcome new author Kate Hathaway, whose *His Wedding Ring* will earn a spot on your keeper shelf.

Until next month—happy reading!

Yours,

Leslie J. Wainger
Senior Editor and Editorial Coordinator

Please address questions and book requests to:
Silhouette Reader Service
U.S.: 3010 Walden Ave., P.O. Box 1325, Buffalo, NY 14269
Canadian: P.O. Box 609, Fort Erie, Ont. L2A 5X3

KATHRYN JENSEN

TIME AND AGAIN

INTIMATE MOMENTS

Published by Silhouette Books

America's Publisher of Contemporary Romance

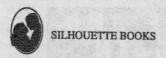 SILHOUETTE BOOKS

ISBN 0-373-07685-1

TIME AND AGAIN

Printed in U.S.A.

KATHRYN JENSEN

has written many novels for young readers as well as for adults. She speed-walks, works out with weights and enjoys ballroom dancing for exercise, stress reduction and pleasure. Now that her children are grown, she lives in Maryland with her two writing companions—Katie, a Chesapeake Bay retriever, and Sunny, a lovable terrier-mix adopted from a shelter.

Having worked as a hospital switchboard operator, department store sales associate, bank clerk and elementary school teacher, she now splits her days between writing her own books and teaching fiction writing at two local colleges and through a correspondence course. She enjoys helping new writers get a start, and speaks "at the drop of a hat" at writers' conferences, libraries and schools across the country.

Chapter 1

A freak April thunderstorm surprised the Vermont weather forecasters that afternoon. Dense, ash-gray clouds boiled up in the west, and the sky turned an ominous green tinged with flame-colored edges. It was a natural phenomenon Kate Fenwick had seen only in *National Geographic* photos of tornado-ravaged skies in the Great Plains.

Minutes later, a torrent of rain unleashed itself on the little town of Chester, accompanied by dramatic bursts of jagged lightning that sliced into the break of silver birch and sugar maples lining the creek behind the two-hundred-year-old farmhouse. She could hear the bolts crackling through the ancient trunks and smell the charred wood. Cringing at each strike, she scurried into the kitchen to brew herself a cup of herbal tea and soothe her nerves.

Storms didn't usually bother her. In fact, she often stood on her back porch, enjoying nature's show. This storm seemed different. Violent winds and stinging hailstones raged and tore at the tiny farming community that was nestled protectively in the lush Green Mountains. The temperature plummeted twenty degrees in less than fifteen minutes. Shivering, Kate clutched the back of a kitchen chair and stood sipping scalding tea, waiting it out, counting the beats between each lightning flash and the following boom.

Eventually, she was making it up to three, then six, then ten. Kate felt the muscles in her limbs unknot. The lightning receded into the clouds, but the rain didn't stop. Setting down her empty cup, she looked at the clock.

"Thank God," she said with a sigh, "they didn't have to come out in that."

Quickly she gathered up plastic ponchos, an umbrella and pulled on her own London Fog raincoat. She ran down the long drive to the main road and met the school bus as it was squealing to a stop. Jesse and Anna stepped off, and she popped a poncho over each giggling head before rushing her children into the house.

Hours after the rain had stopped, as evening settled in, Kate still felt chilled, but she couldn't explain why, because the old oil furnace had cranked out billows of toasty heat all winter long. She lit a roaring blaze in the living room fireplace, then sat in front of it with two baskets full of clean laundry she intended to sort and fold.

Still, she felt deathly cold.

"Jesse," she asked her son, "did you open a window somewhere in the house?"

He looked up at her from the floor, where he'd sprawled on his stomach to work on his homework. His seven-year-old eyes mirrored the disdain of a retiree interrupted during his ritual game of chess, and she hid a smile behind her hand.

"It's cold out, Mom. Why would I open a window?"

With precise movements, he completed a row of cursive *T*s on a sheet of yellow, wide-lined paper.

"Of course," she said. "Sorry to interrupt you." She turned to Anna, who was playing with her two favorite Barbie dolls.

"I can't open windows, Mom," her daughter groaned before Kate had a chance to ask the question. "They're too heavy, 'member?"

It was true. The old wooden frames swelled during moist spring days. Through March and April they yielded only to a bash from a hammer followed by a good hundred pounds of upward thrust. Max had been the only one strong enough to budge them.

Last week, Kate had forced two windows on opposite sides of the house on the first and second floors, with the help of a crowbar. The few inches of space allowed a feather of cross ventilation on milder days. Anna, still Kate's baby although she'd started kindergarten that year, hadn't a hope of opening one even a crack. Second-grader Jesse might try, but if he'd succeeded, he would have admitted it. He shared his father's innate sense of honesty.

Yet the sensation of a cooler band of air, whispering through the rooms, raised goose bumps on Kate's arms as she folded underclothes and warm turtleneck jerseys. She couldn't relax, knowing she'd never be able to make herself settle down for the evening until she located the draft's source.

"I'll be right back," she murmured and left Jesse to his homework and Anna to her dolls.

One by one, she eliminated each door and every window in the massive old house. She checked to be sure the opening to the storm cellar was secured, held her hand in front of electrical outlets.

"I give up," Kate muttered when, at last, every possible opening had been eliminated. She nudged the thermostat up a notch, put on a sweater and decided to make herself another cup of tea. Thankfully, the children didn't seem to be bothered by the chilly currents of air.

As Kate again passed through the downstairs foyer and into her kitchen, she glanced at the antique banjo clock on the wall. *Almost time to put the kids to bed,* she thought automatically. They'd already had their baths and changed into pajamas. The clock ticked softly, and she stood staring at its open, round face. It always reminded her of Max—sturdy, easy to read, dependable. The timepiece, like the house itself, had been in her husband's family for three generations.

Poor Max.

They'd been married for five years before the symptoms became evident to him, and another two before he'd let on to her that he was in pain. The following months had been horrible for both of them, but they'd tried to be sensible about his chances of surviving the cancer. They'd lived each day as best they could. They'd made plans.

Max arranged to sell what remained of his family's poultry farm—with its scattering of outbuildings and two fields—to a woman who bred champion quarter horses. She owned a farm down the road and wanted additional stables to board her pregnant mares until they foaled. The farmhouse, detached garage and a surrounding half acre of land would remain for Kate and the children, paid for, the taxes covered by an insurance policy. All very sensible.

By the time Max died, Kate had started working part-time as a teller at Vermont First National. The transition from married mother of two children to single parent had been as smooth as they'd hoped.

What Kate hadn't expected was the gut-kicking jolt of loneliness Max's absence left behind. Simple, reassuring habits were suddenly no longer there. The comfortable, solid sound of a man's footsteps coming in the rear door from the barn, climbing the back stairs from the mudroom to the second-floor bathroom to wash up before dinner. The way Max whistled off-key as he showered, songs she could never quite figure out. The warmth of his body next to hers in their bed . . .

A year ago, regardless of all their well-thought-out plans, her world had changed. She was alone now, alone with two children to raise. And although Kate knew she could do a good job of bringing up Jesse and Anna on her own, that didn't help the loneliness.

Standing over the stove, cradling a steaming porcelain mug between her palms, Kate shivered once more.

That draft. There it was again. It breezed across her skin . . . no, *through* her skin, as if reaching into her soul.

For an instant, she thought she caught a whiff of a uniquely masculine blend of scents—musk, sweat, cigar smoke and a pungent hair-tonicky aroma that reminded her of the way her grandfather used to smell when she sat on his lap. Bay rum. Wasn't that what he'd called it?

A second later, the smells that had settled around her heart like a warm, comforting blanket were gone. Sadly, she supposed that they, like the draft, must have been creations of her imagination. She obviously was far more tired than she realized.

"Mom! Mom, are you coming back or what?" Jesse called from the living room.

"Or what!" she shouted.

She could hear him giggling, then Anna joining in, parroting her brother although she probably had no idea why they were laughing. *Laughter for the sake of its own pure joy is good,* Kate reminded herself. She'd never been one to mope around feeling sorry for herself. She wasn't about to start now.

Straightening her shoulders, she dribbled a golden stream of honey into her tea. Besides, who could be truly lonely with two great kids like Jesse and Anna?

She peeked around the corner into the living room. Her children were tumbling on the floor like a pair of puppies, pretending to fight over Barbie's pink plastic convertible.

"Why don't you two head upstairs now. I'll be right up for your story," she said. "Pick out a book. It's Jesse's turn." One squabble averted, she thought smugly to herself. As long as the ground rules were laid out in advance, the two children got along remarkably well.

A few minutes later all three were snuggled up on Jesse's bed under a fluffy comforter. The chooser always got to play host to that night's reading. Kate repeated the familiar words of *Bunnicula,* the charmingly humorous tale of a vampire bunny rabbit. Jesse never tired of the tale, and was capable of reading most of it to himself, filling in the gaps from memory when word recognition failed him.

Anna preferred Dr. Seuss's nonsense rhymes. She'd memorized her favorite parts of the *Cat in the Hat* and *Green Eggs and Ham.* When she was overtired, she'd soothe herself to sleep by repeating the lines, word for word, until her eyes drifted closed.

Kate rested against the stack of bed pillows with Jesse and Anna tucked beneath her wings, and read in a soft, hypnotic voice. When she reached the end of the story, the room was blissfully quiet. Only the rain, kissing the windowpanes in a light patter, created a gentle lullaby.

Kate started to wriggle out from between her children.

Jesse stirred, opening one eye. "She's asleep," he whispered.

Kate smiled down at him and ruffled his short blond hair, the identical color of his sister's. "She always is by the time we finish, right?"

"Yeah." He grinned at her drowsily. "One more story?"

"Not tonight. School tomorrow."

He nodded, too tired to protest further. "Want help putting Anna to bed?" he asked, covering a yawn with his hand.

"I'll carry her. You can open doors."

Kate lifted her daughter and pressed the little girl's warm body to her chest as Jesse shuffled ahead barefoot, wearing a self-important grin. He swung open Anna's bedroom door. The little girl's head lolled against Kate's breast, and a sudden wave of tenderness engulfed her.

What right did she have to want more than this wonderful relationship with her children?

Even as the thought crossed her mind, another slipped in. *But wouldn't it be wonderful to love a man so fiercely, with such excitement that passion extended beyond a comfortable, caring friendship?* That was one type of relationship she'd never experienced. Maybe it was one she'd never know. Such things only happened in books and movies, she told herself, dismissing the idea.

She tucked Anna into bed, then returned with Jesse to his room and smoothed the sheets and quilted comforter under his chin after he'd climbed in. "Sleep tight, little man," she whispered into his ear as she kissed his butter-soft cheek.

"Night, Mom," he murmured, then closed his eyes.

She stood over him for a while. His breathing deepened and slowed, sought an unconscious plateau of tranquillity only children found in slumber. Soon he was fast asleep.

Touching her fingertips to his temple one last time, Kate turned and walked from the room. She left the door open a crack as she had Anna's, in case either of them called to her during the night.

Slowly Kate walked down the hall, the wooden floor creaking musically beneath her feet. She was still wearing the jeans, sweatshirt and tennis shoes she'd changed into when she came home from the bank at 3:00 p.m. that day. The bulky wool cardigan had been added to chase off that strange, still unexplained chill.

She sighed, telling herself she was tired, much too tired to do anything but go to bed herself. But it was only 9:00 p.m.

Maybe if she read for a while...

Taking her lukewarm tea with her, Kate walked toward the end of the hall and her own room, intending to search for a novel to suit her melancholy mood, from among those she'd carted home from the library the previous Saturday. She was midway down the hallway when a sudden, bone-gnawing chill coursed through her.

Kate stopped and stared at the attic door on her left. Behind it was a flight of rough wooden steps leading into a huge, open attic, the width and breadth of the entire farmhouse.

"So that's where you're coming from," she breathed, feeling, at last, a little clever for having discovered the solution to her mystery.

Somehow, the storm-cooled air must have found an opening—through a vent, a broken window, or—God forbid!—a hole in the roof. Kate rarely ventured into the attic. There had been few reasons to go up there after she'd packed away Max's personal effects. But now she remembered how her husband had repeatedly fretted over the storage area's contents.

"There's all kinds of junk up there, stuff from my grandparents' time. Probably things they inherited from the previous owners, along with the house," Max had stated.

"We should check it out," she'd said. "There might be something valuable."

"I doubt it. Last time I was up there, all I saw were old trunks full of rotting clothes, stacks of newspapers and old magazines, and lots of cleaning rags." Max shook his head. "Someone stored a can of kerosene up there, too. That's dangerous...the summer heat and all." He'd taken the kerosene down right away, but hadn't the time then for a thorough cleaning.

Kate had offered to do the job, but Max was insistent that it was his family's mess and dirty work. He'd do it.

The cancer had hit him hard right after that. There'd been no time. No time for anything but helping Max die at home, with his family and his cool, logical New England dignity intact. She was glad she'd been able to give him that much.

Now Kate pulled in a deep breath, continuing to stare at the attic door. The image of greasy rags and dangerously flammable chemicals poked doubts in her mind. If she went to bed now, the whole house might burn down around her and the kids while they slept.

It's silly, she argued with herself, *to obsess about a cluttered attic after all this time.* But she couldn't ignore the impulse to throw open that door, march up those steps and at least satisfy herself that all perilous items were immediately removed. It was as if something beyond reason, beyond her normal need for order, was calling to her, beckoning her up those stairs.

Chugging down the rest of her tea, Kate set her mug on the pedestal table that supported a huge Boston fern. She yanked open the linen closet door and removed a few supplies.

As Kate marched back toward the attic door, she caught another trace of male scent in the air. It stopped her cold. After a moment, she swallowed and gripped the doorknob but couldn't make herself turn it. Her insides felt suddenly watery.

What if the damaged window or roof hadn't been a result of the storm? *What if someone had broken into her attic?*

Kate closed her eyes and shivered at the thought. Glancing over her shoulder toward her room, she considered the telephone on the bedside table. Maybe she should call the sheriff's office, let one of his men check out the attic for her.

But wouldn't they laugh if she'd spooked herself and there was no one there!

Gritting her teeth, Kate slowly turned the knob.

He had been calling to her all evening.

Every step Kate Fenwick took through the floors below—as she'd herded her two children inside from the rain, prepared their supper, then cleaned up and supervised their baths and read to them—he'd heard. He'd barely dared breathe for fear of breaking the fragile emotional connection he'd worked so hard to establish between them.

It seemed to him that he'd studied her for a very long while now, but he admitted his sense of time might be somewhat distorted. Time, here and now, held little importance to him. He might have been ensconced in the attic of the Vermont farmhouse for hours, days or years. That didn't matter. What counted was that *other* time and place, the only one that felt real to him.

He sank down in the cracked-leather armchair he'd loved so well when Kathleen had lived here. They'd sat together in her parlor—he in this very same chair, she perched delicately on the wide, rolled arm, leaning against his shoulder, the scent of lilies in her hair.

In the first days following his return from the war, they'd rejoiced in their reunion and picked up where they'd left off, planning their marriage. But his soul hadn't been able to rest, and horrible memories of the carnage of battle drove a wedge into his serenity. He knew he couldn't stay in Chester and live the pastoral life, not until he'd made peace with himself.

Even now his throat tightened and eyes burned at the image of Kathleen begging him not to go. He'd asked her to leave with him. She'd tearfully refused. One warm night in June they'd parted, and he'd never seen her again.

"Oh, Kathleen," he murmured, choking on her name.

Sorrow flowed like molten lava through him, searing all it touched, and he dropped his face into his hands but he couldn't weep. It would be like mourning for himself, and it was *she* he should feel badly for, he told himself. He'd wronged Kathleen terribly, robbed both of them of their futures.

Slowly the sound of footsteps in the hallway directly below reminded him of his newfound hope. For a long time he'd feared there was no way to regain what he'd so recklessly lost. Then he'd found Kate Fenwick.

He concentrated even harder, willing the woman downstairs to come to him.

After a while, his ears prickled at the sound of door hinges creaking. His breath catching in his throat, he pushed up out of the chair and stepped back into the shadows. He wasn't sure she'd be able to see him even if she lit a lamp, but in case she was able, he didn't want to startle her.

As she climbed the stairs slowly, peering into the dark, he observed her from his hiding place, intrigued, for this was only the second or third time he'd seen her up close, really close. Most of the time he watched her from the one of the attic windows as she entered or left the house. She wasn't nearly as plain as he'd at first thought.

In fact, he thought, whimsically, if she wore a dainty lace collar and a more fashionable hair arrangement, Kate Fenwick might be quite lovely.

Kate took each step up the narrow wooden staircase as if she were walking on ice. Before she placed her foot, she listened, felt the rough plank under the sole of her athletic shoe and tentatively shifted her weight onto it, her balance equally divided between a forward and a backward movement.

Should she actually encounter anyone up here, she'd decided, she would throw herself down the stairs, slam the door behind her and ram home the heavy-duty bolt Max had installed during his security-conscious days.

The rest Kate had rehearsed in her mind countless times, part of her emergency-response plan. She'd grab the cordless phone from her own bedroom, scoop Anna from her bed and barricade herself and Anna with Jesse and, from his room, call the sheriff.

That seemed perfectly manageable in the planning stages, before she'd reached the top of the attic steps with her cleaning equipment. But now she wondered. Once she stepped away from the top of the stairs, she would be at a distinct disadvantage. All an intruder would have to do was cut her off from her only exit, and then...

And then what?

She reached up with a trembling hand and tugged on the string dangling in front of her face. The single light bulb overhead flashed on.

And then what? her mind insisted upon repeating. Would he attack and rob her? Terrorize her children?

Feeling for the previous stair tread with the toe of her shoe, she stepped shakily back and down. But before Kate could retreat farther, they came at her again—that breath of cool air, whisking sensually past her cheek, and an accompanying musky scent.

Kate hesitated.

"Is someone here?" she asked.

There was no answer. In the light of the sixty-watt Sylvania she could see quite clearly the area immediately around her. But whatever the presence had been, it wasn't showing itself. She felt another subtle sensation, as if something had passed close by her, so close it might have brushed up against her arm, although it hadn't actually made contact with her skin.

"I've already called the police," she lied, willing her voice not to crack. "They're on their way now, so you'd better leave. The door is open. No one will stop you." She held her breath and stepped away from the head of the stairs, indicating a safe passage.

Still nothing.

Kate sighed. Could it really be just her imagination? She'd heard no footsteps, and nothing seemed to have been disturbed since the last time she'd been up here. When had that been? Probably a few months after Max had died.

She looked around again, feeling more confident. Surely if a burglar had broken into her house and intended to do her harm he would have acted by now. Maybe there were wrens or bats up here, and the stirring of their wings had . . .

No. She surely would have seen them.

Well, Kate thought, *since I'm here . . .*

She was wide-awake now and knew it would take her hours to get to sleep. She'd carried a hand vacuum up the stairs with her, along with a carton of heavy-duty, plastic garbage bags.

"To work," she muttered.

The attic was divided into two large sections. The more spacious of the two, where she stood now, was centered over the original part of the house. It had a plank floor below, bare rafters above reaching up to a peak. String-tied stacks of old newspapers, *Life* magazines, boxes of leather-bound books and several steamer trunks filled the area.

The second section had been part of the addition that, she seemed to remember Max saying, his grandparents had built to accommodate their last three children—whether they'd had seven or eight altogether, she could never recall. This part was deep in shadows, without an overhead light of its own. She promised herself she'd get to that side, after she'd taken care of this end.

The sensible way to make short work of this, she mused, would be to get rid of the obvious trash first. She slid three piles of newspapers to the top of the stairs then tumbled them over the edge. They landed with a thud against the hallway door.

The *Life* magazines she hand carried down and stacked in the hall near her bedroom door. She'd go through these some other evening with the children. The brightly colored pages would be an educational treat—allowing them glimpses of America's past. She might even call Ruth Barkridge, who owned an antique bookstore in town. Ruth could probably give her some idea whether or not any of the books or magazines were worth anything.

Next, there were the trunks. Kate searched through these quickly. They were jammed haphazardly with clothing set aside, it appeared, for mending; cheap costume jewelry; and stained table and bed linens that might have belonged to Max's parents or grandparents. Nothing was of much interest to her.

But rather than fading, her curiosity grew, and she felt irresistibly drawn to continue her job. Kate told herself she wanted to get the job done all in one night, just to get it over with. But she sensed there was another reason, one she didn't understand, but which was important. Her heart picked up its beat, hammering softly inside her breast as she moved slowly out of the yellow circle of electric light, toward the darker shadows of the addition.

Something tripped her up, and she caught herself against a four-by-four wooden pilaster, then reached down to see what she'd kicked. A flashlight—the square, sturdy kind of torch that could sit on its end. Max had used one in the barns after dark; perhaps he had mistakenly left it up here.

She flicked the switch, expecting the batteries would be dead. A strong beam shot across the attic.

"Good," she breathed. "Now let's see what we've got here."

Aiming the light into the dark reaches of the attic over the addition, Kate stepped cautiously between wooden beams and more piles of newspapers. A shiver of excitement rippled up her spine.

The area had been used to store additional trunks of an even more remote age. But what immediately captured her wandering glance was an orderly cluster of antique furniture. A leather armchair, a brocade-upholstered settee, cheval mirror and Victorian reading lamp with a bead-fringe shade, perching on a dusty mahogany table, appeared to have been arranged as though in a normal room.

Approaching the collection of furnishings, Kate marveled at each piece, and at how queerly they seemed to welcome guests into their cozy circle. Yet it was obvious no one had been back here in decades, for the dust lay thick and undisturbed on every surface. Even the brass clasps on the trunks were coated with a dense gray blanket.

Gingerly Kate brushed her fingertips over the back of the leather chair. The rough grain had been exaggerated by age and felt cool and brittle to her touch. However, as she ran her hand down the inside of the back, the surface seemed warmer, more supple. As if someone had recently sat there, sat there for a long enough time to leave his body warmth and the impression of wide shoulders.

"Impossible," she murmured.

Raising her fingertips to her nostrils, she sniffed. That same scent—musk, sweat, bay rum, tobacco . . . and something else.

This additional scent was familiar, a part of her own life, but it took a few moments for her to place it.

Horses! That was it—the pungent, vaguely pleasant aroma of a horse's hide, warmed by the sun. "Impossible," she repeated, shaking her head.

But an uneasy sensation was already growing in her stomach. An impression, of sorts, that what she had discovered was something far more exciting, more mysterious than any pile of yellowing periodicals.

Kate pushed aside warning tingles in her gut and dropped to her knees in front of the first trunk, setting the flashlight on the floor, its beam trained upward into cobwebby rafters. She pried the latches up and lifted the heavy lid to reveal layers of delicate lace; skirts of dimity, gingham and voile; puffy-sleeved and fitted jackets and blouses of baize, jaconet and chintz. The colors were still surprisingly vibrant, as if untouched by time.

"Oh," she gasped. "How lovely."

The trunk had been painstakingly packed with dresses, gloves, pinafores, nightgowns, corsets...layer after layer of women's garments. Kate sat back on her heels, her heart thudding in her chest as she removed each item, touching the tiny buttons, marveling at the exquisitely accurate hand-sewn stitches that finished each garment. Laying each piece aside, she worked her way deeper into the trunk and, at last, came across some men's clothing.

Work pants and a muslin shirt, sturdy denim trousers and two sets of military uniforms, both dark blue with brass buttons and braided trim. She smoothed her hands over the heavy serge jacket, and fancied, for just a split second, some faint connection with the man who'd worn it.

But the feeling was gone almost as rapidly as it had come.

After completely emptying the first trunk, Kate returned each item, just as she'd removed it, and started on the second trunk.

This one was smaller and different in contents—full of a lilac-scented jumble of old letters, doilies, scraps of half-finished tatting, hand-embroidered handkerchiefs and bureau scarves. Each piece rested, in its turn, in her hands. Carefully she touched the tiny, precise stitches and wondered what woman had so lovingly labored with her needle and colorful threads to create such exquisite samples of an almost lost art.

She, herself, had once tried to learn to crochet, but she'd always been a tomboy at heart and had never succeeded in forcing herself to sit still long enough to learn more than a few basic stitches or complete even one item. She'd rather go skiing or hiking, or take riding lessons from Barbara Weintraub, the woman who'd bought the farm. Being outside and active was more Kate's style, although in her adult life she'd had little time for recreation.

But she could admire the talent, the precision and patience such lovely needlework required.

At last she got to the letters. These fascinated her even more than the delightful swatches of fabric that nested them. Carefully Kate untied the pale blue satin ribbon from around the batch that appeared to be the oldest. She opened one envelope after another, soaking in the words etched across each page in a strong, masculine hand.

Each letter began the same, with *My darling Kathleen* . . . and ended with, *Your devoted Jack.* She checked the address: Kathleen McCarter, Chester, Vermont. Perhaps in those days no street number was necessary. Chester would have been an even smaller town back then in—she looked at the date—1867. It would have been no more than a sleepy farming hamlet.

Kate read the first letter, feeling as if she were eavesdropping on a private conversation. Nevertheless, a delicious thrill surged through her as her eyes drifted across the lines.

My darling Kathleen,
I will have to keep this short. Have arrived in San Antonio with Edward. He has introduced me to some very interesting people. One is Major Tom Darcy of Company F—the Frontier Corps of the Texas Rangers. Due to the state of emergency in this part of the state, Darcy says, he is looking for more men to sign on, and this suits me fine.

All I must do to pass enlistment requirements is prove I can ride, shoot and cook for myself. Of course, the war taught me how to handle a gun, and any boy who can stay on the back of my father's mean-tempered plow horse can ride one of these Spanish ponies. I'll have to take a cooking lesson from one of the old hands who hang about the Sweetwater Inn—a deceptively tame name for the local saloon. But that out of the way, I should be able to enlist by week's end. Pay is twenty-five dollars a week, plus provisions, but I must supply my own horse and saddle.

Although Mexicans continue to raid border ranches for cattle and horses, and the Comanches pose a constant threat to settlers, the government's most recent concern is protecting citizens from renegade Confederate soldiers. Some men find peace hard to swallow. I sympathize—you know how I've suffered over my fallen comrades of the 57th Massachusetts.

But these men are no better than base criminals—raiding towns, killing women, children and old men, stealing what they find and burning what they can't take with them. There has to be an end to the violence. The Rangers have been given the job by the governor of rounding up the brigands however we can. It's not a happy task, and ends, more often than not, in more bloodshed. But it needs doing if this territory is ever to become civilized.

My only regret is that you are not here with me. Please reconsider. I can arrange for your safe travel and comfortable quarters for you here in town. I'll even secure leave to come as far north as St. Louis to fetch you. Every breath I take summons up the memory of you in my arms. I want none other.

Please, I beg you, come with me to San Antonio, my darling Kate.

Your devoted Jack

Kate's hand began to shake uncontrollably.

Kate! *My name?* she thought wildly.

It was as if the man who'd written the love letter was speaking directly to her. Kate sucked in shaky lungfuls of air and swallowed over a suddenly parched throat. A wave of confusion and fear washed over her.

The packet of envelopes scattered across the rough planks of the attic floor as she shot to her feet. Grabbing the flashlight, she rushed across the attic and down the stairs. She slammed the door behind her and leaned against the smooth, painted surface, gasping for air.

Chapter 2

Jack Ramsey paced the narrow attic, the spurs on his boots biting into the boards with a resounding crunch. The noise seemed to help him think. Thankfully, no one in the house below could hear him.

"Damn...damn you, Ramsey!" he swore at himself. "You spooked her good."

He laughed bitterly at the word that had sprung to mind—*spooked*. Very apt.

Pausing in front of the mirror on its oak stand, he observed himself critically. Every time he stood here, he was surprised that he could see himself in the smoky glass. Of course, *she* hadn't...well, couldn't see him even if he'd wanted her to. It wasn't time yet. And if he had become visible to her, she'd have run twice as fast. He was quite a sight.

Tight denim riding pants, thick with trail dust. A flannel shirt, torn across one side of his chest. The five-pointed Ranger's star, carved from a solid silver Mexican coin and pinned to his pocket. He ran a hand over his beard—bristly and unkempt, a black shadow across his chin. It gave him a dangerous look.

"Never did like to shave," he muttered. "Pity it took dyin' to make it stop growin'."

The faint Texas drawl sounded foreign to his own ears. He'd picked it up after only a few months in San Antonio, but it had never thickened into a true Western inflection. The Dartmouth patois over New England twang had continued to color his speech, so that his fellow Rangers sometimes called him Yankee—but never to his face. At least, not after the first time when they'd seen his reaction.

Yankee. Johnny Rebel. The hate and killing had to stop somewhere. Name-calling only reminded folks of their hurting.

Jack groaned out loud and spun on his heel. Lord, but he'd handled that woman all wrong. He'd walked right up behind Kate Fenwick and stared over her shoulder at Kathleen's letter, so hungry was he for anything from his own life. He'd tried scores of times to open the trunk himself. Moving around the furniture had taken months of concentrated effort, but the small-muscle coordination required to manipulate the latches on the trunks had been beyond him.

But while he stood close to Kate, he'd felt himself regaining more of his physical capabilities—as if her presence somehow gave him powers he hadn't had in some one hundred and thirty years.

"Why her?" he wondered. "Why is it different with her?"

But The Rules gave him no answer, and he returned to berating himself for being so stupidly careless—standing too close to her, then, on a whim, wishing away Kathleen's name and replacing it with Kate's.

At another time, with less at stake, it might have been a rather clever trick. But seeing her name on the letter had shocked and frightened Kate. He'd tried to hold her back when she'd first started to bolt. But that only fed her confusion and terror.

The worst of it was he'd driven her away when he most desperately needed her. Without Kate Fenwick he'd never be able to accomplish the task ahead.

"Kate! Come back!" he shouted at the closed attic door. He'd tried to pass through it or manage the knob, but failed countless times. "Please, come back!"

Jack waited, watched the door. It didn't move.

Drawing a deep, deep breath, he glared at a space beyond the door, one he calculated would be near where Kathleen's parents' room had been. Now it was Kate's bedroom. He reached down inside of himself and let out a roar of frustration and protest loud enough to penetrate three states.

Kate lay in bed, staring at the ceiling, listening to the house settle around her in its usual symphony of comforting creaks. After closing the attic door behind her, she'd stood for a moment in the hallway and immediately felt much better. Here, on familiar territory, surrounded by her own touches of decor and the kittenish sounds of her sleeping children, she could reason herself out of her panic.

For a moment or two she'd simply been swept up in other people's lives, she'd confused sympathy for two lovers separated by many miles with the reality of her own life. That was all there was to it. Simple.

While she continued talking herself back onto rational ground, she stopped to check on Jesse and Anna. Then she nestled down in her own bed. It took only ten minutes for the electric blanket to warm her goose-bumped skin to toasty perfection.

But she could not sleep.

Kate's heart raced in her breast, and a cold, prickly sweat broke out on her upper lip. She licked it away with the tip of her tongue. The droplets tasted salty and made her feel even more alert. She heard a voice, a man's voice—faint at first.

Suddenly her hands flew up reflexively to cover her ears, shutting out an agonized bellow. She held them there as the seconds passed and her heart raced wildly in her chest. But a moment later, the resonating howl, if it had existed at all, was gone. The house was utterly silent.

In the adjoining rooms, neither of the children stirred, although they often woke to muffled night sounds.

"I'm going mad," she muttered to herself, punching her pillows into submission before collapsing back into them. "I'm going stark, raving mad."

The next morning, Kate awoke, feeling as if she'd actually slept through the night. It had been a tension-drugged sleep, though, so deep she didn't remember turning over once.

She was out of bed by 7:00 a.m. and promptly put a pot of oatmeal on the stove to simmer while she showered and dressed for work. Before blow drying her hair, she woke up the children. All three ate their oatmeal sweetened with maple syrup she kept year-round on the table in a jar, much as folks in other parts of the country kept a sugar bowl on their tables. She used it freely on fruit, yogurt and sometimes in her tea, and the thick amber liquid gave everything a clean, luscious flavor unlike any other kind of sweetener.

By 8:30 a.m. she was waiting with Jesse and Anna for their bus. "If I'm not home from the bank when you get here," she reminded Jesse, "remember to let yourself and Anna in with the key under the back door mat."

Jesse shrugged. "We never use it. Carson always lets us help him with the horses."

William Carson was Barbara's foreman. He was in his fifties, a quiet and solemn man who, Kate swore, could read the equine mind. He never seemed bothered when the children hung around him, but she was careful not to let them pester him for too long. He had plenty of work to do, keeping up with Barbara's growing herd of thoroughbreds.

"Fine," she said. "Just don't get in Carson's way. And you can go inside if the weather is bad again today."

When the bus arrived, Kate passed out goodbye kisses and waved them off. A year from now, she thought wistfully, Jesse probably wouldn't allow her a farewell kiss. He'd think himself too old. How fast they grew.

Kate walked down the driveway and climbed into the Explorer. As she drove the forest-green utility vehicle down the gravel strip to the road, she glanced out the driver's window toward the dark window in the gable at the end of the attic. She thought about Kathleen McCarter's letters from her lover in Texas, and felt a twinge of regret.

It wasn't right that she'd rushed off, leaving another woman's precious tokens strewn on the dusty floor. Besides, Kate felt a growing need to find out what had happened to Jack and Kathleen. She wanted a happy ending for their romance.

By the time Kate pulled into the bank parking lot, she had become obsessed with the idea of reading every one of the letters, and she was toying with the idea of going home for lunch to start on them. Just as quickly as the idea occurred to her, she dismissed it. She didn't want to take the chance she'd have to stay late to make up for missed time during the middle of the day. The letters would have to wait.

Kate slipped behind her desk with a cup of coffee fresh from the carafe in the employee's lounge, and she sat sipping it thoughtfully. *A year,* she mused, *it's been a whole year since Max died.* Maybe that was what was messing with her mind. It was all a delayed reaction to his death. Hadn't friends warned her this might happen? There were emotional issues she obviously hadn't resolved.

"Hey, there, you going to suck on that empty cup forever?" a voice demanded. "You look like you could use more sustenance than caffeine and ironstone."

Kate looked up to see the sunny face of Barbara Weintraub. Barbara was thick-boned, strong and adored quarter horses. She loved their natures and their aesthetic grace, but above all, she was a keen businesswoman who understood the value of fine breeding stock.

A new foal from one of her prize mares, two days old and barely standing, was worth at least five thousand dollars. Once broke and properly trained, the sky was the limit.

"I haven't seen you at the farm lately," Kate said, standing up to give her a warm hug. "Where've you been?"

"Traveling," Barbara said. "I hate it. I like letting the buyers come to me. But I'd made a deal to personally deliver two of my babies to a stable in West Virginia, and there was no getting out of it." She glanced at Kate. "Hey, I was just teasing before, but you do look a little pale. Something wrong?"

"No," she lied. "Just had trouble getting to sleep last night."

Barbara frowned at her. "You shouldn't be alone in that big old house." It was an old complaint they constantly debated.

"I'm not alone. I have Jesse and Anna."

"Children are fine company some of the time. Others, a woman needs adult companionship."

Kate forced out a laugh, shaking her head. But she admitted to herself that maybe, just maybe, Barbara was right this time. Anyone who imagined drafts, after-shave and screams in the night might arguably benefit from the reassuring presence of another person in her house.

"Seriously," her friend persisted, "I don't see how you can keep to yourself so much. It's not healthy. You're a young woman, barely thirty."

"So who are you going to try to set me up with now?" Kate asked good-naturedly. "How many cousins from New York do you have?"

Barbara laughed. "This one's from New Jersey."

"Wonderful."

"You should meet him."

"Undoubtedly."

"He owns a meat-processing business . . . very successful."

Kate shook her head. "No way, but thank you."

Barbara caught an irritated look from the boss and sighed. "Well, there must be some reason you're not sleeping. Meet me for lunch at my place, and we'll talk about it."

"I only get one hour," Kate reminded her.

"That's better than nothing. I'll be waiting for you."

They sat in comfortable wicker chairs, in the sunny den off the back of Barbara's home. The main house at Willow Creek Farms was a modern ranch-style structure, one level, built in the shape of a letter *L*, with the short wing off the rear serving as its owner's office. Barbara kept her stallions and mares with her until after breeding, then transferred the pregnant mares down the road to Kate's place to wait out their term and foal.

She'd converted Max's old chicken houses, gutting the interiors, lining them with cedar paneling and siding them in vinyl. Running water and heat serviced each triple-size stall.

"The Hilton of horse hotels," Kate often teased her.

"Quality care pays off in contented horses and healthy foals," Barbara countered in her most businesslike tone.

But Kate suspected her friend spoiled her horses because she liked to, pure and simple. There was a soft, loving side of Barbara few people ever saw. Most men viewed her warily, from a safe distance.

"So tell me what's really up?" Barbara asked, pushing aside Kate's plastic-wrapped cheese sandwich and placing a plate of Caesar salad and crusty bread in front of her.

"Nothing. I was just restless last night."

Barbara said nothing, just watched Kate as she thrust a forkful of romaine lettuce into her mouth.

"No, it's more than that," Kate admitted after a few chews.

"You've met someone. Good. That kind of sleepless night is okay."

"Not someone, exactly . . . more like, some *thing*."

"He's that bad?"

Kate giggled and started eating with more relish, feeling herself relax now that she'd decided to confide in a friend. "Shut up and I'll tell you what happened."

"I'm all ears."

Kate laughed. "I can see that." She swallowed and took a deep breath. "Last night I decided to clean out the attic. No, wait—there was something else first. Before I did that, I felt sure a window or door had been left open. I kept feeling a draft and smelling something strange."

"Wasn't your oil burner acting up, was it?" Barbara asked.

"No, I checked, and I eliminated all the other obvious possibilities, too. I decided the draft might be coming from the attic."

"Did you hear sounds up there? I got squirrels breaking in on me all the time. A damn nuisance—the little buggers can sure cause a pile of damage. You'd better call an exterminator to—"

"It wasn't squirrels," Kate inserted before Barbara could rattle off the phone number of every exterminator in town. "It was something else, something I couldn't see and can't explain."

Barbara studied her with a higher level of concern. "It's Max, isn't it? You're fixating on him."

"No," Kate said slowly. "This morning I thought maybe I was, but I really haven't been thinking about him, not any more than usual. I mean, I miss him and all, but you know how it was with us. We were more like brother and sister, living in the same house, working together to keep the farm running, raising the kids. Partners."

"Thrilling."

"Marriage doesn't have to be a circus," Kate said tightly.

"Forget I said anything. So you weren't pining away for dear Max last night."

"No. You see, I went up into the attic, looking for the source of the draft and smells. I thought maybe a tree branch had smashed through the roof in the storm, or something was leaking up there, letting out that strange odor. And I started up toward the attic, but it was so...so weird..." Kate couldn't find the words to explain how she'd felt.

"Weird how?"

"I don't know. It was almost as if something was calling to me, wanting me to come up there. I know it sounds crazy, but it's true. I felt as if I *had* to go up there, as if I didn't have a choice.''

Barbara chuckled. ''I get like that with mucking out stalls—no putting off *that* chore.''

Kate sighed and chewed on a piece of bread. ''Listen, I didn't find any opening that would let in the outside air, other than the usual vents you find in any attic, but it was fascinating up there. I waded through junk Max's parents and grandparents had stored away. Then I found some other stuff that was much older.''

Kate described in detail the contents of the two trunks.

''It was really eerie. I could almost sense another person's presence up there. I felt as if it were circling me, moving in closer. At first it didn't frighten me. I felt excited . . . stimulated.''

''That's called being horny,'' Barbara informed her bluntly.

''Knock it off. That's not what I mean.'' But what did she mean? Wasn't that sort of the way it had been? Her pulse racing, her breathing strained and short? Hadn't she felt a little flushed? Hadn't she lain in bed minutes later, perspiring, unable to sleep?

''There were the letters,'' Kate blurted out, shutting off her mind from the direction it was taking at Barbara's outrageous prompting. ''They were written by a man in Texas—I think the date would put them just after the Civil War, to a woman he loved in Chester. She must have lived in my house at one time.''

Barbara leaned forward over her table with more interest.

''Letters? Like love letters?''

''Exactly.''

''Well, what did they say?''

''I only read one, then I bolted.''

''Doesn't sound like you, scared of an attic.''

''It wasn't the attic that frightened me. It was the letter. It had my name in it. *My name, Barbara!*''

''Kate Fenwick?''

''No, just Kate. He called her Kate.''

''And that wasn't her name?''

''Her name was Kathleen.''

Barbara made a face that would have pleased Jesse. ''Well, there you have a great mystery. Why anyone would call someone named Kathleen, Kate, I have no idea.''

Kate groaned and put down her fork. "I know it's a common nickname for Kathleen or Katherine or a lot of other variations, but he only called her that once, at the end of the letter. He was asking her to join him in San Antonio, Texas, and I felt—no, I *knew* that he was talking to *me.*"

Barbara pushed her half-finished salad away from her. "That's illogical. You know that letter has nothing to do with you."

"I—I—" Kate couldn't argue with her. Barbara made everything sound so cut-and-dried. Simple.

"You're alone too much," Barbara continued. "You probably shouldn't have stayed in that house. It's upsetting for you because of Max."

"It's not upsetting! I'm very happy there!"

"So why is your voice shaking, and why do you look like you're going to burst into tears any second?"

Kate turned away and drew the back of her hand across moist eyelashes. "Maybe you're right. Maybe...maybe..."

"What?"

"It was so romantic. His letter. I couldn't help wondering what it would be like for a man to love me that passionately, so deeply that he was miserable without me. He was a Texas Ranger, you see...he'd gone down there after the war, and she wouldn't go with him, and..."

"*He's a fantasy,*" Barbara stated, a no-nonsense edge creeping into her voice. She caught Kate's wandering gaze and held it with her own eyes. "You read a letter written over a hundred years ago, and now you're dreaming up macho riders on the wind. You're imagining all the things a man could be that Max wasn't."

Kate blinked then stared at her clenched fists in her lap. "Max was a good man. I don't regret our marriage for one minute." She swallowed. "But maybe...maybe I am fantasizing."

"Why don't you wait for this weekend to finish the cleaning? I can come up in the attic with you, and we'll get the job done quick, together. It'll be easier on you that way."

"Thanks."

"Then I'll introduce you to Paul, my cousin from New Jersey."

"Don't push your luck," Kate grumbled.

Chapter 3

Jack waited anxiously until the middle of the afternoon, then stood at the dusty window overlooking the driveway until he saw Kate's vehicle turn in from the main road.

In his own time, a carriage that moved without horses or steam power would have been viewed as magical or the Devil's design. He'd watched with interest, from his isolated perch in the attic, the progress of the modern invention called the automobile. After decades of refinements, they still fascinated him. He itched to try his hand at driving one of the shiny contraptions.

Unfortunately, The Rules stated in their insistent, silent way that he was unable to leave the attic. And it was unlikely anyone would drive an automobile up the stairs to him.

As soon as Kate parked in the garage behind the house, Jack sat down on the top step and concentrated on the door below. "Come to me, Kate. Come to me tonight. I won't hurt you," he murmured.

He knew he no longer had to shout for her to hear him. He only said the words aloud out of habit. Now, merely by willing her to share his thoughts, he could make her hear.

However, he expected she wouldn't open the attic door until she'd laid her children down for the night. He'd learned her habits and priorities; the boy and girl always came first—feeding them, playing games and working with them on their letter writing. Then they'd bathe—every night, for goodness' sake!—and she'd read to them.

Sometimes he'd sit at the bottom of the stairs, listening raptly to the stories. Some were silly, made no sense to him at all, but he luxuriated in the silky tones of her voice.

His favorite tale was by a French author whose name was unfamiliar to him: Saint-Exupéry. His book was called *The Little Prince.* In the story, the child prince wished to return to his home, but was lost in worlds so strange to him, he didn't understand them. Jack could identify easily with the little prince. He, too, yearned to return home.

He also liked another story about a stuffed bear named a Winnie-the-Pooh. This character was favored by Kate's daughter, while the boy liked another creature in the same stories, called a Tigger.

Tonight, the children's bedtime story was a short one, and Jack wondered if Kate had chosen it herself, making it intentionally brief.

As soon as he heard her soft footsteps passing through the hallway, he began his summons again.

Kate! I need you. Come to me. Don't be afraid. Come now.

It was only moments before the door beneath him opened, and he sprang to his feet, reacting out of instinct, forgetting that she couldn't see him.

Come, he said when she seemed to hesitate. *Please don't be afraid. We've so much to do tonight. Time is short.*

"I'm coming, I'm coming," she muttered to herself as she tromped up the stairs, carrying her lantern and an armful of thin-skinned green bags with her, all business tonight.

He staggered backward a few steps, staring at her as she brushed past him. Had she heard his actual words? His voice?

She gave no sign of being startled or overly wary now. She crossed the expanse of the main attic, holding her flameless torch in front of her as she walked, stepping over and around boxes, trunks and support beams until she'd reached the still-open trunk that had contained his letters to Kathleen.

She looked at the floorboards around it, and a puzzled frown creased her pretty face.

Yes, she was pretty. He could see that now. Her hair was a soft, sensible brown and her eyes a darker, pensive mahogany.

Her skin glowed, and traces of freckles remained where last summer's sun had warmed her cheeks. He knew she didn't carry a parasol to keep her skin white as Kathleen had. Somehow the subtle tan suited her.

Kate's eyes searched the floor closest to her feet, then drifted again toward the trunk.

I tried to close it myself, he thought. *But it's too awkward and I didn't have the strength after picking up the letters. I couldn't just leave them lying about.*

"Now where did they go?" she asked out loud.

Over there, on the reading table.

Immediately her glance shifted to the leather armchair, then to the small claw-footed table beside it. With a gasp of surprise she dropped the flimsy sacks from her hand and ran to the table where he'd managed to roughly stack the envelopes and drape the pale blue ribbon over them. Tying them into a neat packet resembling Kathleen's had been an impossible task for him. But he hadn't known how long it would be before Kate returned, and he couldn't bear to see his love letters lying abandoned on the floor. Retrieving them one by one had taken most of the night.

Now Kate picked up the whole pile with trembling hands. "Impossible," she breathed. "They were down there...then they..." She stared at the table, then slowly took in the makeshift room around her, squinting into the deepest shadows. He could almost hear her mind working, trying to make sense of the inconceivable.

Don't be afraid. I won't hurt you. I just wanted you to know I'm here. I need you, Kate.

Still gripping the torch and letters, Kate's hands slowly lowered to her sides. Her shoulders remained rigid. He ached to reach out and knead them until the tense muscles unknotted. He restrained himself, fearing he'd terrify her.

"There *is* someone here," she said firmly. "Where are you?"

Jack stepped forward, facing her so she wouldn't feel threatened, even a little, if she began to see him. He didn't want to startle her. *I'm here, Kate. Right in front of you.*

The sensitive muscles in her face quivered, and she bit down on her lower lip. She blinked.

"I'm hearing things. Words in my head."

No! Jack cried. He was overjoyed. This was more than he'd hoped for from their first real meeting, more than he'd been led to believe could happen. She was reading his thoughts perfectly! *No, you're not insane, sweet woman. You're hearing a soul's cry for help.*

"Rubbish," she said.

He laughed. *Rubbish?* Where he'd last been in life, the expletives were a good deal earthier. Half the women he'd known in San Antonio had been able to curse up his one side and down his other.

Chuckling, he stepped closer, until his lips nearly brushed her ear as she tucked smooth brown tendrils behind the lobe.

Sit down, Kate. Sit down and listen to what I have to say. Please.

She glanced back over her shoulder toward the top of the stairs, and he held his breath, praying she wouldn't run away again. If she did this time, he wasn't sure she'd come back, ever.

Clenching his fists at his sides, he wondered if he had the power to physically detain her. But as soon as the notion flitted through his mind, he realized any use of force would negate her usefulness to him.

A willing mortal, those were The Rules. Kidnapping her wasn't going to do the trick.

Sit, he whispered. *Listen.*

Taking tiny, stiff steps, Kate crossed the attic extension and lowered herself by stages into the leather chair. Jack remembered it as a rich, red Corinthian leather. Now the upholstery was nearly black. Rows of age-dulled brass tacks rimmed the back and arms, holding the brittle leather in place over a rickety wooden frame. The chair creaked plaintively as she sat in it.

Kate set the lantern on the table. Resting the letters in her lap, she tenderly arranged them according to the dates at the top of each, inked in his own hand.

Then she came across the last one . . . the only one he hadn't written. Major Darcy had sent his condolences to Kathleen, along with his uniforms, after—

"So talk to me," Kate whispered, still staring at the official-looking letter embossed with the lone star of Texas. "If you're really here, if you're real at all . . . talk to me." She closed her eyes and rested her head back against the chair. "I'm too tired, too confused to know what to think anymore. Maybe Barbara's right—I've spent too much time alone since Max died."

Jack's heart went out to her. *It takes time to mourn. You owe yourself that much. Another man will come into your life.*

"How can you know that? How can— Oh!" A whimsical smile teased her lips. "I forgot, you're not real. You're a soul."

A soul yes, and real. I was once a man, a man with dreams and ambition and a love for a woman that even death couldn't still.

He crouched down on the floor at her feet and looked up into her face. Her eyes remained gently closed, as if she were letting herself drift between consciousness and sleep. Perhaps that was the only way she could deal with the illogic of this moment. To her, it must have been like talking at thin air.

"You are the man who wrote the letters to this Kathleen McCarter?" she asked at last.

Yes. Jack Ramsey.

"Why did you leave her?"

The war.

"No." She shook her head and slowly opened her eyes. "No, you apparently fought in the Civil War for the North. I saw the Union uniforms, read about the Massachusetts regiment. But you came back to Vermont after that, then you walked out on your fiancée."

He could feel the anger and frustration building inside. He hadn't known such emotions still burned within him, although he'd had a temper to reckon with when he'd been alive. But now it was crucial he control his reactions.

I asked Kathleen to marry me and come with me to Texas. She was timid, afraid of the vast distance—a fragile woman.

Kate brushed her fingertips slowly across the yellowed vellum of the top envelope. "Are you sure it was the distance?"

What else would it be? he asked, dumbfounded by her question.

"Not to hurt your feelings or anything, but . . . well—" Kate shrugged "—maybe she chose not to leave Chester because she wasn't in love with you."

He smiled. *I may have wondered about that back then. But I know now that she loved me as steadfastly as I loved her. I wouldn't have stayed away much longer anyway. I enlisted in the Rangers for two years, then, no matter what her decision, I planned to return home to Vermont.*

"Something happened to keep you from coming back," Kate murmured.

Her eyes shifted, seeking something solid to focus on, but ended up gazing straight through him. Just as well, he thought. He wasn't a very pretty sight, under the circumstances.

Yes. Something happened.

"What?"

He grasped the arms of the chair on either side of her and leaned in to study her face. He was still unable to tell if she believed she was really communicating with him—with a ghost, for he supposed that was what he was although he'd never felt the need of labeling his condition of deadness. Maybe she thought she was just playing along with her imagination.

There was a gunfight. I was shot.

Kate's face went pale. Her hands convulsed in her lap. "You were murdered?"

Yes. Shot in the back.

"How awful. And Kathleen?"

She was heartbroken. He couldn't help grinning just a trifle smugly. *Of course, if you'd seen me back then, you'd realize how much she'd missed out on. I wasn't a bad-looking gent if I do say so—until the end.* He shook his head. *Facedown in the black San Antonio dust with a bullet in my back. Want to see where it went in?*

He'd intended merely to lighten the moment, by shocking her just enough to make her laugh. She apparently was still unable to see him. Anyway, he knew the wound no longer showed.

Unfortunately, his teasing had the opposite of its intended effect. Tears pooled in Kate's soft brown eyes and she blinked rapidly, as if to chase them away.

Hey, don't cry! he pleaded. *That all happened long ago. It has nothing to do with you.*

"How can you say that?" she snapped.

To his astonishment, she stared straight at him. *At* him! Not *through* him! Her features contorted with fury and pain. She shot up out of the chair, dropping the letters from her lap to the floor and rushed forward, knocking him out of his squatting position and onto his rump.

"You make yourself at home in my attic, barge into my life, bless me with the tragic details of your lost love...and you...and you have the *nerve* to say I shouldn't take it personally!"

"Well, I never intended—" Jack stopped. He'd heard his own words. He'd moved his mouth, and actual words came out.

He gulped and looked up at Kate from his rather awkward seat on the floor. She was staring at him with as much astonishment as he himself felt.

"My God, now I'm seeing things, too! Barbara's right." Kate squinted at him critically. "I didn't know ghosts were so, so dirty... and smelled."

Smelled? He glared at her, a little offended, then shrugged. "Reckon we stay the way we were when we last lived. I'd been on the trail for six days straight. Who is Barbara?" he asked, brushing himself off as he stood up.

"My friend. My very wise friend who advised me to seek professional help in not-so-many words." She started moving toward the steps. "I was demented enough not to listen to her."

"Wait! Don't leave! There's so much we have to talk about." Jack reached out, but stopped his hand from touching her. *Too much, too soon,* a voice warned.

Kate turned and looked at him. "I have no idea what's going on. None. Just let me sleep on it. I'll be back tomorrow. I promise."

With a pang of regret, he let her leave. It was true he couldn't physically force her to help him, but there were other ways. And he was desperate enough to use them.

Sleeping on it was an extremely optimistic goal, Kate realized. She tossed and turned all night, afraid that the man who'd appeared to her in her attic would call out to her again. She was terrified she wouldn't be able to resist his rich, mesmerizing voice.

The past twenty-four hours had been far too weird for her, Kate decided. She had always been sensible and cautious in all of her social relationships. Hadn't she married Max more for practical motives—to have children, share a stable home—than for love? It always seemed to take her a long time to warm up to people. She kept a few close friends, but most lived at a distance and had evolved into pen pals, an arrangement with which she felt comfortable.

Kate would never dream of inviting a stranger into her house. Even in rural Vermont there was the fear of a trickle-down ef-

fect of urban violence. Drug lords and gangs would soon over-
flow the cities, seeking out new territory to poison—or so the
local newspapers claimed.

No, Kate thought, *I like being alone, for the most part. I enjoy my privacy.* She didn't yearn for a carnal rendezvous with
her married boss. She didn't relish resuming the awkwardness
of teenage dating. She'd do fine on her own, with Jesse and
Anna. Most of all, she didn't need to share a tormented nineteenth-century couple's heartbreak.

And yet, there he'd been. Jack Ramsey, or so he claimed,
lived in her attic. And she didn't know what to do about him.

When she'd first started sensing the shape of his words,
they'd seemed to come to her through her subconscious. There
had been no feeling at all that they were part of normal speech,
issuing from the attic. No, they'd felt as if they originated from
within her.

That much she could almost accept. People during times of
stress sometimes imagined voices, occasionally felt consoled by
the words of loved ones who'd passed away.

Who could say what spiritual bonds linked people in death
as in life? She could close her eyes and let herself believe she
was dreaming. His voice had seemed comforting...inter-
esting...appealing. A Texas Ranger. How fascinating!

Then the timbre of his words had altered slightly, deepened,
become richer and intrusively intimate. It had happened in the
blink of an eye, as his story of his own death suddenly and irrationally moved her to tears. His voice became a real voice,
like anyone else's. And she'd *seen* him! She'd actually *seen* him!

Kate lay in bed, shuddering. What was happening to her?
Why her? If this Jack person was a creation of her imagination, he certainly was a spectacular fantasy. Sure, she'd chas-
tised him about being dirty and smelling funny, but beneath the
grime there'd been a strong, lean man somewhere around six
feet tall, with eyes as piercingly blue as an August day. He'd
towered over her slight five-foot-three-inch frame. He exuded
masculinity, and suddenly she found herself recalling what it
felt like to be held in a man's arms, to release herself to him,
totally and for all time.

"Oh, God," she whimpered. "Don't fall for a specter, Kate.
Even one of Barbara's cousins would be better."

* * *

Kate kept her promise. The next morning she packed the kids off to school in record time, then she telephoned the bank. Annette Appleby, an older lady who alternated between receptionist and teller duties, answered the phone.

"Tell Brian I won't be in today," Kate said. Brian Stone was her boss.

"Are you all right?" Annette asked. "There's nothing wrong with the children, I hope."

"They're fine. I'm just not feeling up to par this morning. I think a day's rest will help a lot."

"I'll tell him," Annette said. "You just take it easy, dear."

Kate hung up. At least she hadn't needed to lie. She really wasn't feeling her normal self.

She started to brew herself a cup of orange-spice herbal tea. On second thought, she prepared another mug then placed both on a tray with a plate of toasted wheat bread and a glass dish of strawberry preserves she'd put up the previous spring. Maybe ghosts got hungry, too.

Kate had already dressed, taking a little more care to select an outfit than she would have any normal weekday. She wore a pair of cream-colored knit pants and an oversize sweater with pink rosebuds embroidered over the front. Setting down the tray on her bureau, she brushed her shoulder-length hair out loose and applied a touch of makeup. She felt a little silly, but what the heck. It wouldn't hurt to take time for herself once in a while, just to perk up her own spirits.

She grinned at the word. *I'm primping for a ghost,* she thought.

Balancing the tray on one hand, Kate turned the brass knob in the hallway door and started up the attic stairs.

"Jack?" she called softly when she didn't see him waiting for her at the top.

There was no answer.

She climbed the creaking wooden staircase and turned to the right, tugged the string dangling from the bulb to light her way then scrambled across the main attic. As she balanced the tray and stepped over obstacles, Kate made a mental note to wash the two small windows, to bring in more light during the daytime. She set the tray on the pretty mahogany table and found her flashlight where she'd left it sitting on the floor the night before. She turned it on, and the space around her was bathed in a dim yellow glow.

But the Ranger was nowhere to be seen.

Feeling surprisingly hollow inside, Kate sat down and sighed. So it had been either an overactive imagination or fluctuating hormones that had dredged up the lanky Texan from the past.

Picking up her cup, she sipped, trying to convince herself she was glad it was over. Now she could return to her normal life. No more ghosts. No more mourning nineteenth-century lawmen and their brokenhearted ladies. No more—

"Who's the second cup for?"

Kate's fingers spasmed and hot tea splashed down the sides of the cup onto her sweater.

"Jeez, you scared me! What are you doing sneaking around like that?"

"I wasn't sneaking, I was observing. You look nice today."

He stood in the darkest end of the attic, lounging against a glass-fronted lawyer's bookcase that was filled with leather-bound volumes.

Hastily Kate stood up, seized a napkin and began brushing amber droplets from her sweater. "This will probably stain, too," she muttered.

Jack stepped forward and peered at her outfit. "Doesn't look like it'll be a great loss. The thing doesn't even fit you."

"Sweaters like this are supposed to fit loose," she fumed. "It's comfortable . . . and stylish."

He tilted his head to one side in a doubtful gesture. "Doesn't make much sense. Sort of like wearing a blanket. A man can't see your figure at all."

"My figure be damned, why would I want to parade my figure when I'm at home alone with two kids in a farmhouse?"

He nodded. "Guess you're right. Old widow ladies like you—"

She flashed a furious look his way.

He shut up, but the beginnings of a smile teased the corners of his lips.

"Anyway," he began again, eyeing her waist, "wearing something like that, it's a wonder a woman would bother with a corset."

She looked up at him from beneath her eyelashes, sure he was expecting a reaction from her. Maybe the women of his day would have blushed or run off tittering to themselves at the mention of underclothes.

"I'm not wearing a corset," she announced bluntly.

His eyebrows rose with interest. "Really."

"Or a bra."

"Bra?"

"Never mind." She wasn't about to give him an education in the improvements made in the past century on women's undergarments. "Would you like some tea and toast?" she offered, sitting back down again.

He scratched his jaw, looking puzzled. "It smells really good, and it's a nice thought. But—"

"I made the preserves myself."

He shook his head. "I'm sure they're delicious. But I haven't felt the need for food or drink since . . . well, you know . . ."

"Oh," she murmured. "Sorry."

"Not your fault." He came over and sat on the floor at her feet.

Kate leaned back into the chair cushions, slathered a slice of toast with jam and munched contentedly on it. She'd learned she could leave off the butter and put on as much of the strawberries as she liked, and not gain an ounce. It was a happy indulgence.

"So why are you here?" she asked, getting to the point that had kept her awake most of the night. "Why are you in my attic, talking to me?"

"I'm here because this is the house I was meant to return to."

"To Kathleen."

"Yes."

Kate ate slowly, thinking about his words. "You were *meant* to come back here. Does that mean that all people who die return to haunt the place they'd been headed for when it happened?"

"No." He flicked a speck of dried mud off of his boot, but she couldn't find it on the floorboards. "My case was sort of special."

"How?"

"Well, you see I was chasing these fellas who were fixing to make more trouble than they'd a right to. I expect you wouldn't know what it was like after the war. Up here in the North, well, there were hurting families and bitterness. Lots of folks had lost their boys. But Vermont soil wasn't desecrated by her sons' blood. Down South, where I marched with the regiment, well, it was ten times worse."

Her eyes scanned his face. His were the most expressive features she'd ever seen on a man. Even when he wasn't conscious of his own mood, she saw the dark shadow of pain in the chiseled lines around his nose and mouth. "*You* survived," she pointed out.

"Yes, but not a whole lot of my friends lived to come home with me. Petersburg was bloody awful, and I hear places like Gettysburg were far worse, though it's hard to imagine."

She thought of the movie by the same name. She'd sat through four long hours of the passion of war and wasted lives. The death toll it depicted was beyond imagining.

"The Civil War was a great tragedy in the history of our country," she murmured.

"Yes. Terrible." He swallowed, and his eyes misted over.

She looked away to give him a moment to pull himself together.

In a little while he continued. "After the war, coming home was all I wanted to do. Come back to Chester, marry Kathleen and raise a family. But once I got here, I couldn't sit still, couldn't stop thinking about the boys who'd died in the fields beside me and how I hadn't done enough to change things."

"I'm sure there was nothing you could have done," she said consolingly.

"Maybe. Maybe not. Still, it's a question a man asks himself." His hand rested on the leather beside her knee, the fingers wide and callused. A subtle tension coursed through them, then they relaxed. "One of my old classmates from college…" He looked questioningly up at her. "Dartmouth—it's still around, isn't it?"

"Yes," she assured him. "A fine university."

He nodded, looking a little pleased. "Anyway, an old chum, Edward Cushing, came home. He'd been down in Houston, Texas—went down there to teach before the war and ended up staying and editing a newspaper called the *Houston Telegraph*. During the war, he bought into it, and by the end of the war he was sole owner. Anyway, he came back East to purchase a new press and check out his old state, see how the war might have changed her and what the political atmosphere was like."

"You must have been happy to see a familiar face," she commented.

"Yes, and it was Edward who told me what was going on down in Texas. How the war wasn't over there yet."

Kate frowned at him. "That's not what my history books said. Once Lee surrendered—"

"I don't mean the War Between the States, I mean the war between the settlers—the Mexicans, the Indians to the Confederate boys who didn't know how to stop fighting once they'd learned to kill. The State had its hands full during Reconstruction. Women and children weren't safe anywhere outside of the larger towns or the forts. And those were few and far between. Most families lived in nothing more elaborate than wooden lean-tos or one-room log cabins. A house like this, you only found in Galveston, and it was the palace of a rich man."

"So you left to join the Rangers, to help bring peace to a state two thousand miles away."

"Yup, that's what I did." He sighed. "Might not have made sense to Kathleen, to her parents or to anyone else in Chester...but I knew I had to do it. I had to help this country, all torn apart by the war, and I had to have time to heal myself. It was what I needed to do. I didn't feel like I had a choice."

Kate watched his face, transfixed by the wash of emotions passing over it. He was a man who cared deeply for other people. All he'd asked was to live long enough to do his duty and return to his love.

Jack caught her staring down at him. "I guess, being a woman, you think that was foolishness, taking off like I did."

"Not at all," she said softly. "I think you were very brave."

"Kathleen, God rest her soul, she was pretty mad at me, and upset. Said I was tempting fate, coming back whole from the war then going off again."

"She didn't want to lose you," Kate said. "I can understand that. But you still had to make your own life. She had the choice of going with you or staying behind."

Jack shook his head. "Looking back, I wouldn't have wanted her in San Antonio. After I'd been shot, she would have been all alone out there. No family, no friends. As ruthless as some men could be in those days, they might have killed her, too. No telling."

Kate chewed her lip and thought, trying to build a logical framework from the past for what was happening now. "So maybe Kathleen was right. Your fate was to return to Vermont, and something went wrong down in Texas. You weren't supposed to die there, not when you did at least."

Jack's face brightened, and his blue eyes sparkled faintly, hinting at how intoxicatingly brilliant they must have been during life.

"You're a smart one, darlin'. That's just how it works. I'm not sure of the details or reasons. It's not like Saint Peter or He Himself sat me down and explained The Rules. But somehow I know that the only reason I'm here in your attic is to make things right."

Jack leaned closer to her, and she pressed back into the chair, still a little uneasy with the thought of conversing with a dead man.

"You see," he went on, "I was supposed to come back here and marry Kathleen. We had, or would have had six children. She and I would have lived clear into the twentieth century and died of natural causes long after our first great-grandchildren were born." Jack gazed intently up at Kate. "That's where you come in."

Kate straightened in her chair. "I have an awful feeling I'm not going to like this."

"Just keep an open mind," he encouraged.

"It's open."

He took a deep breath and frowned at her for a moment, as if trying to read her mood. At last he said, "I need you to come back with me to Texas, in 1867. Come with me and help me find my killer before the day of my death—then we can make history right."

Kate felt a nervous giggle bubble up inside of her, then saw that Jack was serious. She rearranged the curve of her lips into a solemn line. "That's preposterous."

"It's not," he insisted. "It can work because that's what's supposed to happen, only, I can't take just anyone with me. My travel mate must be a mortal who believes in me, who. . ." he looked away as if uncomfortable continuing. "Someone who *cares* about me."

Kate started to open her mouth. The words *no way* were already forming on her lips.

Jack covered her mouth with the palm of his hand. Miraculously, she felt, actually *felt* the rough calluses on the insides of his long fingers.

"Oh," she breathed against his skin. Her heart thudded, rising into her throat.

Slowly Jack bent forward. Lifting his hand from her lips, he kissed her gently. She breathed in the musky outdoors smell that had trailed through her house for days. He tasted pleasantly of sweat. A warm glow melted a path through her veins, and the lovely melding of sensations was so pervasive, so welcome, she felt incapable of drawing away from him.

"Please, Kate, come with me to San Antonio," he repeated huskily.

"I . . . I—"

He kissed her again, and her insides dissolved into warm puddles. Marvelously, hopelessly, her body tuned itself to his touch.

"We'll make a good team," he ground out. "And I promise you'll benefit as much from this venture as will I."

"How?" she gasped.

His eyes were afire with some deep emotion she could no longer read. "Just say yes, Kate. Just come with me."

She felt her head bob up and down.

Chapter 4

Still trembling and feeling the pressure of Jack's lips on hers, Kate rushed down the attic stairs then the second flight to the sunny normalcy of her kitchen. Breathing too hard, her fingers shaking as they gripped the vellum envelopes she'd carried away with her, she sat for several minutes and tried to compose herself.

At last she stood up, walked over to the telephone on the wall, picked up the receiver and mechanically punched in Barbara's phone number. The line rang twice before her friend's throaty hello interrupted.

"It's me," Kate said without introduction. "Can you come over?"

"Where? Work?

"No. My place . . . now. I have to talk to someone."

"All right. Sure, I'll be right over," Barbara agreed, her voice sounding strained.

Kate hung up and put the teakettle on to boil. She pulled out the decorative tin of herbal and imported teas she kept in her cupboard. Snatching up two glass mugs, she set them on the table along with a plate of lemon cookies she'd made earlier that week.

By the time the kettle was whistling, Barbara had let herself in through the back door. Her boots clomped across the wooden floor of the rear hallway. Her wide, ruddy face thrust itself around the corner of the kitchen door several inches ahead of the rest of her formidable body.

"You sounded awful on the phone. What's going on?"

"Come in. Sit down."

During the few minutes it had taken Barbara to arrive, Kate had weighed the consequences of telling her the whole truth... at least as much as she knew or thought she knew. Though physically very different than Kate, Barbara shared her cool common sense and practical view of life. A view that didn't allow for phenomena such as UFOs, gremlins, leprechauns or ghosts. If someone had confessed to Kate that he'd seen ghosts, she'd have initiated tactful inquiries into psychiatric help for that person. Barbara was more direct. She'd commit her own mother within twenty-four hours.

So Kate knew she couldn't confide totally in Barbara. The woman had breezily dismissed Kate's concerns about a hundred-plus-year-old letter with her name in it. Why would she take a ghost seriously? But there might be a way Kate could ask her help, in a roundabout way.

"I don't want you to worry," Kate began. "I'm fine. The children are fine, too. Now, I said sit down—and choose your poison." She pushed the tea-bag tin toward her.

Barbara pulled off her denim jacket and sat, eyeing her suspiciously. "So why'd you drag me out here if life is so rosy?"

Kate perched on the edge of her chair and selected mint tea, hoping the aromatic brew would settle her queasy stomach. "I've decided you're right, I need a change of pace."

"Really? You want to date my cousin? I'll ring him up right from here and—"

"Not that kind of break. I'd like to go away for a while—just a short trip."

Barbara leaned forward across the table, looking interested. "Alone? Or with a *friend?*"

"With a friend. And, yes, you can assume that means a man."

"Who?"

Kate sipped her tea, trying to look suitably mysterious, which really wasn't difficult given she knew almost nothing about

Jack, what he had in mind for their proposed trip back in time
or even if his scheme had a chance of working.

"A friend . . ." Barbara mused, plopping a tea bag into her
cup.

"That's all I can tell you for now," Kate said. "The thing is,
I can't very well go off . . . somewhere . . . if I'm worried about
the children."

"Say no more." Barbara held up both palms in a gesture
graphic enough to stop a runaway stallion. "Just give me a call
when you've ironed out your plans. I'll grab a toothbrush and
move right in. The kids won't even know you're gone—oh,
better bake a couple of batches of cookies before you leave,
unless you want them eating store-bought. You know I can't
cook worth a damn. How long do you think you'll be away? A
week? Two?"

Kate realized with a shock that she hadn't a clue. Jack hadn't
indicated how long his investigation was likely to take. And
what about travel time? Would spanning over a century and
several thousand miles take seconds, hours, days or far longer?

"I don't know," she said vaguely, sipping her tea. "I guess
it all depends on how things work out."

Barbara waved off the matter. "Doesn't make any difference." She narrowed her eyes expressively. "Just remember
when you do go off with your mystery guy, I want details. It's
been so long since I went with a man . . ." She sighed wistfully
then chuckled. "Well, I guess it's pretty obvious why. I'm not
the ideal of feminine grace, am I?" She glared disdainfully at
her muscular thighs inside well-worn jeans.

Kate reached out a hand and placed it over Barbara's.
"You're a striking woman who's smart, a hard worker and has
a heart of gold. Why don't you send out some signals? You
never know who might be interested."

Barbara shook her head and slid down in her chair with a
smile. "Naw. I'll just live vicariously through you for a while
longer." She toasted Kate with her tea. "I've got a feeling
something pretty exciting might be brewing in your life."

Jack could barely hear the two women, talking in the kitchen
two floors below. Kate had asked her woman friend to come
over. They'd chatted for a while, in hushed voices so that he
could only pick up a few words here and there. Then he heard

Kate's feather-light footsteps ascending the stairs to the second floor.

Jack prayed she hadn't changed her mind. There was no alternate for the job, no other person who fit the prerequisites for his return ticket to San Antonio. He'd already waited so long, so very long to make things right.

After decades of patience, he ached with frustration at the loss of his sweet Kathleen. He'd been without her for so long. The compulsion to recapture his life and try again had become overpowering.

Yet he knew The Rules wouldn't allow him to force Kate to accompany him. Well, he hadn't exactly forced her, but he hadn't been completely honest with her, either, and he'd—

Damn! Why had he kissed her?

Because, he answered his own question, *you're too damn impatient.* He couldn't make himself wait for her to grow slowly fond of him, to fall in love with him, even though that was what had to happen. His ticket home would be a woman willing to love him selflessly, trust in him without limits—although she understood he was destined to belong to another.

He'd already seen too many decades pass to believe such a miracle could happen more than once. Families had come and gone from the farmhouse, leaving behind more memories, more junk in the attic. Not one person had responded to his pleas for help.

Then Kate had come along and he'd sensed a rightness about her. Regretfully, she was married, too involved in an ordered, well-planned life with her husband and children to even be aware of his existence.

So he'd waited a little longer. Waited and watched Kate Fenwick. Learned to see through her calm exterior to a heart that cried out for passion and excitement. And when he'd at last managed to coax her up into the attic and she'd hovered precariously between rushing off with him or scurrying back to her own world and shutting him out forever... Well, had he any choice? He'd taken a risk. He'd touched her and kissed her—seduced her, really. There was no other way to look at it.

Jack sighed and rubbed at the spot in the middle of his forehead that used to ache at times like this, when he'd been alive. At least he'd told her the truth about one thing—she *would* benefit just as much as he and Kathleen if he could turn the past around.

All he had to do was get through *that one day*, the day he'd been shot. He could then return to Kathleen, live out his life as fate had intended, raise his children, send them off to pursue their own destinies. . . .

Jack dropped down into the leather armchair and stared unblinkingly at the scuffed toes of his boots.

And what about Kate?

His mind grew cloudy, and the answers no longer came so readily. Apparently, he was allowed responses to some of his questions. Others of his concerns received no acknowledgment. Information came to him as a vague shadow, half-understood, mistily glimpsed as moonlight flowing across the landscape of his mind.

"Damn her," he muttered, rubbing the spot. "Why'd she have to be so good-looking?"

A plainer, less intriguing woman would have made limiting their contact to an occasional kiss or mechanical touch so much easier. He could measure out affection just sufficient to encourage her to stay with him until he no longer needed her.

In life, he'd been faithful to Kathleen, at least faithful in his heart. He had no intention of being otherwise in death.

He recalled Kathleen's porcelain-white arms, her tiny, corseted waist enclosed in a lovely pink beribboned gown, trimmed with lace cuffs and collar. Her pale blond hair swept up over her brow. How sweet, how fragile she'd looked as they'd parted. Tears shimmered in her eyes, even as she refused that last time to leave her beloved Vermont for him.

Then, to his astonishment, another face swam into his vision—Kate's. Her tears had been no less real when she'd heard of his death, but a strength glimmered through that Kathleen had never possessed. Kate lived by herself, keeping her house without the help of servants, raising two children on her own and even filling a man's shoes by working days in the town.

No male family member—father, uncle, brother or husband—made decisions for her. She was quite remarkable, both in spirit and physical appearance. She'd laughed at the idea of cinching in her waistline, he remembered, chuckling. Without realizing what he was doing, he summoned up the thought of a single, loose layer of fabric she'd called a sweater, covering her naked flesh. . . .

Jack felt himself respond to the image. A familiar warmth spread through his loins, and he stared at himself in amazement. He hadn't believed he was capable of that sort of reaction. How odd!

Yet, when he'd kissed Kate the night before, he had actually *felt* her. His fingers hadn't slipped through her body as they'd melted through the latch on the trunk. Touching her had been a natural and wholly pleasant sensation.

Too pleasant . . . given his determination to only take things so far.

A muffled sound came from somewhere nearby. Startled, Jack realized someone was in the attic room with him. He looked up at Kate from where he was sitting, his hands balled in tight fists on his thighs, both heels dug into the floor. Something inside of him quickened. She'd changed out of the creamy sweater outfit and was wearing blue jeans and a man's plaid shirt.

"When had you planned on leaving?" she asked.

"Leaving?"

"You know, to go to Texas, to your time."

"Oh, yes." It took considerable concentration to move his eyes away from the paths they were roaming—over her slim blue-jeaned hips; up to her small, high breasts within a plaid men's-styled shirt and farther up the delicate line of her throat.

"Well," he choked out, "we should leave as soon as possible, as soon as you're ready."

She nodded, her eyes wide with a mixture of fear and anticipation. "I have to ask you one thing."

"Yes?"

"You've done this before, haven't you? I mean, you *know* it works."

Jack stared at her, thinking fast. If he told her the truth, she'd certainly change her mind. But if he blatantly lied, she might see through him.

"Actually, no . . . I haven't done it before. But," he added quickly, "I *know* it will work."

She crossed her arms over her chest and gave him a teacherly scowl. "How do you know?"

He shrugged but couldn't look her in the eye. "I can't explain because I don't understand myself. It's just one of The Rules. I understand it's true. Something tells me I needn't question it." He paused, watching her doubtful expression. "You know when your children will arrive on their yellow coach. You know that each spring, the field beyond that window will turn blue with chicory blossoms.''

"But that knowledge is based on experience," she objected. "Something is likely to happen again because it's happened so many times before." Kate paced the floor, impatiently sweeping cobwebs from the rafters above with her hand. "If you've never done this before—"

"It will work. *Trust me!*"

Kate spun around and glared at him hotly. The blaze in her eyes made him back off a step. "*Trust you?* I don't even *know* you, and you ask me to leave my children and all I know and love for you. Don't you think that's expecting an awful lot? What if this grand plan of yours doesn't work? What if I leave and *I can't get back!* Did you ever think of that?"

Tears welled in her eyes, and he rose from the chair and took a step toward her, wanting to hold her for just a moment, to reassure her that he'd never ask her to sacrifice her children or her own life for his. But before he could close his arms around her shoulders, her fists shot out, pounding him soundly in chest.

He gasped, shocked. "I just wanted to—"

"Tell me how it will work!" she demanded. "Give me a guarantee I'll be able to come back to my children."

"I—" He didn't know what to say. He couldn't give her proof if all he himself had was faith. Faith that had rippled through his soul like the waters of a mountain brook—constant, cool and reassuring in its perpetuity. He'd felt that way ever since she'd climbed the stairs to his attic retreat the other night.

"I have an idea," she said when he found no words. "You go first. You go and come back, then I'll know that it works."

"I can't," he said hopelessly. "You're my passport. I can only return to San Antonio with you."

She squeezed her eyes shut and blew a long puff of air between her lips. "All right. We'll go for just a few minutes. We'll hop back there, check out the place and come back. It'll be sort of a trial run."

"But how can I find the person who killed me if we—"

"It's *my* way or not at all," she said firmly. "After I see that it works, I'll tell Barbara to come and stay with the children for a few days, a week, whatever it takes."

He glared at her. She was a stubborn woman, but he couldn't fault her logic. She wasn't willing to risk her own life or jeopardize her children's welfare for a stranger. Her lack of trust hurt, but he understood.

"Fine." He nodded. "We'll go now. You'll be back before the children return from their school."

"And no fooling around," she said.

"Fooling around?"

She blushed, but he looked genuinely puzzled by the expression. Thank God he hadn't caught the double entendre. "No running off to scout out some gunslinger or meet up with old sidekicks. This is just a dry run, Jack. There and back. No fancy stuff."

He grinned, feeling a boyishly mischievous thrill. "Right. No fancy stuff."

Turning away from Jack, Kate took one last look around the attic. Half of her was sure she'd never leave the spot where she stood now . . . at least, not for some fanciful journey through time.

The other half wasn't sure of anything, and that terrified her.

In fact, the unknown had always frightened her. She needed to control her life and, whenever possible, the world around her. Now, here she was, relinquishing that control to a stranger. Trusting him with her very existence. Because he'd told her she should.

Did Jack Ramsey deserve that trust? She wondered.

From the moment Kate had met him she'd sensed there was something dangerous and strong and reckless about the man. Yet, when he had the opportunity to coerce her to cooperate, he'd been gentle, intelligently persuasive and lost his temper with her only once. Aside from kissing her that one time, he'd been painstakingly careful to behave as a gentleman and do nothing to unnerve her. He'd seemed a good man, a man who deserved another chance, and her help.

When he'd told her he was sure they could travel safely to his past and back, she wanted desperately to believe him.

Kate felt Jack step up behind her, snapping her attention back to the moment at hand, and she stiffened reflexively. He wrapped his arms around her in a warm bear hug.

"I have to hold on to you," he murmured in her ear. "It's important. We don't want to be separated in the transfer."

"Separated?" Her voice cracked, and a wave of fear engulfed her. Dread—black and suffocating—washed over her, and she tried to turn to face him. "Jack, maybe we should just wait until—"

"Hush," he said, gripping her harder to keep her from moving. "Let me concentrate."

"No, listen to me! I've changed my—"

"Stand still!"

She did, because she had little choice.

Kate found her shoulder blades pressing hard against Jack Ramsey's chest, her hips aligned with the rigid muscles delineating his thighs. Her body was so hypersensitive, she could feel the row of buttons running down his shirtfront, and the other shorter line, lower down, securing his denim trousers.

But she couldn't feel a heartbeat, and that saddened her.

Of course, she thought. *He's dead.* Ghosts don't have heartbeats.

A pleasant dizziness stole over her, as if she'd treated herself to one glass too many of a good wine. The attic rafters and beams spun around her, and suddenly the sensations became more intense and she felt short of breath. Kate thought of all the science-fiction flicks she'd seen as a kid. Perhaps the trip would be painful, eat away years of her natural life or alter her physically in some horrible, irreversible way.

"Jack!" she cried out in terror.

But he only held her tighter, until she was sure he'd crush the life out of her.

The scent of him—musk, man and faint traces of horse—engulfed Kate as he bent protectively over her, pressing his cheek to the top of her head. She clutched his arm, holding on for all she was worth as the sense of leaving behind everything she'd ever cherished overwhelmed her.

Tears pooled behind her lids, and Kate squeezed her eyes shut to block out the wildly altering panorama around her. How would Jesse and Anna grow up without her to protect them? Without her to soothe away their fevers, or hug them and read stories each night, or warn them against the evils of the world?

Evils that were, perhaps, as deceptive as Jack Ramsey.

How could she have listened to him? How had she allowed him to draw her into such a crazy scam, whatever it might be?

"Kate. Kate, can you hear me?"

She became vaguely aware of Jack's honeyed drawl, slicing through her vertigo, anchoring her gradually to reality.

It must have all been in my head, she told herself. The sensation of movement left her. Gravity reasserted itself.

Without opening her eyes, she tentatively scuffed her right athletic shoe and felt the familiar wooden boards of her attic beneath its sole. The surface felt unusually gritty. *I should sweep,* she thought, just as she opened her eyes.

A scream surged up through her throat the second her surroundings swam into focus.

Jack's hand clamped roughly over her mouth. "Quiet!" he rasped in her ear, dragging her back into the shadows of a stucco building, one of many that lined the unpaved street where they stood.

Kate's heart thrummed wildly in her chest as she scanned the parched landscape. A blazing orange sun beat down from a sky that seemed to stretch out forever. Several horses with riders and mule-drawn wooden wagons moved lazily down the strip of dirt.

"Are we... is this—?" she stammered between Jack's fingers.

"San Antonio, yes," he said. He eased the pressure of his hand away from her mouth. "Keep quiet now, understand?"

Kate looked up at him. His eyes—bluer and brighter than at any time in her attic—danced rapidly from one building front to another, then shifted to take in each of the riders as he backed the two of them farther into an alley.

Kate sucked in a shaky breath of hot air. "Well, that wasn't so bad. We made it." She tapped her foot on the ground and touched the side of one of the buildings, needing to prove to herself that everything around them was real. "Fine. You've convinced me. We can go back now."

Jack didn't seem to be listening. He released her and started moving stealthily out of the alley and toward an open doorway of what looked like the entrance to a dingy, little store.

"Jack?" Kate whispered hoarsely. The heat was beginning to penetrate her shirt. She felt steamy inside of it, despite the dryness of the air. "Jack, come on. You promised. Trial run, remember? One quick trip then back to Chester."

He ignored her, continuing silently down the raised planks that formed a crude sidewalk. When he was almost to the doorway, she dashed forward to catch up with him and seized him by the shirtsleeve.

"You're not going in there, are you?"

"I said be quiet." His expression was suddenly different, harder than it had been in her attic. The once-easy smile lines were taut and sharp around his mouth and eyes. The blue of his eyes had darkened and turned predatory. "We're not going back—not yet."

"Why not?" she persisted.

In a lightning-fast move, he backed her up and pinned her against the chalky stucco wall. Pressing his face toward her, he ground out, "Because *I don't want to die!* Can you understand that? I don't want to leave my work here undone, and I refuse to leave my family because some trigger-happy gunslinger feels like popping me in the back. Have you got that?"

"But you promised!" she stated, refusing to back down, even under the intimidating blaze of his temper.

He groaned. "I'll get you back home when I'm ready. I have to find out what day this is and catch up with the boys."

The boys, she thought. His fellow Rangers. Her heart leapt precariously. What he was suggesting could take days...weeks!

"No, Jack! We're going *now.*"

He glowered at her. "You don't have any choice."

"I do. I do have a choice," she insisted, not really sure how she knew, but she did.

He looked at her, a shadow of disappointment passing across his eyes, as if he, too, had known but had hoped she wouldn't discover his secret.

"You said that you had to be accompanied by a *willing* mortal, someone who cares for you."

"You do care," he said, moving closer to her until his chest nearly brushed hers. "I can see it in your eyes, even when you're furious with me." She was aware of the rhythmic clopping of horse's hooves. Jack was intentionally blocking a passing rider from seeing her.

"So I care. Sue me!" she snapped. "The thing is, I also have to do this of my own free will. You said so yourself. If I change my mind, if I decide finding your killer isn't worth sacrificing my own interests..."

Jack winced. "Don't say *that!* Don't even think that."

"So I'm right. If I stop thinking of you as my first priority, back we go."

This seemed to jolt him. Jack stared at her, drew his tongue over his lips and looked morosely off into the distance.

"You're not sure, are you?" Kate asked. "We might zip back to Chester and you'd have lost your one chance of catching up with fate."

He rolled his eyes and, at last, dropped his hands from her arms, although he still took care to block her from anyone who might pass by them. "I don't know for certain," he admitted. "It's possible."

"So," she said, smiling at him sweetly, "you'd better keep me happy, don't you think?"

He raked one hand through his shaggy black hair. "I guess so," he admitted.

"Then, I want to go home. *Now*."

The look of sheer desolation that swept over his face broke her heart. It was as if she'd given him a puppy to hold, then told him she was sending it back to the pound.

"Now?" he asked weakly.

"I have to be there when Jesse and Anna come home. We can arrange a longer trip later, as soon as Barbara is around to watch them."

Jack gazed pleadingly at her. "It's my life, Kate. Please. Now that we're here, let's just look around a little. Maybe we can find out how many days I have left." He briefly touched her cheek, and she felt the warmth of his fingertips linger even after he'd taken them away.

Kate couldn't look him in the eye and say no. She couldn't deny him such a simple request, not when so much depended upon it.

"All right," she grumbled, to make sure he understood she was just being gracious, "we'll stay for one hour. That should be enough time for you to get your bearings."

He let out a raspy breath. "Thank you."

"But first," she suggested, "we'd better do something about the way I look."

"What's wrong with the way you look?"

"I'm wearing Levi's with a zipper and Reeboks."

He stared at her as if she were totally mad. "Reeboks? Is that anything like a bra?"

Kate lifted a foot. "Athletic shoes, circa 1996. And zippers, unless I'm mistaken, haven't been invented yet. I'm a walking anachronism." Her glance shifted to the Mickey Mouse watch

Barbara had helped the kids pick out for her Christmas present. "This, too." She took off the timepiece and thrust it into her pocket. "Anyone who sees me will know I'm not from around here. They'll be suspicious of you, too, because you're with me."

"You're right."

He looked up and down the street, then grabbed her hand and ran across the low, plank porch in front of the next building and down another alley.

"We'd better fix you up a little." He tossed a wicked grin over his shoulder, and she suddenly wished she'd kept her mouth shut.

Jack pulled her up short in front of a watering trough. A pinto pony, tied to a short hitching post, shuffled its hooves in the dust and snuffled softly into the hot wind.

Jack lifted a buff-colored hat off the saddle horn and plopped it on Kate's head.

"Hey, that's not yours!"

"You're right. It's yours...now." He started untying the horse. "And *he* is mine."

"That's stealing! I thought Rangers upheld the law."

"In my day, darlin', Texas law was rather flexible. Besides, this pony belongs to Pete Graves, and for sure he's settled in for a good long afternoon of cards and whiskey at the Sweetwater. He won't even know we borrowed Pecos. Now, see if you can tuck your hair up under that hat so it'll stay, and splash some water on your face to get rid of your rouge or whatever you've got on your face."

"Why on earth should—"

"Do it!" he barked.

She decided now wasn't the time for explanations.

Cramming fistfuls of shoulder-length brown hair up under the greasy band of the hat, Kate eyed the murky water in the trough. She glanced sideways at Jack, to see if he was watching her. He was busy going through Pecos's saddlebags.

Gingerly she scooped up a few tablespoons of water and sprinkled it on her face. "There," she said, crinkling her nose at the stink as muddy droplets skidded down her cheeks, "are you happy now?"

"Immeasurably so," he said, spinning her around.

She saw the fistful of dirt, but what he intended to do with it didn't register until it was too late to duck. With the proficiency of an experienced makeup artist, Jack smeared the brownish-black grit across her cheekbones and forehead.

"What on earth are you doing?" she squealed.

"Darlin', you ask way too many questions. You're the one who pointed out we have to disguise you. This is the best we can do for the time being."

"My clothes aren't any different! I'm just dirty now, you idiot!"

"Take off the shoes."

"My Reeboks? I'm not letting you smear mud all over seventy-dollar cross-trainers."

"I'm not going to get them dirty."

She glared at him warily, but started unlacing them.

"Socks, too," he instructed. "You'll be more believable barefoot."

As soon as she handed him the shoes and socks, he tossed them under the side of the nearby porch.

"Someone will take them!" she cried in protest.

"Probably not. The rattlers will discourage any thief."

"Rattlers?" She stepped back quickly from the low platform. "How will *we* get them out of there?"

Instead of answering, Jack stooped beside her and started rolling up the bottoms of her jeans. His eyes wandered with interest up her legs, stopping about crotch level.

Kate's eyes widened, and her pulse raced.

He noticed her reaction and chuckled. "Don't get all excited, darlin'. Just wondering what to do about that zipper contraption."

With a huff, she tugged her shirt out of her pants to cover her hips. "Better?"

"It'll do." His piercing gaze continued its inspection up her body and stopped at her breasts.

"If you're thinking of making me look like a boy, we've got a problem, Tex. I can't just take them off like a pair of Reeboks."

Jack didn't seem to hear her. With a distant, speculative look in his eyes, he reached toward her.

Kate stepped back quickly. "Hey, watch where you're touching, mister!"

Jack's eyes flickered up to hers and his cheeks flushed. "I was just, um…just wondering if you were wearing your—" He pointed.

"My bra. Yes, as a matter of fact, I am wearing one," she said demurely. "Though I really don't know why my undergarments should be your concern."

"It's tight?"

"Huh?"

"Tight. The thing holds you."

As irked as she was with him, she almost laughed out loud. "A brassiere supports a woman's breasts, yes."

He raised his brows and nodded, obviously intrigued. "Then if you rearrange it slightly..."

She understood then what he was getting at. "Right."

Kate turned her back on Jack and reached up inside her shirt. Stretching out the sports bra she often wore in comfortable preference to the more lacy types, she eased it over her breasts so that the strongest band of elastic pressed firmly across the fullest part of her breasts. If she'd been built much larger it might not have worked. But as things stood, when she smoothed the shirt back into place, she looked as close to flat-chested as she'd been on her twelfth birthday.

"An improvement?"

Jack smirked. "Depends upon one's point of view, I guess."

"Shut up. Now what? Remember you only have an hour, and it's already..." She pulled her watch out of her pocket and looked at it. Barely a minute had passed since they'd arrived. She tapped the watch against her other hand and listened. It seemed to be running. "Never mind," she grumbled. "Let's get this over with."

Jack nodded, mounted the horse and pulled her up onto the saddle behind him. "You're my sister's boy, come out West to visit," he muttered.

"No one will believe I'm a boy," she said.

"People believe what they're told and think they see. Don't talk, and keep your hair under your hat. We'll be fine as long as—"

She felt him stiffen in the saddle. The muscles across his shoulders strained inside his shirt. She realized she'd wrapped her arms around his waist in an very unboylike gesture, and quickly released him.

"What is it?" she whispered.

"Yancy Kennard and his sidekicks."

"I take it he's not a friend?"

"I've got an order for his arrest," he ground out.

"But, Jack, we don't have time to—"

With a sense of horror, she felt him kick Pecos into a trot out through the alley and into the street, directly toward the three men who were mounting their horses in front of a white-washed building with a sign over the swinging doors, Sweet-water Inn.

One of them looked over his shoulder at them and said something to the other two. They turned, hands gravitating toward the pistols strapped to their hips.

It was only then that Kate realized something was missing from her and Jack's outfits. Neither of them was armed.

Chapter 5

Jack measured the quantity of liquor in the three men's eyes. A pint or more of whiskey apiece would render quick reactions and steady aims impossible. On the other hand, one or two shots made a man reckless. And a man emboldened by spirits, with a gun in his hand, was not something he took lightly. Ever.

"Howdy there, Ranger," the youngest of the three called across the road.

"Hello, Yancy. Surprised to see you still 'round here. After the big mess down in the salt flats, I figured you'd be lyin' low."

Kennard lifted one corner of his lip and sucked on a space between his teeth. "Reckon if a fella had anything to do with it, he would be, that's for sure."

He grinned, and Jack thought to himself, *He's not much more than a boy. Maybe nineteen or twenty-one years old, tops.* Sandy-colored hair fell forward over one eye, and a meager attempt at a mustache lined his top lip, partially hiding a scar.

"Hey, Ranger, my sister's been asking for you."

"Has she?"

"Pamela's done gone sweet on you."

Jack laughed tightly, keeping his eye on the young man's gun hand. It looked almost too relaxed, dangling at his side. "Can't imagine Pamela Kennard being sweet on anyone, other than herself.''

He hadn't meant any harm by the comment. In fact, he respected the woman. But Yancy stopped smiling.

Jack felt Kate pull back behind him after peeking over his shoulder. *Smart girl,* he thought. *Best to stay out of sight.* But Yancy's glance shifted with reptilian interest at even this small movement.

"My sister's boy from Vermont, come out to see the West,'' Jack said before anyone could ask.

Kate poked him in the back and whispered something in his ear. Jack ignored her. His every sense was involved in reading Yancy—the tone of his voice, the flicker of an eyelid, the telltale flexing of the fingers in his left hand.

"Is he now?'' Yancy muttered. He shot a look over his shoulder at one of his friends. "Surprised you have time to show the boy around, what with huntin' down those desperadoes done killed the colonel.''

Resolving the Great Salt War, as the press had come to call it, had been just one more task given to the Rangers. Lake beds that had provided free salt for centuries to whoever could cart it away, had been bought up, then fenced off and guarded by a Colonel William Walker. Mexicans, Texans and Indians alike had been furious, and more than one man on the talking end of a gun threatened to run straight over Walker's guards to get to the beds, which had become a lucrative source of income for many.

The short version was bloody fighting had broken out and Walker requested intervention from the governor. Since the old man had important connections in the state capital and Washington, as well, the governor dispatched a division of Rangers to ride south and settle things down. Before they could reach the flats, a man fitting Yancy's description had shot and killed the colonel and dragged his body through miles of brush before leaving what was left of it in the desert for the buzzards.

Walker might or might not have deserved killing, but Jack took flaunting justice seriously.

"I'll find time. Family always comes first,'' Jack said. "Now I think you'd better ride with me to have a word with my captain. We've been looking for you for days, boy.''

Yancy's lip curled in a sneer. "And what if I don't want to ride with you, Ranger?''

Kate nudged Jack more forcibly in the back. He couldn't for the life of him imagine why the woman wouldn't leave him alone to do his job.

"If you don't give me your gun and come peacefully," Jack said, easing his right hand toward his hip, "I'll have to insist."

Yancy squinted into the sun, tracking Jack's hand inch by inch. An amused smile tugged at his thin lips.

"You've got no gun!" Kate whispered. "Take us back to Vermont! Now! He'll shoot you!"

He already knew about the gun, of course. *No,* Jack thought, in a sudden flash of intuition. *This isn't how it ended. I wasn't mowed down today, in town, by Yancy and his boys.*

But did fate inevitably take the same twists and turns? He had to risk that it did.

Slowly Jack pressed both of his hands farther down, toward the pommel of the saddle. "You don't think I'd come after you unarmed, do you, Yancy?" he muttered low in his throat.

"Sweet Mary," the younger of the two men beside Yancy breathed. "He got two pistolas hid under that saddle. I can see 'em."

"Yer a blame fool, Ranger," Yancy said with a snicker, "likely to blow your horse's head off."

"That ain't where I'm aimin'."

To Jack's satisfaction, Yancy was no longer smiling. His younger companion looked back over his shoulder, as if eager to get out of range but equally afraid of what might happen if he ducked out on his friend.

The man on his right had a familiar face, full of sun-etched wrinkles, with a jagged scar running from one ear to his chin. He studied Jack for a moment, in silence, before shifting his glance past him. A muscle in his cheek twitched. "Give it up, boy. Here comes trouble."

In the next second all three had wheeled their horses. Spurs dug into horsehide. Hooves thundered through San Antonio as a detachment of dusty Rangers tore past Pecos and after the three riders.

Kate couldn't believe what had just happened. The well-mannered, educated Union officer she'd met in her attic seemed an entirely different person from the lawman who'd just called the bluff of three dangerous gunslingers. Back in his own element, Jack seemed absolutely sure of himself—determined and fearless. And, she thought with a thrill, he looked magnificent astride a horse.

When they'd first approached the three riders, Kate had been too absorbed in Jack to pay much attention to what was going on. She liked the way it felt—riding behind him, pressed up against his back, feeling his muscles work as he expertly guided Pecos forward. His every movement seemed so natural and masculine. She momentarily forgot time and home.

Then she realized they had no gun, and a horrible thought struck her. What if Jack got himself killed now...right *now* while she sat there on his horse. Or even worse, what if both of them were gunned down by these past-life miscreants? Either way, she'd never get back to Jesse and Anna.

A river of ice flashed through her veins, but there was nothing she could do! Her heart raced. Sweat dribbled down her chest, catching between her compressed breasts, and she prayed, prayed as she hadn't since she'd been a child. Not until the other Rangers showed up did she breathe again.

"Where you been, Jack?" one of the riders shouted as they raced past in a cloud of dust.

Kate let out a sigh of relief and dropped her cheek against Jack's back. She felt him tense and kick his horse into a gallop.

"Don't you dare!" she screamed.

The horse seemed to stop of its own volition, or maybe Jack was so surprised by her objection, he yanked on the reins.

"They don't need you to track down that man," she pointed out. "You don't even have a gun!"

Jack shrugged, looking more amused than disappointed. "You gotta admit, that was a pretty good bluff."

"It was stupid. You nearly got both of us killed. How could you forget you're not wearing a weapon?"

"I didn't actually forget," he said as she crooked one leg between them, swung around and jumped down from the saddle. "I guess I'm still a little disoriented by the trip back. It's been over a hundred years, remember?"

"It's pretty hard not to remember."

Kate studied the town surrounding them. Some of the flat-roofed shops and houses were built of stucco, washed in blues and yellows that reminded her of pictures she'd seen of villas on the Mediterranean. A church, bank and several businesses appeared to have been constructed of square-cut blocks of white limestone, as were some of the more prosperous-looking homes. These last were trimmed with graceful balconies, vivid red jalousies and pretty potted plants.

Many of the buildings were without doors, but some sported bright-striped blankets strung across the openings to keep out light or dust, or perhaps to provide a little more privacy. A cluster of houses at the end of an adjoining street had a distinctly rural Mexican appearance—mud brick with thatched roofs of river grass.

Despite her rush to return home and reassure herself that this time-travel business would work both coming and going, Kate was enchanted by the picturesque surroundings. She'd always thought of the Old West in muted sepia tones, but splashes of brilliant hues surprised her from every direction—in the clothing of passersby, carts loaded with produce, the brilliance of the sun and colorful pieces of pottery sitting in a casual display in front of one shop.

Jack rubbed his beard-stubbled chin and dismounted. "Sure could use a drink."

Kate snapped out of her trance and shook her head firmly. "No way. It must be getting late. Your hour must be up by now. You promised we'd leave."

He looked at her from beneath long, black eyelashes. "And you promised we could come back."

She felt pinned under his intense gaze, and had to turn away. Common sense warned her she should swear to anything that would make Jack take her directly back to Chester. Once safely there, she could refuse to let herself be spirited off to the past again. They'd been lucky this time. Only chance had brought those other Rangers along at the very moment they'd most needed them.

Kate blinked, then turned to stare suspiciously at Jack. Or was it chance?

"You were stalling for time, weren't you?" she demanded. "That business about concealing guns in your saddle was a ploy! You knew your fellow Rangers were on the way. How?"

A faint smile lifted one corner of Jack's lips. He shrugged.

The truth hit her with the impact of a lightning bolt. "You *know* what date it is because this is a day you've already lived through! You confronted those three before, and your friends showed up then, too."

"Figured it out, did you? You think I'd have risked your life if I hadn't known how the situation would turn out?"

Kate launched herself at him with an unladylike snarl. She pounded him on the chest with her fists. "You scared me half to death, you jerk! You terrified me! I thought they were going to kill you!"

He held her off at arm's length with one hand. "That's impossible."

"Why?"

"Because between now and the day I die, well, we know that I continue living."

"That's not funny," she snapped.

"Relax," he said, patting her on the arm. "Apparently I'm invincible until that day, and it's almost a week away."

She glared at him, feeling suddenly drained of terror. What remained was a vague feeling of annoyance with Jack and, conversely, a rather pleasant exhilaration and euphoria unlike any she'd ever experienced. She'd just taken part in a dramatic moment in history, one that anyone else from her century could only read about.

Kate looked around, wishing she could talk to some of the people in the town. A woman with exotic Mexican features walked past, and Kate longed to stop her and question her about the details of her life. She felt insatiably curious. Where did she get her clothing? Did she have a family? How did she view her own life? What were her hopes and dreams?

This was like stepping into the pages of a history book, and Kate drank in the rich atmosphere.

Then the sane, safe half of her personality kicked in. She turned toward the setting sun. "It *is* getting late. The children must be home from school, wondering where I am."

"Give me just ten minutes," Jack said, handing her Pecos's reins as he started away from her.

"Jack."

"Ten minutes . . . across the street at the Sweetwater," he called over his shoulder. "I promise I'll behave myself, and you'll appreciate the result."

She threw up her hands, at a loss for what he meant. "You'd just better be back here in time!" she shouted after him.

Bending down, she picked a pebble from between her toes. "I'm not waiting one minute longer for you!"

He lifted a hand in laconic reply without turning around, and ambled into the saloon.

Kate led Pecos back to the water trough and sat down on the ground, for lack of a better place, to wait for Jack. He probably intended to question customers in the drinking establishment, she reasoned, to gather information and narrow the field of suspects for his killer. She drew shapes in the dust with her finger. Personally, her money would be on that punk Yancy who'd just ridden off with the Rangers on his heels. He looked capable of anything, probably wouldn't blink at shooting a man in the back.

Kate looked at the row of hearts she'd sketched in the dirt, then brushed them away in exasperation. What on earth was she thinking?

Sometime later, she looked up from where she knelt in the dirt, trying to snag her Reeboks from beneath the porch with the pointed end of a stick. She couldn't believe her eyes.

A tall, long-legged man strode toward her. He was clean-shaven, square-jawed, and his glossy ebony hair had been trimmed neatly over a pair of shockingly blue eyes. His pants and shirt both looked fresh and new. The muscles of his strong neck worked in subtle coordination with his easy gait, but she thought she could see a little knot of tension in his brow—as if he were a little worried about her reaction.

She decided she'd better not overdo her enthusiasm. No sense feeding his already-healthy male ego.

"Well, you don't look half-bad cleaned up, Ranger." She stood up and brushed off her hands.

"Thank you, ma'am." He grinned and set a black Stetson on his head, tugging down the brim rakishly over one eye. "The bartender moonlights as a barber. He can even rustle up some new duds for the right price. Sure you don't want to take time out to grab yourself a quick bath? You could use one."

She tried to look highly offended. "Thanks to you and your handiwork with Texas dust." She pointed at the opening under the porch. "I can't reach my shoes."

He shook his head. "Impractical monstrosities. Imagine—white leather. Sure you want them back?"

"You bet I want them back."

He knelt down on the ground and reached beneath the planks with one long arm.

"What about the rattlers?" she gasped, horrified at the thought of his bare hand disappearing into the dangerous shadows.

"Diamondbacks prefer rocks for shade. I was just trying to make you feel better about leavin' them."

"You creep!"

"Now there you go, name-callin' again."

He straightened up with her shoes in one hand, socks in the other.

"I could come up with some better names for you, believe me," she sputtered, sitting down on the ground to hastily pull on her footwear. She didn't bother lacing the athletic shoes before springing to her feet. "Now, do your thing."

Jack looked around regretfully. "We really can't stay a while longer?"

"No."

He hesitated, suddenly solemn. "Kate, what if we can't get back? What would you do then?"

She had the distinct feeling that he was testing her.

"I don't know what I'd do," she said, her eyes locking with his. "Everything I know and care about is back in Chester, nearly a hundred and thirty years from now—my children, my friends, my job..." She involuntarily shuddered. "Jack, please don't mess with my mind this way. I've kept my part of the bargain so far. I'll help you again. Just, just please—"

The words dried up on her lips. Jack stepped forward and silently wrapped his arms around her. His embrace was warm and, once again, he rested his chin on the top of her head, as if to enclose her body with his from as many angles as possible.

Slowly the familiar reeling sensation overtook her, spinning her, pulling her through the years. As before, she felt compelled to close her eyes against the frantic blur of images, colors and motion. Lives by the thousands and the poignant dramas of decades unfolded and rushed past, assaulting her senses. Around her, Kate sensed the joy, grief, dreams and pain of all humankind. And still she didn't look, couldn't bear to chance even a glimpse, for she sensed such a profound experience would be too much for one person to bear.

Her fingers dug into Jack's muscled arms, and she felt his reassuring presence close more tightly around her. *Without this . . . him, holding me . . .* she thought wildly, *I'd be lost.* The abject fear of flying off into eternity—never again to see her children, the farm, her house—consumed her.

Life is short, so very short, she thought. One moment a new life began. A beat in time later it was over.

Gradually her vertigo eased, time slowed and a natural heaviness settled over her body. She felt a firm surface beneath her feet. Slowly, slowly, she opened one eye.

They were in the attic. Her attic. And, remarkably, afternoon sunlight was streaming through the windows.

"We're back!" Kate cried, breaking out of Jack's arms.

She ran around the room he'd fashioned for himself, touching the sagging leather chair, leaping to reach errant cobwebs with her fingertips, swinging around to hug an antique doll that sat on a trunk.

Kate faced Jack, her cheeks tingling, excitement frothing through her veins.

He looked at her, his face solemn, eyes a shade duller than she remembered them being in San Antonio.

"What's wrong? It worked!" she shouted. "It worked. Isn't that fantastic? We're back, and—"

Jack swerved away to stand at the window. She closed her mouth and waited for a moment, thrown by his change of mood, unsure of how to approach him.

"Jack? What's wrong?" Tentatively Kate crossed the attic and looked up into his strong face. "You're angry," she stated when he didn't respond.

He shook his head, staring at the black felt Stetson, which he'd taken off of his head and now gripped by the brim.

"But it went so well, Jack," she continued. "I know you wanted to stay, but—"

He wrenched around abruptly to face her and pressed his hand over her mouth. It was a gentle pressure, but the quick warmth suffusing her lips from his rough palm surprised her. Kate moved a step backward and bumped into a post.

"Stop talking," he said gruffly, his eyes a darker, more intense blue than she'd imagined they could ever become. "This has nothing to do with my wanting to stay in San Antonio."

She crinkled her eyebrows questioningly.

Jack's hand moved, as if he'd determined to drop it away from her lips. Instead of leaving her skin, his fingertips trailed across her cheeks and down her throat. His eyes never left hers.

"You can't possibly know how much what you're doing means to me," he said tightly.

Kate forced a tremulous smile, confused by his behavior, but not frightened. "No big deal. I want things to work out for you."

"Do you?"

She concentrated on the words passing between them, trying not to let the evocative path of his hand distract her. His wide fingers brushed lightly from her throat, across her shoulder and down her arm, raising delicious chills in their wake.

"Why sh-shouldn't I want your life to w-work out for you?" Kate stammered. "You seem like a nice person—" she smiled "—I mean, ghost. You were murdered. That certainly wasn't fair and . . ."

Kate knew she was babbling, but she couldn't help it. His eyes were doing strange things to her insides.

"I mean," she continued helplessly, "keeping that from happening again, stopping someone from shooting you, well, that's just a decent thing for one human being to do for another. Don't you think?"

He nodded. "It is decent. And selfless. Remarkably selfless, Kate Fenwick."

The words were soft—just a husky whisper from his throat and no more than a statement of fact—but Kate couldn't ignore the taut melody underplaying their deceptively simple lyrics, or the tension in Jack's face. His eyes delved into hers, seeking some other answer.

"I'm not being totally selfless, I guess," she admitted softly. She drew her tongue across her lips, and they felt summer chapped—strange for April in Vermont—a reminder of the Texas heat. "I like you, Jack. Of course I don't want you to die."

"Even though you know I must someday?"

She swallowed. "Yes, but not that way, not alone in a dusty desert town with a bullet in your back." Damn it, she wouldn't cry for this man, this stranger . . . not again, and certainly not in front of him!

"Kate," he murmured. "For God's sake, don't fall in love with me."

Lifting her chin, she stared at him. The urgency of his words, if not their actual meaning, snapped her back into focus. She took a breath and composed herself. "What makes you think I'm falling in love with you, Jack Ramsey, a ghost!"

"I didn't claim you were in love with a ghost. I'm not sure that's possible. But you might be in love with a man's soul."

Kate tried to duck out of the tight space between Jack's chest and the post she'd backed into.

He reached out, seized her by the upper arms and drew her firmly back into the circle of his embrace. "Just as a man can fall in love with a woman's soul," he continued as if she had done nothing to interrupt him, "which is wholly another matter than enjoying the way she looks, how she feels in his arms and all the many pleasures of her body."

Kate swallowed, looking up into the marvelously varied contours of his face. "I—I'm not— I don't know what you're talking about," she choked out.

He pressed closer to her, until his breath caressed her quivering lips. "You married Max," he said. "But you were never in love with his soul." He gazed deeply into her eyes, as if through them he could read her most intimate thoughts.

Kate closed her lids, unwilling to let him see more, unable to think while he was so close. A thousand sensations swam through her veins, and overpowering them all was an unsettling heat that built inside of her. Low down. An aching, needful heat that she hadn't allowed herself to feel or satisfy for over a year.

"I loved Max, I cared deeply for him," she argued weakly. "He was the father of my children."

"That's different," he whispered. "We were meant for each other, you and I, Kathlee—" His voice cracked, and a horrified expression contorted his features.

Flinching, Jack quickly stepped back and released her.

Kate reached for his hand and held on. "That's the problem, isn't it, Jack?" she said, pushing her own hurt aside to confront the issue head-on. "You're afraid of my falling in love with you, or your falling in love with me—or maybe both. But you and Kathleen are fated to mate. I have nothing to do with your life, your future. I'm an interruption, a necessary detour along the way. That's why you were warning me, right?"

His eyes brimmed with pain, and he looked away from her. "I'm sorry. What an awful thing to do, come out with her name like that." He turned back and touched her cheek tenderly with the side of his thumb. "You're right. The only reason I'm allowed another shot at surviving that day is Kathleen."

She stared up at him, at the eyes that refused to leave hers even as he swore he belonged to another woman. "I don't believe it," she whispered. "God help me, but I don't believe you were meant for a woman who refused to follow you when you really needed her."

"I am—it must be," he insisted. "I can't explain it, Kate, because I don't myself understand the reason why things sometimes happen as they do. The Rules..." He shook his head. "I do know that Kathleen and I were meant to marry and raise our children, and that it's important for some reason beyond my or your understanding that this come about."

Kate stared at him. He meant what he was saying, meant it from the depths of his being. Yet he seemed just as torn by their predicament as she felt.

Nevertheless, she couldn't ignore the way his eyes devoured her.

"Then you have no desire—" she murmured "—to kiss me?"

Jack's expression softened as he pulled her into a reassuring embrace, his arms enclosing her much as they had during their travel through time. Even as he tried to comfort her, she was aware of his arousal—the shallowness of his breathing, the thin sheen of sweat that rose on his upper lip.

"I didn't say anything about not wanting to kiss you," he said tightly. "But I won't do it."

The certainty of his tone triggered a perversely impish impulse in her. "Are you sure?" Kate asked, then immediately kicked herself. What did she want from him? He belonged to another woman, and she respected that. He'd told her he meant to return to Kathleen, thwarting the powers of death if need be. Why was she flirting with him like a schoolgirl?

Because you're aching for a man. The answer came to her. *You're just as aroused as he is, and there he stands, looking like a damn Western hero. John Wayne, Clint Eastwood and the Lone Ranger all rolled into one!*

A wave of embarrassment washed over Kate. She withdrew her arms from around his neck and veered away. "I'm sorry. Jack, I don't know what's gotten into me." She laughed, but her voice sounded strained to her own ears. "Must be jet lag or something—"

She was dashing for the stairs even as he shouted for her to come back.

Chapter 6

Kate's foot hit the third riser from the top of the staircase at the same moment Jack locked his arms around her and lifted her effortlessly back up to the attic floor. She was trembling uncontrollably when he turned her around and enfolded her in a cocoon of muscle, denim and flannel.

"I was lying," he said gruffly, his words muffled as he pressed his lips into tangled brown tendrils at her crown. "I *do* want to kiss you. I want—"

He replaced words with action, cradling her in his arms, brushing his lips over her cheek, her jaw, the delicate point of her chin, then sweeping them up to her mouth. Testing her lips with his tongue, he parted them and tasted her.

Kate lifted her arms around his neck, welcoming his kisses, shutting out all reason, all question of tomorrow, blocking out the powers of fate. Only that moment existed, and for that single blip in time, Jack would be hers and she his. . . .

With blind hunger, Jack fed on her lips and throat. Pulling open her shirt, he sent buttons rattling across the floor. His mouth found her breast and sucked feverishly at the pink nipple, moving his tongue across and around its hardening bud, savoring her as though he'd been waiting all of these many decades for her alone. For this chance to love Kate Fenwick in a way she'd only mistily sensed a man could love a woman.

Max had seemed to possess a limited sense of passion, and unleashing what he did have was something his nature didn't allow. He had been her first and only love. As tender partners, they'd carefully satisfied each other. They'd made love, always in their bed, never too loudly, never past the point of absolute control. And now Kate realized that those times had been only a fraction of what a man was capable of doing for a woman.

Heat sizzled through her veins as she felt Jack's moist lips again and again draw the sensitive flesh of her breast into his mouth. He devoured her between his own moans of pleasure.

"Stop me!" he choked out suddenly. She couldn't tell if he was addressing her or some great, distant power.

From a dim corner of her mind, the thought crept in that they might well have crossed some forbidden line. The mortal and the spirit, clashing in passion, bordering on the most intimate of human acts. Kate pushed her fear of the unknown aside, this one time. Her need for Jack was as unquenchable as his for her.

Later, she thought fleetingly, *later, we'll sort all of this out.*

With a groan of pleasure, he cupped her breasts in his palms, nuzzling, kissing, caressing both supple globes with a frenzied need. A bolt of heat shot through her, following a straight line from her erect nipples to her liquid center.

Remarkably, Kate felt the short, sharp rush of her first orgasm in over a year. It slammed into her with such force, it left her weak-kneed and gasping for breath.

Kate gripped Jack's shoulders and staggered back against the top of the stair rail. Closing her eyes she shuddered deliciously.

"Tell me to stop, Kate. I swear I will!" He stared at her, still clutching her to him as if he were helpless to stave off his craving for her flesh without a command from her lips.

Kate's fingers followed the muscled line of his neck into the short hairs at his nape. "Please, Jack. Make love to me." Her voice dropped away to a whisper.

For a moment, he looked into her eyes, as if trying to be sure that she meant what she said. He must have found something there that convinced him. Slowly he moved his right hand away from her breasts, unfastened the button on her jeans then managed the zipper. The pads of his fingers felt cool against the heat of the burning flesh inside her briefs. Although the heavy denim tightened around her hips, he worked his hand downward with sure intention.

Anticipating the imminent contact of his fingertips with her most intimate self rocked Kate to her bones. He was almost there, almost *there!* But he hesitated once more.

For a second, Kate feared he would withdraw; then he gently touched the already-wet folds and plunged his fingers deep within her. She drew a sharp breath. The erotic pleasure shocked her, and pleasured her in the same moment. This, she sensed, was what she'd unknowingly longed for—this unpredictable wildness, the animallike alter ego of a gentleman that harkened back to time immemorial when men took their women in battle or barter and made them their mates—body, heart and soul.

Yes, Jack could be tender, calm and reasonable—but he could also fill the hidden hungers in her.

Kate clung to him, her lips buried in the hairs on his chest, hazily realizing she must have torn open his shirt in her own frenzied response. Wanting to spur him on, to make sure he continued doing the wonderful things to her he was doing, she kissed the muscled mounds, flicking her tongue delicately over his flat, brown nipples, testing his response.

A low moan of pleasure escaped his lips. She drew her teeth across a hardening circle. With a guttural cry, Jack thrust his fingers deeper still, lifting her, moving within her in a relentless, primal rhythm as they stood, body to body in the dim attic.

Wave after wave of delicious sensations, so intense they verged on pain, released within her.

Kate felt all awareness of her muscles drift away. Her limbs trembling, she leaned against Jack, uttering whimpers that lengthened to a prolonged cry of ecstasy. Jack's mouth crushed down over hers, cutting off her scream.

Riding each surge of her orgasm, Kate dug her fingers into the muscles of Jack's arms. At last, her body's quaking gentled and settled into a sated hum. Still she clung to him, breathing too hard, caring too much and knowing the most wonderful and most awful thing had just happened between them.

* * *

Jack held Kate against him, shaken to his roots by what he'd just done.

Not long after he'd dragged her back up the steps and started kissing her, he'd realized that his capabilities were limited. He knew he'd be unable to fully respond to her, as any mortal man certainly would have, by consummating their passion.

Reckon that's as it should be, he thought now with a clearer head. There were lines between life and death that simply shouldn't be crossed.

Yet he had felt all the familiar urges. The hunger had reached down inside of him and grabbed hold, refusing to let go until he acted.

At first it had seemed as if it would be enough to kiss Kate, just sample her sweetness—then he'd force himself to release her.

But he'd lost control, completely and without regret. He'd desperately needed to make Kate share his agony, to make her understand how hopelessly she aroused him. Only, he hadn't counted on going as far as he'd gone. If he was still capable of reading a woman's reactions, Kate had come out of the experience a many-times satisfied lady.

Oddly enough, that made him feel worse. He'd treated her like a common saloon girl. He'd denied her the respect she deserved.

Jack didn't know what modern women thought of men who backed them into corners and brazenly assaulted them. But, where he was from, what he'd just done to Kate was cause for a father or older brother to break out the shotgun.

Kate shifted in his arms, reminding him he had to say something.

"I'm so sorry, darlin'," Jack murmured, annoyed when the words came out still husky with passion. He coughed once, hoping that would help. "I don't know why I let myself go like that."

"I don't care," she said.

"You should care. I took advantage of you. You were leaving. I stopped you and forced myself on you because I was terrified you wouldn't come back."

To his amazement, she looked up at him and giggled.

"That'll do the trick every time, Ranger."

Jack reached down and leveled her chin up to make her look at him. "I'm serious, Kate. I didn't plan that. I didn't want that to happen."

She stiffened, and a wary shadow crossed her brown eyes. "You didn't?"

"No, I...well, I did, obviously, *want* that and more. But the way I acted was pure hot-blooded selfishness—"

"You're dead, Jack," she said dryly. "I doubt you have blood—hot or otherwise."

"Y-yes, of course, but—" He was stammering. Why was he stammering? He never stammered. "I just mean, I don't want you to think I intended to trap you up here and rape you."

"The idea never entered my mind," she said, smiling at him in an all-too-permissive way. "I liked everything you did to me. *Everything,*" she repeated with emphasis, as she pulled away just enough to tuck her shirt into her jeans.

He watched her hands move, smoothing the fabric beneath the waistband, and felt himself begin the dangerous climb back up to lust. Jack forced himself to turn away, clenching his fists, trying with little success to get a grip on himself.

They stood quietly for a moment, then he felt Kate move over to stand behind him. Her hands rested flat against his shoulder blades.

"You didn't have an orgasm, did you?" she asked.

He was shocked that she'd even ask, that she'd bring up such things. But he reminded himself of the conversations he'd overheard through the decades he'd spent in the attic. He'd learned that women and men spoke much more frankly these days about sex.

"It's not important," he said quickly.

"It *is,* if you want it," she said. "You should have let me—"

"No!" He spun around and glared at her. "It's not a question of what I want. I just can't...not here...not while I'm—" He threw up his hands in exasperation. How could he explain The Rules when he himself only had the foggiest sense of them. "Listen, darlin', I don't know for sure, but making love seems to be one of those things that a ghost can't do. Apparently, I can touch you and...well, please you, but the ability to satisfy my own needs—"

"I see," Kate said, removing her hands. She tucked her fingers inside his clenched right fist, easing it open to make room for her hand. "I'm sorry. I'd have liked to return the favor."

"It's not important. I should be concentrating on other things—maybe that's the reason I'm not allowed."

"But you shouldn't feel guilty about making love to me like that," she whispered. "I don't regret it. You shouldn't. It was an exciting gift. I'd almost forgotten how wonderful—"

Kate's eyes flickered open wide in alarm.

"What is it?" he asked.

Then he heard the sounds, too—high-pitched childish squeals, and a slamming door somewhere in the house below. "Mom! Mom, where are you? Jesse's got my hat and won't give it back!"

"Jesse and Anna," Kate said with a sigh, a sheepish smile spreading across her flushed face. "I'm a terrible mother. I'd almost forgotten I had kids, I was enjoying myself so much."

Jack couldn't help smiling. She had a naughty streak in her that he liked a lot. She liked games, and love was the most enjoyable of them all—even better than a good hand of poker. But for it to be right, really right, love had to have special players, those dedicated to sitting out the game to the very end. That was one promise he knew he couldn't make or keep for Kate.

"You'd better go to them," he said sadly. "After they're in bed tonight we'll talk."

"Yes." Standing on tiptoe, she kissed him lightly on the cheek and smiled. "I'll be back."

Jack watched her go, this time stopping himself from reaching out to hold her when she walked down the steps and through the door. When she'd closed it behind her, after looking back one last time with a sweet smile, he slumped into the leather chair and dropped his head into his hands.

Wrong... wrong... wrong!

What had he done... to Kate and to Kathleen? Kate Fenwick had generously offered to help him. But what she really needed was a mortal man capable of meeting her needs and being her partner for life. Kathleen was the woman he was fated to marry and with whom he'd have children. He must be stronger, keep his priorities straight. He had to do better than this!

There was no avoiding Kate, though. No getting around the fact he had to use her to return to San Antonio. He vowed he would steel himself against succumbing to her again. He would make sure they didn't end up in each other's arms, even if he had to hurt her feelings to do it. Much as he longed to touch her, even now, he must restrain himself, for both of their sakes.

"I'm sorry, Kate," he whispered into the musty half-light of the attic. "I wish I could be the man you're waiting for...."

Kate stepped into the hallway at the same instant two small bodies torpedoed into her. Jesse struck her waist-high, and Anna tackled her around the thighs.

"Where were you?" Anna shouted. "We been looking all over for you."

Kate pulled the two fireballs along with her into the kitchen. "Have you been looking for very long?" she asked, feeling guilty. She was thankful they'd had the good sense to stay on the farm. They'd probably wandered down to the barns and passed the time bothering Carson, as Jesse had said they would.

"Ever since we got home."

She looked at the kitchen clock and was shocked to see that it read only 3:30 p.m. She and Jack had probably been back for an hour. That meant they'd only been gone for thirty minutes or so, modern time! She looked out the window. It was still light outside.

Weird, she thought.

Yet maybe time was relative to where one was in history.

"I'm hungry!" Jesse wailed. "When's supper?"

"Not for a while," Kate said, although she herself was famished. "But we can have a snack."

She lovingly freed herself from her offspring's clutches. Kate pulled a gallon of milk from the refrigerator and placed the cookie jar on the table—a signal Jesse took seriously. He immediately dropped his book bag and rushed for a chair.

"Wash your hands first, you two. Then you can eat," Kate said, placing two large molasses cookies on a napkin at each child's place.

She poured their milk and sat down with them, taking a couple of cookies for herself and munching as she listened to their happy tales of friends and school, and complaints about the mean teachers who gave them too much work, and the usual bullies who wouldn't leave them alone.

Jesse had his father's blond hair, as did Anna, but both children shared Kate's features. Their eyes were a rich, intelligent brown, set wide apart. Their noses were small, centered over firm, rounded chins. Although they had long arms and legs, their bodies were compact and sturdy. The effect was deceptive. When standing apart from their classmates, they appeared tall for their ages. Beside their friends, they were only average height.

"I'm going to beat up Eddie Johnson one of these days," Jesse muttered darkly between bites of cookie.

Kate's attention immediately focused on her son. She'd been preoccupied with thoughts of Jack. In fact, she hadn't been able to stop thinking about him since she'd left the attic. The sensation of his hands on her flesh and the yearning in his eyes haunted her. Physical and emotional connections between them seemed to strengthen, rather than weaken, in his absence. She tried to brush all of that aside and pay attention to other, more controllable parts of her life.

"Why would you want to beat up Eddie?" she asked Jesse.

"'Cause he's so mean," he stated. "The creep deserves it."

"Maybe you could set a good example for him," she suggested.

Jesse scowled at her. "Like how?"

"Oh, I don't know…" She fished around for examples. How had Jack handled those nineteenth-century punks? He'd threatened to blow their heads off. Not exactly the example she was looking for. "You could offer to be his friend."

"I would hate it if Jesse were Eddie's friend," Anna burst out. Her lower lip quivered as she looked, wide-eyed, at her mother, tears pooling beneath her long, pale lashes.

Kate reached out and patted her hand. "Why is that, sweetheart?"

"H-he calls me names," Anna said with a sniffle.

"He pushed her down, too," Jesse added solemnly.

Kate looked from her son, back to Anna, who was nodding in agreement. What had been going on that she'd been totally unaware of? Children playing, even a little roughly, was to be expected. But if this boy had targeted Anna as a convenient victim for violent pranks, she needed to be there for her, to protect her and make sure things didn't get out of hand. Jesse must have had a reason for feeling he needed to stand up for his sister.

Kate grilled them both and found out there had, indeed, been a series of "attacks" and they were taking place exclusively on the school playground, during lunch break. Apparently, the supervision of parent volunteers wasn't as effective as she'd been led to believe by notices sent home from school.

Kate felt a bitter twinge of guilt for not being there herself. But her work hours coincided with the school day, so she'd had to find other ways of helping out. Her contribution had been to organize weekend fund-raisers, to enable the school to purchase computers and sports equipment. So far, she'd been quite successful at it.

But that still didn't resolve the problem of a bully harassing her children.

Kate decided she'd write a note to Anna's teacher, letting her know of her concerns. Mrs. White would hopefully speak to the playground monitors. Yes, that was the way to handle it. It would work just as well as requesting a parent-teacher conference, which might seem an overreaction.

In the back of Kate's mind she wondered if she wasn't looking for ways to avoid entanglements in her children's lives, right now when she was contemplating going away again with Jack. She felt torn and uneasy with her decision. Yet, part of her grew more and more excited as she felt herself being drawn into his life.

Kate felt terribly brave and adventurous. How wonderful it had been to witness and take part in a remarkable period in history. Besides, Jack needed her. Without her, he'd never fulfill his destiny. Without her, he'd die a senseless death, still a young man.

Kate looked up from her napkin where two cookies had lain. The napkin was bare, but for a few sugary crumbs. She didn't remember eating the cookies.

Jesse itched around on his chair, looking restlessly toward the kitchen door. "Can I go out, Mom? I want to go see Aunt Barb's fat horse."

This time of year, as spring began to warm Vermont, Barbara's pregnant mares roamed out of their cedar-lined stalls into the meadows, fresh with new clover. The children had started taking keen interest in the birth process after Barbara delivered a graphic explanation of the steps by which horses produced babies.

Kate had laughingly told Barbara later that she suspected her children understood less than half of what she'd told them. But the expectation of the newborn horses virtually in their backyard had been enough to set their minds whirling. Jesse and Anna spent most of every afternoon down by the barns, talking soothingly to the mares and stroking their velvety noses.

"Okay, you two run along. Just stay out of Carson's way. He has work to do."

"We won't bother him!" Jesse shouted as he tore across the room toward the door.

Kate leapt up and headed him off. "Coat." She pointed to his down-filled jacket, hanging on the back of his chair. "It's cold out."

He grumbled, but slipped his arms into the parka before rocketing through the back door, Anna close behind.

A whisper of chill air slipped in from the unheated mudroom. Kate closed the door firmly to conserve precious heat.

With a sigh, she sat down at the kitchen table, pulling a writing tablet and pen from the narrow drawer under the maple tabletop. She wrote a carefully worded note to Mrs. White—brief but to the point. She didn't want the woman to feel as if she were accusing her or her aides of negligence, but she did intend for them to realize she felt the situation might become serious if the errant Eddie wasn't controlled.

When she'd finished that, she crossed the kitchen to the phone and picked it up. Today was Friday, a lucky happenstance. Jack would want to return to San Antonio as soon as possible. Over the weekend she wouldn't have to find a way to get out of work. She would, however, take Barbara up on her baby-sitting offer, and dialed her friend's number.

The phone rang four times, then Barbara's answering machine picked up.

The recorded throaty voice made Kate smile. Barbara was a wonderful friend—never complaining, independent, smart, hardworking and loyal. Unlike Kate, she never seemed timid about any new situation. Go For It! seemed to be her motto. And off she steamrolled through life. That was how she'd built herself a thriving business.

The only thing that seemed to be missing from Barbara's happily active life was a man. She'd apparently never been married, and although that might suit her in some ways, Kate had wondered.... Was it by choice she remained single? Or did she find it difficult to relate to men with her own forceful personality?

Whatever... Barbara's go-for-it philosophy was what Kate decided she must adopt this time. As she'd sat listening to Jesse and Anna complain about their troubles, she'd made up her mind that she could do no less for Jack than she was doing for her children. Standing up to the bullies of the world, whether the inevitable elementary school brand or the more dangerous gunslinging brute of an earlier time, was important. Her fair and just nature demanded no less.

But why risk everything she had to help a stranger? she asked herself for the hundredth time. Somewhere in the background she heard the answering machine beep after Barbara's voice had invited her to leave a message. Why indeed? Was her motive simple compassion for another human being? Or was there more to it? Was she in love with Jack Ramsey, as he'd suggested she might be?

The suspicion struck her with such impact, she couldn't speak, couldn't even mouth the words of her message for Barbara.

In love? Surely not. How could she *love* Jack? He wasn't even a man! He was a ghost.

No, she couldn't—wouldn't—allow herself to dwell on that possibility. On the other hand, he was definitely appealing—charming and polite in his Vermont embodiment, masculine and tough in his world as a Texas Ranger.

Oh, yes, she could definitely fall for a man like that...a man who was capable of arousing deeply buried feminine instincts. Because Jack could do what he'd done to her—unleash marvelous, forbidden feelings—she had to be careful, very careful of him. Whether or not he intended to do so, he had the power to destroy her. He could work his way into her heart, use her to gain his ends, then ditch her in this century to nurse her shattered heart.

I refuse to let him do that to me, she thought. *I won't confuse love with what can only be lust. I won't do it!*

"You won't do what?" a voice asked in her ear.

Kate turned her head and stared blankly at the telephone receiver in her hand. "Barb?"

"Yeah, is that you, Kate?"

Kate laughed. "I didn't realize I was talking out loud. Did I say anything else?"

"I don't know, I just walked into the room and you were leaving some kind of message on my machine. What won't you do? You sounded furious. I hope I haven't—"

"No, of course I'm not angry with you. I was just . . . just babbling, I guess. Listen," Kate said, quickly changing the subject, "I've decided for sure that I want to go away for the weekend."

"This weekend?"

"Yes." She hesitated. "I know it's awfully short notice but—"

"Don't worry about it! When do you want me over there?"

Kate thought fast. She couldn't very well ask Barbara to come to her house, then disappear up the attic stairs right under her nose.

"Anna has a gymnastics lesson at nine tomorrow morning," Kate said. "Could you pick up the kids at eight-thirty and take them to the Y? I'll say goodbye before you leave and plan on being back Sunday night."

"May I ask where you're going?"

She didn't want to lie to Barbara. "One of those outdoorsy places where you can ride horses and get lots of sun."

"Like a dude ranch or spa?"

"More like a survival weekend," Kate muttered.

"Oh, one of those team-effort, learn self-confidence escapes? You'll have to tell me if you like it—sounds right up my alley."

Kate shook her head, wondering what she'd let herself in for. She might have to do some inventing after all.

"And your 'friend' is going with you?" Barbara asked pointedly.

"Yes, *my friend* is going with me," Kate mimicked her, good-naturedly.

"Will I get to meet him?"

The question threw her. Could anyone but she see Jack? "Maybe someday," she said hastily. It hurt that she couldn't share Jack with her best friend. She sensed that Barbara and he would have hit if off famously.

"The shy type, huh?" Barbara laughed. "Well, when I do get to meet him, I promise to be on my best behavior and not scare him away."

Kate took a deep breath. "Thanks, Barb. I really appreciate your being here for me."

"No trouble."

"One other thing..."

"Yeah?"

"You remember I asked you once about the kids—you know, if something ever happened to me..." They'd had a serious discussion a week after Max died. Kate had asked Barbara to be the children's guardian if the need ever arose. After getting the nod from Barb, she'd had her wishes added to her will.

From the other end of the line came a soft scraping sound, as if Barbara had moved the receiver closer to her mouth. "Is something wrong, Kate?"

"No, I just—" Kate bit down on her lip. How could she explain the fears that had tormented her when she'd traveled with Jack? "If anything every happened to me, is taking Jesse and Anna still all right with you?"

"Of course, but...Kate, are you all right? You're not sick or anything, are you? You aren't flying to some clinic in Mexico to try some experimental drug or anything?"

Kate forced out a laugh. "You have a wild imagination. No, I'm not dying of some incurable disease."

"You sure you're okay."

"I'm fine."

She could hear the other woman let out a long breath.

"Well, that's a relief. I worry about you sometimes. Why are you suddenly checking up on your kids' auxiliary mom?"

"I guess...I just don't travel much. Got the jitters. You know how I hate flying."

"Take a Dramamine—you'll be fine."

"Sure," Kate said. "I'll be fine."

But Kate wasn't sure at all. Because every second she spent with Jack in his world, she was risking her own life. He might be temporarily immortal, although she had some doubts about that. But she was reasonably certain that she was just as vulnerable in 1867 as she was in her own lifetime.

Kate hung up the phone with a hollow feeling in her stomach. It was still there when she climbed the attic stairs later that night.

Chapter 7

All evening, as Jack waited, he paced the attic floor. He could faintly hear Kate, moving around her kitchen, clinking pots and pans. Eventually, the aroma of cooking food wafted up the stairs. Warming milk, the sharp tang of Vermont cheddar cheese, the fresh buttery scent of golden corn—corn from cobs he'd seen Kate pick from her garden last fall.

"Oh, boy, macaroni and cheese!" her little boy shouted as he bounded up the stairs to the bathroom to wash before eating.

Jack admired her knack for gardening and using the fresh vegetables and local dairy products in dishes she cooked for herself and her children. Kate was a clever woman—capable, strong even when she seemed insecure about her own abilities.

She'd always "hung in there," he thought, conjuring up one of her own pet phrases. "Hang in there, Anna. You'll get it right next time," she told her daughter before driving her to the lessons they called gymnastics. "Hang in there. You'll do okay," she'd say to her son about his schoolwork.

He sniffed again, letting simple, homey, kitchen smells he'd forgotten fill him up. Oh, how he longed to sample her cooking. Although he'd had no appetite for food since he'd passed from the living world, he'd found himself ravenously hungry when they'd taken their short trip back to San Antonio. Returning to life must have awakened more than one dormant function.

Now, the luscious bouquet of Kate's cooking beckoned to him, and he descended the creaking stairs, fighting the urge to throw himself on the door at the bottom of the flight.

He got as far as the last step and reached out for the knob. The thing simply dissolved through his fingers. He couldn't grip it, turn it, shove it. Nothing.

Then he felt the warning tingle course through his arm and into his shoulder and chest.

"Forbidden territory, right?" he muttered. "I know, I know. I figured out my boundaries long ago. But so much has changed," he said with a sigh. "I had to try again."

After all, he'd been able to use his hands quite effectively to please Kate. It made sense he'd be able to employ them in other ways. But perhaps, he thought, there had been some reason he was unaware of, some purpose behind his being allowed to please her.

Slowly the dull gnawing in his stomach subsided. He wished Kate would come to him, though, and they could leave again, right away. Rediscovering his taste for food gave him one more reason to return to Texas.

He paced the floor, restless, brooding, no longer as secure as he'd once been in his belief that Kathleen was the only woman for him.

Jack planted his feet and stared down at the age-cracked trunk that contained his uniform and personal effects that someone, perhaps Kathleen herself, had packed tenderly away. He had learned it had taken over a month for word of his untimely death to reach his fiancée.

After that, Kathleen had continued living with her parents in Chester. She never married, never bore children—the children they should have had. She cared for her aging parents until their deaths, then she herself passed quietly away—creating barely a ripple in the pond of time with her own uncomplicated life. She wasn't practical and tough spirited like Kate, but she had been lovely and sweet, and he'd loved her because a young man cherishes the very things he is not and can never be.

Jack remembered, again, the war.

He'd fought for the North and been shocked and sickened to find he was killing young men just like himself. The only difference was the flag they fought under and the color of their uniforms. Their death cries carried the same agony; their blood ran just as red. It was more than he could forget.

Returning home, he'd vainly longed for a way to wipe away the haunting memories. At first it had seemed impossible, then, one day, Edward Cushing, an old friend from college, showed up. They sat over a bottle of port and Edward told him of the brave struggles of his adopted state of Texas to create a safe frontier for settlers and bring peace between them and the Indian and Mexican cultures in the area. Jack decided that very night he'd return with Edward to Houston and make his atonement by enlisting in the Texas Rangers.

He hadn't counted on going out there alone, though. Taking Kathleen with him had immediately become part of his plan.

A lump swelled in his throat, and he blinked away an unbidden image of Kate. No, he mustn't let this other woman into his heart. He had to focus on his goal: to survive his death day and return to Kathleen. He couldn't allow himself to become sidetracked by Kate, regardless of how appealing she might be.

Jack kicked violently at one corner of the trunk, but it barely shivered at his ghostly assault.

What a wretched, wretched feeling to be so close to Kate, yet unable to act on his instincts.

He kicked again, smacking the trunk with the toe of his boot. Why was he being tormented like this? Was this some kind of test? Yes, he thought, pacing the width of the attic, that must be it. He was being tested to determine his worthiness for a second chance. Well, he'd very nearly failed once. He'd best watch himself from now on.

Jack sat in a cane-back chair beside the window and looked out across the lush, rolling hills of Vermont. The evergreens looked fresh and lovely against the darkening sky. Silver birch and budding sugar maples added a dramatic contrast to the scenery and signaled spring was not far away.

He watched the sun settle into a deep crimson puddle on the horizon, then turned his chair to face the top of the stairs and concentrated on the door below. The door that separated him from Kate.

Come to me now, my lovely traveler, he called silently. *Come to me now. I can't wait much longer.*

* * *

Kate felt as if she were being rushed through the dishes. She found it impossible to relax as she read Jesse and Anna their bedtime stories. She knew why.

"Stop it, Jack," she muttered as she finally turned out Anna's light and closed her door. "I have a life to live, too, remember!"

But the relentless tug refused to release her, and it was all she could do to run around the house, checking locks on doors and flicking off electrical switches before heading upstairs again. She climbed to the attic with precious little dignity intact.

"You're such a nag!" she fumed, looking around for Jack when she at last stood beneath the bulb dangling in the middle of the main section of the attic. "Where are you, Jack? Show your face, you pest!"

A mellow chuckle issued from the far end of the attic, and she stormed toward it.

"You have a temper, lady! I'd thought your pounding on me in San Antonio was an aberration from your normally passive personality."

"Look, you!" She shook a finger at him, as if she were scolding her nearsighted paperboy who'd tossed the *Tribune* onto the roof for the third time in a week. "I'm doing you a favor."

"And a mighty big favor it is," he added, still softly laughing at her, his blue eyes alight, arms crossed over his wide chest as he lounged against a support beam.

"Exactly. An enormous favor. The least you can do is wait patiently and let me take care of my kids."

He looked contritely at her through long, black eyelashes. "So when do we leave? An hour? Jesse and Anna should be asleep by then."

"Not tonight. Tomorrow morning at nine."

"What?" He lurched toward her. "But that's over twelve hours from now! We're wasting precious time."

"Look, Ranger," she snapped, refusing to be intimidated. "I know how important this is to you. But I won't leave my children without a proper sitter. Besides, it would take a lot of explaining to make my friend understand why I had to take off with just a few hours' notice."

"I don't care what you tell her. We should be moving out—"

"And I don't care what you say. We're staying here until morning. You can't go anywhere without me, remember?"

He rolled his eyes and groaned. "Fine. We wait."

"Besides, we've got plenty to do between now and then."

He frowned at her. "Like what?"

"To start with, finding me appropriate clothing. I think your idea of disguising me as a boy stinks."

"You do?" A spark of amusement returned to his eyes.

"I do. It's ridiculous. If we're going to be in Texas for any length of time, someone will figure out I'm a woman."

His eyes ran suggestively up and down her figure, wrapped in a flannel robe. "Reckon yer right about that, ma'am."

"Knock off the phony accent, Jack. You're a Vermont boy. You couldn't have picked up that drawl in such a short time." She tugged the lapels of her robe closer together at the neckline. "I know what you're doing."

His eyes widened with mock innocence. "What am I doing?"

"You're trying to charm me. It won't work."

"Worked just fine earlier today."

Kate's mouth dropped open, and she felt her cheeks burn. It took her a moment to recover. "It won't happen again," she assured him.

"Pity."

She sighed, unable to tell if he was serious or teasing. "I agreed to accompany you to find your killer. I'm not interested in starting a short-term affair with you, Jack Ramsey. It was insane, the way we behaved earlier."

"But you enjoyed yourself."

"Yes, I did," she admitted, then stomped her foot in frustration. "So what! It's been a long time."

She wasn't about to tell him it had never been that way for her. Not ever.

In a way that seemed quite remarkable. She'd learned something about herself that afternoon. Kate shot a questioning look at Jack, wondering why she felt different, as if she'd discovered a part of herself she hadn't known existed. It was a strange and troubling idea, to realize she'd reached thirty years of age and not once experienced the height of pleasure her body was evidently capable of giving her.

"What are you thinking now?" Jack asked, squinting suspiciously at her.

Thank God he can't read my mind, she thought. *If you knew what was going through my head now, Ranger, I'd be lost.*

She was remembering something that had flitted through her mind only a few hours earlier—that it might be rather fun to repay the favor, to bring Jack some degree of the pleasure he'd brought her. The idea amused her, but only for a moment. It was, after all, impossible. Jack had said as much himself.

"Come on," Kate said briskly, "we have work to do. Then I need some sleep before we make this trip." She strode past him. "Do you sleep at all?"

"Me? No, not here." He turned to follow her across the attic, stooping to avoid hitting his head on rafters as they approached the far gable. "What are you doing?"

"Searching for a better disguise," she said, lifting the lid of Kathleen's trunk. She glanced up at him. "Do you think she'd mind?"

"I expect not, given the nature of our mission."

He stood back as Kate sifted through layers of lace and muslin and pretty gowns. "That one there," he suggested. "The homespun dress in blue and white."

Kate held it up. The fabric was coarse but of lovely, muted shades that had hardly faded at all. "Why this one?"

"It's simple, functional—more like the dresses Texas women wore. The ones who didn't work in the saloons, that is."

"Might be fun to be mistaken for one of them," she said, winking at him.

"You'd be damned dangerous in one of them places."

"How so?"

"Every cowhand, sheepman and rambler within a hundred miles would be fightin' over you."

"They would?" It wasn't so much the concept of men competing for her as Jack's believing it would happen that pleased her.

Jack scowled at her. "Don't go getting any romantic notions. Most of those fellas smelled pretty bad and weren't much to look at in the bargain."

She batted her lashes at him. "Jealous."

He laughed, but stopped abruptly when she held up Kathleen's dress in front of her. Kate winced at the pain that crossed his face.

Quickly she refolded the dress. "Maybe I'd better find something of my own to wear."

"No," he said tightly. "Wear it. Nothing I've ever seen you in would be appropriate, and nothing else of Kathleen's is right for the West Texas plains."

She saw by the set of his jaw there would be no arguing with him. "All right. This is what I'll wear. I just hope it fits."

He tipped his head to one side and observed her figure. "The two of you aren't so different in size, as long as you wear a corset."

"No corset."

"Have it your way. You'll be up all night letting out the dress."

To hell with his comparisons, she thought irritably. "I won't be up all night," Kate snapped, "because it doesn't have to be let out. Now I'm going to bed."

She picked up the dress; then, as an afterthought, plucked the boned corset from the top of the pile of dresses. "Just in case," she muttered, and stomped down the stairs.

Kate woke the next morning an hour before the time she'd set her radio-alarm clock to go off. She lay between the sleep-warm sheets, staring at the glowing digits in dawn's pearly light. Time, she thought. How much time will we have?

If time worked on a similar basis for their second trip as it had their first, a weekend of her time would be about the same as almost two full weeks of Jack's. To be safe, they should stay in Texas no longer than ten days. She hoped that would be enough. To stay away longer, she'd need to impose upon Barbara and ask her to watch the kids into the middle of the week, which would mean getting them off to school and supervising homework.

Barbara would do it, she knew, because she'd never refuse Kate anything . . . just as Kate would do anything for her. Anything except go on another blind date with one of her relations, she thought ruefully. All the same, she'd rather not have to complicate Jesse and Anna's life by staying away any longer than necessary.

Kate tossed the sheet and blankets aside and climbed out of bed, suddenly restless and stirring with energy she rarely felt on other mornings until she'd downed her first cup of coffee.

She was excited, prickling with anticipation. The journey itself... She didn't look forward to that. Passing through time had been terrifying the first trip.

But the rest—what had happened once they'd arrive in San Antonio—was wrapped in a wonderful sense of adventure. And as difficult as it was managing Jack once he was in his own element, she'd loved seeing him alive—a real man, not a ghost trapped for eternity in an attic with only his memories for company.

She couldn't think of him now without picturing him astride a horse, his hat pulled rakishly over one turquoise-blue eye, that taunting grin on his full lips as he dared three gunslingers to call his bluff.

Kate sighed, gathering up a pair of warm sweats to wear while getting the kids off. She'd change after Barbara picked them up.

While showering under a scalding spray, Kate mentally organized her morning. Cereal and milk for the children. She'd put homemade applesauce on the table, too. Sometimes she could get a little fruit into them that way. Anna was especially finicky about her fruits and vegetables.

By 7:30 a.m. Kate was out of the shower and dressed. She roused the kids with a kiss and a reminder of the day's fun. "Aunt Barb's coming to stay with you, remember?"

They were out of bed like a shot, and she left them to dress in the clothes she'd laid out for them the night before. Above the kitchen, she could hear them shouting back and forth to each other, plotting ways to convince Barbara to let them ride one of what they called "the baby horses." Anna had taken a special fancy to a sleek black colt she'd dubbed Licorice.

Kate laughed. "Fat chance, guys," she murmured to herself. The lanky colts wouldn't be broken for riding for many months, and they were too skittish to try mounting before then. Besides, there was the risk of injuring an animal that was worth thousands of dollars.

However, she knew Barbara would probably take them on her own horse for turns around the paddock. They'd be satisfied with that.

"Thank God for friends like you, Barb," she whispered to the teakettle when it finally whistled. Kate knew she could never in good conscience leave the children to help Jack if it hadn't been for Barbara.

Arriving half an hour early, Barbara was all smiles.

"So, do you need any help with last-minute packing?" she asked.

"No. Thanks anyway. It's all finished."

Barbara nodded, glowing a little less brilliantly. "I wish your Jack was coming earlier for you. Like I said, I'd like to meet him."

Kate winked at her. "And that's an understatement if I've ever heard one."

"So what if it is? I'm naturally curious about this man who's captured your heart when so many have failed."

Kate giggled, feeling like a schoolgirl swapping boyfriend statistics with her best friend. "Well, it's not going to happen today, so just chill, as the kids say."

"I guess I'll get a peek at him sooner or later, if he hangs around long enough." She looked pointedly at Kate.

"What's that supposed to mean?" Kate asked.

"It means, if history repeats itself, you'll chase him off, or start comparing him with Max, and he'll come up short on your checklist of male attributes. Then you'll dump him. Same difference."

Kate laughed. The thought of comparing steady, pleasantly featured Max with Jack's flash and masculine aura was ludicrous. They were two entirely different men from two different worlds. Then a chilling thought struck Kate. Actually they *weren't* from separate worlds any longer...they were both dead.

"What's wrong?" Barbara asked. "You just turned stone gray! I was teasing about comparing your boyfriend with Max. Don't take me so seriously."

"He's not my boyfriend, and it's not that," Kate assured her. She gave her friend a weak smile and lied through her teeth. "I just remembered something I forgot to pack."

Jack watched through the attic window as Kate strapped Jesse and Anna onto the bench seat of her friend's vehicle—the type newspaper advertisements called a pickup truck—then kissed both children on their foreheads and waved the three of them off. He immediately swiveled around to face the attic door, but endless minutes ticked past before he heard Kate's steps rising to meet him.

He had been ready for hours.

Throughout most of the night he'd planned the stops they should make, decided on the people he needed to interview, who would most likely provide clues to the identity of his killer. Now he was ready to pull her up the last few steps, wrap his arms around her and go.

Jack stared in disbelief at Kate. She was still in her bathrobe. Her feet were bare, and her hair was a tousled mess.

"You're not ready!" he boomed.

"No, I'm not," she bit off. "This *thing* is impossible!" She shook the corset at him. "Kathleen's dress is so tiny in the waist, I can't button it unless I wear this contraption. And I can't lace it up by myself. I've been in and out of that dress a half-dozen times. It just doesn't work, and I have nothing else to wear." She glared at him as if he were supposed to do something about the situation.

Jack laughed. "The ladies I knew either had womenfolk or a servant to deal with the complications of their garments."

"Oh, well that solves everything!" she cried. "I'll just ring for my entire fleet of upstairs maids."

He shook his head at her, but didn't dare risk another laugh. "Come here. Let me help you with it."

Kate stepped back. "No."

He found her vacillations between prudishness and sensual abandon amusing. The memory of her enthusiastic reaction to his touch the day before flashed across his brain, stirring up an instant and forceful response from his own body.

"This is no time for false modesty, darlin'," he stated. He reached out, grabbed the corset and jerked it out of her hand. Tossing it onto the leather chair, he moved his hand to the collar of her robe.

"Wait!" she cried. "I'll take it off myself, thank you. You don't need to manhandle me."

Jack stepped back obediently and waited—aware that he was holding his breath as his eyes fixed expectantly on Kate's hands. After a moment's hesitation she peeled off the robe, exposing delicate, lacy underthings so insignificant, they bared vast stretches of soft, pink skin.

Jack was shocked. "Wh-where are your bloomers? Your chemise?"

It was her turn to laugh at him. "Ladies' undergarments have changed. A bra and bikini panties are all I ever wear."

He swallowed, reining in the heat that suffused his body. With effort, he removed his eyes from the slim, satiny flow of her body.

"I thought you were going to help me get dressed," she said, sounding almost nonchalant now. She smiled rather wickedly.

"I was—am, I mean." Jack swallowed again, but it didn't do much good. Damn these modern women, he thought. Their men must go around hard all day long!

She picked up the corset and lapped it around her middle. "There. Start lacing at the bottom. I've figured out that much."

Jack stood behind her and set to his task with energy. But an agonizing tingle raced through his fingertips whenever they brushed against her flesh. His eyes drifted helplessly from her waist, down to the luscious swell of her bottom at the upper edge of the tiny triangle of pink satin. Through the silky, translucent cloth, he glimpsed a mesmerizing valley he ached to investigate. Jack could imagine himself cupping her full hips, backing her toward him, then tucking himself into her warmth. Lord, he could almost feel the surge of male power. It had been so long, so very long.

"What's the problem?" she asked. "I thought you were in a hurry. We only have a couple of weeks or less, your time. About two days of mine."

Jack cleared his throat, getting better control of himself, and concentrated on alternately hooking and crossing the laces up the curve of her waist and back. "You figured that out, did you?"

"Yes."

"That's more time than we need anyway."

"Huh? Hey, that's too tight!"

"Sorry. I mean, we only have a week or so before I die."

"Oh," she breathed, looking as if he'd slapped her. "Then we really had better get going."

"Agreed. There, you're done. Now on with the dress."

The indigo blue-and-cream homespun hung softly from Kate's shoulders. Dozens of narrow, hand-sewn tucks ran in precise lines from the collar to her pinched-in waist. The sleeves buttoned tightly at her wrists.

Jack took her in, suddenly feeling dazed. His eyes filled with tears.

"I look that much like her?" she asked softly.

"No. You are two very different women." He turned away, unwilling to reveal to her how that difference made him feel. It was as if he'd been struck with the realization he'd chosen the wrong woman. Yet fate responded with a clear message that all was happening as it should. Kate was merely his tool to reach Kathleen. He felt confused and sick.

"Come here and stand close to me . . . for the trip," he said gruffly.

Kate looked up at him, a hurt look in her rich coffee-colored eyes, as if she understood how he was distancing himself emotionally from her. He thought, *Reckon I'm the worst rogue there is.*

Then he shut his eyes, enfolded her in his arms and drew a picture in his mind of the raw desert landscape due west of San Antonio.

As before, Kate felt the floor drop away from beneath her. The fierce whirlwind of time swept her up, beating around her like a violent storm. She hugged Jack's waist as he held on to her.

This time, she tried to keep her eyes open. Vivid images of faces swam toward her and veered away into bright, white space. People of all descriptions and races—plain and beautiful, young and old, famous and common—appeared, then were gone too swiftly for any one of them to register in her mind. They were born, lived their lives and died . . . and time sped heedlessly on.

Hills, flowers, snow, rude cabins, a covered bridge, high-rise apartments. . . She and Jack were traversing the country, as well as decades, at speeds faster than light. Try as she might, Kate could no longer force herself to watch. She felt as if her brain might explode with the effort of comprehending it all. The overwhelming sensations reminded her of trying to cram for her college world history final exam. But this was ten times worse.

At last the wild spinning slowed, and Kate felt a familiar heaviness return to her body.

"You all right, darlin'?" Jack asked.

"I'm fine. You?"

"Made it again."

She sighed a little regretfully as his strong arms dropped from around her. Kate looked around. They stood in the middle of a flat stretch of desert, near the foot of two sandy, scrub-covered mounds about fifty feet high.

"Where are we?"

"Just outside San Antonio, on the road south to the Mexican border."

She nodded. "What now? Will you run into Yancy again? Or does something else happen?"

He looked a little embarrassed. "It's not as if I know everything before it happens. It's more like driving a road you've been down before, but you can't remember the landmarks until you come to them. Then you suddenly know where you're at."

"After nearly one hundred and thirty years, I'd expect your memory might be a little foggy." Kate sighed and looked up. A blazing sun was climbing the eastern sky. Its heat was already beginning to penetrate her dress. "Must be over a hundred degrees out here, and dry as a bone."

"Guess that's why they call it a desert," he commented wryly. "Come on, the horses should be over here."

"Horses?" Kate walked as fast as she could in Kathleen's laced, high-top shoes, trying to keep up with him.

"Yup, that's why I wanted to come back to this day, this time. I recalled I'd been riding out from town to join my boys, after a few days' leave. I had my favorite horse with me and a broke mustang I inherited from an old boy who got shot by Comanche."

"Indians?" she asked, scanning the horizon. "Out here?"

He nodded. "They've been driven this far west by settlers, ranchers and the army. With the start of the Civil War, the government didn't have time or manpower to keep track of 'em anymore. When Texas seceded from the Union, most of the men hereabouts joined the Confederate army and were sent east to the great battlefields."

"And that left no one to hold the fort, so to speak," she said.

"Right. All the tribes wanted their lands back, which is pretty understandable. Never did seem fair to me, what we did to the Indians, forcing them into reservations so we could steal their land. But once it was done, there had to be a way to make peace between our people. That couldn't happen as long as we were killing each other."

Kate chewed her bottom lip thoughtfully and listened, enthralled by Jack's living view of history.

"At any rate, the Comanche, Kiowa, Apache and a bunch of other tribes took advantage of the lack of protection. They did to white settlers what some whites had been doing to them—burned their homes and killed their women and children while their men were off soldierin'."

Jack looked so incredibly sad, she had to reach out and touch his arm. The sleeve of his shirt already felt lightly damp with sweat.

"You were awfully brave to believe you could help by coming out here," she whispered as they continued hiking across the sand toward the twin buttes that were the only rise in the landscape for miles.

Jack shrugged. "I learned you can't escape human nature. Men of every race can be cruel or kind, depending upon circumstances. But you can't sit still and let that sort of thing go on. The Rangers were given the job of guarding the home front during the war—protecting settlers as best they could, holding off the Mexicans who'd have liked to take back part of Texas for themselves. The Rangers did the job best they could, with precious few men. After the war, when I enlisted, we were charged with rounding up Confederates who hadn't gotten their fill of killing and turned into renegades, robbing and killing for whatever they could get."

"It sounds like an impossibly difficult job," she murmured.

"We never completely got a handle on things, not while I was alive." He gazed sadly at a mesquite bush and stuck his hands into his pockets as he led her across the sand. "But from what I could see in the books and newspapers stored in your attic, looks like civilization's come a long ways."

"It has," she assured him, "and a lot of that was the doing of brave men like you, Jack."

He flinched, and an uncomfortable expression filled his eyes. For the life of her, she couldn't figure out why her admiration should make him uncomfortable.

"The horses," he said abruptly. "They're around this way."

Tethered behind the first of the two buttes, they found a pretty sorrel mare and a mottled gray-and-white mustang stallion with wild eyes. Both had blankets, canteens and basic supplies strapped down behind their saddles. The wooden stock of a Winchester rifle stuck out from a long, leather holster alongside the mustang's shoulder. Glancing quickly at Jack, she saw that he wore a pistol, and ringing his belt was an ample supply of ammunition for both the rifle and his pistol.

Jack gave the horses water from one of the canteens strung to the chestnut mare's saddlebag. He turned to Kate as he was cinching up the saddle on the mustang.

"You'll ride Sunny Girl," he said indicating the other horse. "She was my mount before I picked up Apache. She won't give you any trouble. The mustang will never be more than half-broke. I'll ride him."

Kate stared at Jack. Until this moment, she hadn't thought about transportation. "You didn't tell me I had to ride."

Jack laughed. "Of course you have to ride. We don't have automobiles, you know."

"I know that," she snapped defensively. "But I figured I'd ride on the back of your horse, like before."

"We have too much ground to cover to ride the same horse. He'd be worn out in half a day." He hesitated. "You do ride, don't you?"

Kate took a deep breath. "In a manner of speaking." Which meant, around Barbara's training ring and a few times with Barb through the surrounding fields. "I'll manage," she assured him.

Chapter 8

After the first hour, things got better.

Kate kept an eye on the way Jack let his heels settle into his stirrups and how he held his reins loosely in one hand. She copied him and remembered Barbara's many pointers. Despite her attention to detail, she fell off Sunny once. Kate stood in front of the mare and held a brief sisterly discussion with her about taking it easy on beginners. To Jack's amusement, they got along happily after that.

"Sunny's really a lovely horse," she said after they'd ridden for another hour. She stroked the mare's silky neck and coarse blond mane. Kate even liked the way she smelled.

But as they rode, Kate caught herself thinking more about Jack than about her mount. She observed with fascination the rippling muscles in his shoulders as he guided the spirited mustang. She remembered how those same muscles had knotted under her hands as she'd clutched him to her in the attic.

Kate had to keep reminding herself that he was off-limits, not only because he'd pledged himself to another woman. He was no more a part of her world, of her time, than last year's tulips, Model T's, or . . . or corsets. It amazed her that he'd been able to touch and move her as he had. That particular thought sent lovely, primitive chills up her spine, and set her wonder-

ing if there might be factors at work in his mission that even he
didn't understand. Had he been allowed to seduce her as a
means of guaranteeing she'd come with him? Was fate that
calculating?

They rode for nearly another two hours, Jack leading the way
and not speaking at all unless she asked him a question.

Cacti of a myriad of shapes, the occasional dwarf scrub pine
and mesquite shrubs lined their way across the chaparral. There
was no road that she could discern, but Jack guided Apache
forward without hesitation. From the path of the fiery sun
above, she guessed they were moving to the southwest now.

"We're heading away from San Antonio, aren't we?" she
asked at last.

"Yup. If we followed this trail to its end, we'd wind up at the
Rio Grande." His drawl was creeping back again, the crisp New
England accent fading. She liked the drawl better: his baritone
voice rumbled pleasantly in his gut.

She rubbed the insides of her calves. The leather was beginning to abrade the bare skin where her skirt pulled up. "Are we
crossing into Mexico?"

"No. We're not going that far. In another five miles we'll
come to Rancho del Sol." He turned in his saddle to look at her.
"Are you getting tired?"

"No."

"The heat might be too much for you. You're not used to it."

She shook her head. "The sun feels wonderful after a long
Vermont winter. My bones need thawing out."

Jack grinned, losing the contemplative look that had closed
over his features since they'd mounted up and started their ride.
"Just let me know when it gets too much. And keep that hat
on—the sun's stronger than you think." She was wearing a tan
felt hat that had been tied to Sunny's pack-saddle.

Kate looked around. Distant purple-and-rust hills rimmed
the desert. "Is the ranch beyond that rise?"

"At the foot of the hills. You can't see it from here."

"Why are we going there instead of into town?"

"That's where Yancy Kennard hails from."

Kate frowned, feeling her stomach tighten with tension. She
rode up alongside Jack so she could see his face better. "Don't
you think the other Rangers would have caught him by now?"

Jack's eyes darkened and fixed on a distant point. "No, they
didn't catch him. And Yancy won't be at del Sol. He's not en-

tirely stupid. But his sister, Pamela, runs the spread, and she's the one I need to talk to."

"What's she like?"

Jack grinned. "Knows everything that goes on in this part of West Texas. Everything. The woman's sharp. I think you'll like her. In a way, the two of you are a lot alike. Pamela's a very independent woman. She's run all three thousand acres of del Sol single-handedly since her old man died. Her mother was killed by a renegade raiding party when she and Yancy were young. Dad was a tough old guy, wouldn't take crap from anyone. Pamela took after him."

"And Yancy?"

"He's a spirited kid, all right. But he's got no direction and less sense. Just makes trouble for himself. He'll get himself killed yet."

Kate slanted a look at him. His tone was confident, and final. "Yancy will die young, won't he? You know that."

"Yeah, I know."

Jack refused to talk any more about Yancy or his sister.

Kate rode in silence, soaking up the exotic landscape, wondering when the cactus buds that she saw hugging the spiny, contorted green bodies would bloom.

Rancho del Sol came into view slowly, a low line of red tile roofs emerging out of the desert floor, gradually rising to reveal stark white adobe walls and a surrounding split-rail enclosure. The Spanish-style ranch with its rambling main house and many out buildings was impressive. After seeing the crude stucco and stone structures of San Antonio, Kate hadn't expected anything so grand.

"Oh, my," she breathed.

"It's beautiful, isn't it?" Jack said, guiding his horse closer to hers.

"Breathtaking. Is this the sort of place you'd have had if Kathleen agreed to join you?"

He laughed. "No, darlin'. Del Sol isn't in my price range. Kathleen would have lived at Fort Deal, while I was out on jobs. If we stayed after my enlistment was up, we'd have started out in a one-room cabin with less than a hundred acres." He gazed wistfully across the sunbaked stretch of bronze-and-tan earth. "Kathleen would never have been happy here. I realized that the first week I was in Texas."

Jack looked thoughtfully at Kate, then turned away.

"What?" she asked.

"Nothing." He kicked Apache to a trot. "Let's finish off this last mile."

Kate nudged Sunny in the ribs with her heels, and she broke into a smooth gallop, overtaking the mustang. Jack matched his pace to hers.

Although Kate had rarely ridden hard or fast before, she felt remarkably at ease with the sorrel's liquid gait. Bending low over Sunny's neck and letting her body feel one with the horse as it ran, she was reminded of times she'd ridden an inner tube down the gentle rapids of the stream behind the farmhouse. But here, sand swept away beneath her for miles, and the hot wind rushed at her face, leaving her breathless.

Jack's mustang ran with her like flowing smoke, the silvery mane flowing out behind the muscled piebald neck. Jack shot a surprised but approving glance her way.

All too soon, they'd run out of desert and reached the ranch's gates. Apache and Sunny huffed and snorted to a jouncy halt. Kate rested her palm on the mare's neck to settle her.

Three hands rode out to meet them. Kate didn't like the looks of the men. One, she thought, resembled the older of the two men who'd been with Yancy the other day, but she couldn't be sure if it was him.

"Howdy," Jack called out in a friendly voice. "Miss Pamela around?"

"Mebbe," the man in the lead said. He spat on the ground and eyed Jack, then let his glance slip away to take in Kate. "Who's askin'?"

"You know me, Hornsby. We met the other day in town. You and Yancy and one of his young tagalongs..."

The man nodded slowly. "Guess I do recall, now that you mention it, Ranger. But there ain't no warrant out on me, and I don't know where Yancy's got to. What you want with Miz Kennard?"

"Just need to talk to her about her brother."

"She hasn't seen him in weeks. He took off. Probably headed for California."

"That so? Well, maybe I should ask her myself, seein' as how I'm the one investigatin' his part in Colonel Walker's murder."

"Miz Kennard's got nothing to do with her brother. She throwed him out, you know," the hired hand said placidly.

"No, I didn't know."

Kate watched the older man, trying to read some form of truth from the weather-ravaged brown face. Jack sounded to her as if he didn't believe what the man was telling them.

The hired hand continued. "You might as well turn around and go back the way you came. She told young Yancy she wouldn't be havin' him around the ranch no more. Reckon she just got tired of him comin' to her to pay off his gamblin' and drinkin' debts. Always in trouble, he is."

"Well, you should know. You're with him half the time," Jack said.

Hornsby scowled at him.

Kate sat on Sunny, her heart hammering in her chest as she watched the two men face off.

As if to give their boss more room, the two junior hands flanking Hornsby backed their horses away.

"Take your horse over there," Jack directed Kate, his voice low as he pointed with his chin toward a nearby shed.

Kate gripped her reins, desperately trying to think of a way to avoid the inevitable showdown. If only she could think of a way to distract Hornsby... or to make it appear they had another reason for being there.

"This is *so* disappointing!" she wailed out loud.

Kate felt four pairs of eyes latch on to her.

She forced a smile and blurted out. "Pamela will be awfully upset if I don't get to see her, don't you think, Jack? I promised I'd drop in." She turned to Hornsby, who was looking puzzled. "You see, I'm Jack's other cousin from Vermont. And I won't be in the area for very long."

The man rubbed his grizzled beard with finger and thumb. "You know Miz Kennard?" He studied Kate's face, then dropped his eyes to her bare knees. She'd had to lift her skirt to allow her to sit astride the saddle. A dark, appreciative smile curled his lips.

"Well, yes, we've written to one another."

The three cowboys seemed to ease back into their saddles. "Don't want you to think we're not neighborly, miss. It's just these are hard parts and rough times, not like where you're from out East."

"We gotta protect a lady like Miz Kennard from unscrupulous types," one of the other men added.

"Like lawmen?" she asked sweetly.

"Like she needs protectin'," Jack muttered under his breath.

Kate glanced at him, then back to Hornsby who, thankfully, seemed not to have heard this last comment. "I understand completely," she murmured. "And we'll go if you like, but I'll feel so very rude, having given my word."

The three men exchanged confused glances. No one appeared willing to take responsibility for making the wrong decision.

"We'll take you on up to the house," Hornsby agreed at last. "You'll leave your pistol at the door, Ranger."

Jack tipped his hat.

They dismounted in the dusty yard between the ranch house and two barns. Behind them were several bunkhouses and storage sheds. On the fourth side of the yard was a large corral, penning some of the sleekest, most regal-looking horses Kate had ever seen.

"Good Spanish stock," Jack murmured when he caught the awed expression on Kate's face. "The woman knows her horseflesh."

"Barbara would die for one of those stallions," she whispered.

Hornsby disappeared inside, but soon returned. "She wants to see you in her parlor. The maid will show you the way."

Jack unbuckled his gun belt and draped it over one arm while he held out his other for Kate. They climbed the few steps to the veranda and then into the cool, dark interior of the house.

A servant appeared and took away Jack's gun. A second later, a proud Mexican woman motioned for them to follow her.

Kate looked around in amazement as they passed through a shadowy foyer and into a well-lit grand hall lined with oil paintings in dark, refined hues.

"The family gallery?" she whispered to Jack.

"Some. They're not all portraits." He pointed to a landscape that might have been a very early Cézanne.

Kate raised her brows and blinked at him questioningly. "It's real," he said. "And I'll bet so is that Rembrandt and the Lorrain over in the corner. In your day, they'll be priceless."

Feeling her excitement grow, Kate studied every painting, vase and sculpture displayed in the pristine-white hall as they slowly approached a pair of ponderous, carved wooden doors. The maid opened both in one motion, then stepped aside, as if she were presenting royalty.

Jack led Kate into a room brilliant with sunshine. Lace panels drifted gracefully across tall windows, created of many small panes. Although the sun radiated through the curtains in delicately etched patterns across the clay-tile floor and furnishings, most of its heat seemed to remain outside.

A slender woman in her late twenties, with hair as black as polished obsidian, stood up from behind a Spanish escritoire. She wore a man's riding gear, in black, with silver belt and earrings of the same metal, set with turquoise stones. Her eyes sparkled, dark and vibrant, as she smiled at Kate. Then she turned toward Jack.

"Welcome, Ranger Ramsey. I understand you've brought someone to meet me." If one of Pamela Kennard's employees had related Kate's story about their correspondence, the young woman showed no sign of it. She extended a long-fingered hand toward Jack, who accepted it and kissed her fingertips lightly. Somewhat reluctantly, Kate thought, Pamela withdrew her hand then looked curiously at Kate, who introduced herself as Jack's cousin, but used her real name.

"I'm glad to meet you," Kate said quickly. "I'm afraid I told a little fib to your foreman. I said we were friends. You see, Jack has told me wonderful things about your ranch, and I just had to see it for myself. It's absolutely breathtaking."

Pamela Kennard laughed a clear, tinkling laugh. "My dear, you're forgiven your little subterfuge—men can be so heavy-handed, don't you think?" She sighed. "Anyway, del Sol is hardly breathtaking. Fontainebleau is breathtaking. A château in the Alps is breathtaking. My little ranch is simply a pleasant oasis in the middle of a barren wasteland. A study in contrasts."

She grasped Kate's hand in a strong grip. "Tell me, what has brought a lovely young Easterner all these many miles? Surely not the hope of touring my home."

She motioned to a sumptuous gold-brocade settee, and Kate joined her there while Jack crossed the room and looked out the window. Kate sensed he was uneasy here, and she didn't blame him. Although Hornsby claimed Pamela had banished her

brother from the family property, there was no guarantee he
wouldn't steal back to hide out on familiar turf. He might even
have followed them across the desert with the thought of eliminating one Ranger to discourage others from continuing the
manhunt.

"I've come to teach in Galveston," Kate said. Jack had told
her that Galveston was the most advanced city in the state.
Houston was just a backwater town, plagued by fever-bearing
mosquitoes. The Dallas and Fort Worth areas were hardly more
than dusty way stations on the way north. Even Austin, the new
capital, was still in its planning stages, with most of the land
parceled out to a few families.

"To teach," Pamela repeated, her precisely rouged lips
twitching with shared excitement. "I think that's marvelous.
And will you be starting your own private school or taking a
position with the town?"

"I'll be looking into the possibility of founding a school for
young ladies," Kate ad-libbed. "I believe there might be some
interest among the more established families."

"Oh, absolutely . . . absolutely!" Pamela cried. "I only wish
we had enough families of quality in San Antonio to support
your effort. If we had, I'd snap you up this very minute for the
benefit of our young women. But the men of these parts—" she
shot a withering look at Jack's back "—they're so blind to
modern ways. They think educating women is a waste, as if all
we're good for is cooking, birthing and occasionally filling in
for the lame plow horse."

Jack turned around and shook his head. "No one could
claim you'd fallen into that rut, Pamela. You can outthink and
outride any man on this ranch."

She looked pleased. "Why, thank you, Ranger." Pamela
turned back to Kate with a gracious smile. "Please say you
won't leave San Antonio without dining with me one day. You
can even bring your cousin, if he agrees to leave his gun and
smug male attitude outside my dining room." She winked at
Kate, a woman-to-woman conspiracy.

"I'd like that very much," Kate said.

"Perhaps this Sunday?"

Kate looked at Jack.

He hesitated and hooked his thumbs through his wide leather
belt. "You may not be so eager for our company when I tell you
why I've come."

"Then it wasn't to introduce Kate to me?" Pamela asked, not sounding terribly surprised.

"Not entirely. I'm looking for Yancy. He's wanted for Colonel Walker's murder. I'm sure you've heard the rumors."

"I have," she said stiffly. Kate could almost feel Pamela's tension filling the elegant room.

"We have witnesses," Jack continued. "They saw him fire point-blank at the colonel. Then Yancy and some of his friends—we're not sure which ones—dragged Walker's body around, bragging about what they'd done."

Pamela stared at him. "Yancy did that?"

"That's what witnesses claim." Jack rocked back on his heels, observing her expression. "The governor's pretty miffed, seeing as how he ordered the Rangers to protect Walker. Now we have to bring Yancy in to face trial."

Pamela pushed herself to her feet, her face flushed with anger. Kate guessed they were about to be thrown out, but the woman surprised her.

"I *knew* his behavior would come to something like this! Absolutely disgraceful!" She stalked across the room, picked up a crystal decanter of amber liquid and poured herself a stiff shot from it. "The foolish, foolish boy! Of course he'd been hauling salt off the flats and selling it. Everyone did. But Yancy had come to think of it as his private source of income."

"The flats are very close to your land, aren't they?" Jack asked.

"They border del Sol on the extreme southern edge." She set the decanter down hard, shaking her head. "That was maybe why Yancy felt so protective of that land. Still, I didn't believe he'd do anything this drastic."

"You don't sound as if you doubt he did it," Kate remarked.

"Oh, don't get me wrong, I'll get my brother the best defense lawyer west of the Mississippi." Pamela tapped her nails in a nervous tattoo against the sparkling crystal goblet cupped in her hands. "But I do know what he's capable of. Yancy's headstrong, young and has our daddy's temper." With a sudden jerk, she spun around and dashed the glass to the floor. "The fool!"

Kate winced at the crash of shattering crystal. "You couldn't have known. Probably couldn't have stopped him."

"True. But I feel responsible for Yancy. I'm eight years his senior. Ever since Daddy died, I've been looking after him." She stared, dry-eyed at the shattered crystal and droplets of liquor spotting the red clay tiles. "I knew he'd find a way to destroy himself. And now it's happened."

Kate felt terrible for the woman. Pamela was such an elegant, refined woman—and her brother was no more than an Old-West version of a modern street-gang member.

"Maybe there's something that can be done to—" Kate looked at Jack for support.

He glared stonily at Pamela. "I'm sorry. I have to bring Yancy in—you know that."

Pamela sighed. "I suppose I do."

"If you see him—"

"No," Pamela shot back, her eyes aflame, "you can't honestly expect me to turn him in. I won't do it." She paced two steps one way, then spun around in the other direction, her silver earrings flashing in the sunlight. "I'll do this much—if he shows up, I will try to encourage him to give himself up and stand trial *if he insists that he didn't do it.* But as I expect you're right and he did kill the colonel, I won't turn my brother over to be hanged."

Kate's mouth was suddenly drier than it had been while they were crossing the desert. A wave of compassion for Pamela Kennard settled over her. The woman's parents were dead, her brother appeared to be a criminal headed for the gallows, she was unmarried, without children, and managing a sizable working ranch in hostile country. All she had was del Sol…the land and her horses and cattle. How lonely it must be, Kate thought.

Jack nodded. "I guess I can understand that. Just warning you, it wouldn't be smart to try to hide your brother here on the ranch. Sooner or later someone will run him to ground. It would be easier on you if it didn't happen on your daddy's spread."

Kate stood and reached out to touch Pamela's arm. "I'm sorry. Perhaps we should just forget Sunday and—"

"No," Pamela said, lifting her chin, her eyes bright with dignity. "Sunday we'll dine here. The three of us." She looked pointedly at Jack. "Yancy won't be joining us."

"If you're sure," Kate murmured.

"Yes, come by noon. We'll eat at one, have a nice visit and you'll leave in time to get back to town before nightfall."

Kate smiled at her. "I'll look forward to it."

Jack bowed his head to her. "We'll be here."

"Consuela will see you out." Pamela waved them toward the door, evidently wishing to remain in her parlor.

As soon as they were on their mounts and headed north toward town, Kate kicked Sunny to walk beside Apache. She and Jack rode side by side in silence until the red tile roofs of the ranch sank into the heat waves rippling over the sand.

"She's an exquisite woman," Kate murmured, "so in control of her own life. It must be terribly difficult for her, saddled with a brother like Yancy."

Jack didn't answer her.

"Did you hear me?"

He nodded, his eyes riveted to the horizon dead ahead.

"What's wrong?" she asked.

"I'm not sure. I just don't trust that brother of hers. I expect, she, like Hornsby, thinks Yancy has left for good. But I can't help feeling he won't run far. He'll hang around, looking for another fight."

"You said he dies young," Kate said. "Do you know from having seen it happen? Or is it something you just kind of understand the same way you know what happened to Kathleen after you died?"

"That's not clear to me yet," Jack admitted. He frowned at a tumbling branch of sage and adjusted his hat lower over his eyes. "I'm beginning to get a feeling your being here with me might change what happens. Back at del Sol, I remembered having that same conversation with Pamela about Yancy, including her losing her temper and smashing the glass. It wasn't until we were in the middle of it that it all came back to me like a flash flood roaring through a canyon."

"Really," Kate breathed.

"Yeah. But this time Pamela said things she didn't say before, because you were here to ask questions and turn the conversation in different ways. It was strange—like remembering a play you've seen performed before, and you know the actors' lines so well, you can recite them. You know exactly what's supposed to come out of their mouths, only this time the lines and even their actions are a little different.''

Kate stared at him. "Maybe I'm here for a more important reason than to be your ticket back through time. Maybe I'm some sort of catalyst of events, or I'll be the one to actually find your killer. Maybe—" She scratched her fingers through Sunny's pale mane and sighed. The possibilities were endless, certainly too many for her to sort through just yet, with so little information.

Jack observed the long, low horizon.

Kate followed his gaze, which seemed to lock into a grim stare. Dark clouds were piling up in the west.

"Looks like a storm heading this way," he muttered. "We'd better get moving."

Chapter 9

The Texas norther ripped across the desert, driving sand and brush before it with a wicked vengeance. Chill gusts outran the horses and would have won a race with the devil himself, had he dared shown his face.

Even though they rode at a gallop, before Kate and Jack came within sight of San Antonio, evil black clouds crowded directly overhead. Then the skies split wide, unleashing needle-sharp droplets that lashed Kate's face and stung her arms and shoulders through the sleeves of her dress. Sand, like tiny chips of glass, blasted away at the two riders, clinging to wet skin, clothing, horses. It was almost impossible to breathe, even though Kate took the bandana Jack offered and tied it over her nose and mouth. She could see only as far ahead as Sunny's ears, flattened against her head in terror. They were forced to slow down for fear of one of the horses catching a hoof in a prairie dog burrow.

"I didn't think it rained in the desert!" Kate shouted above the wind.

"It doesn't . . . much. But when it does, there's no holdin' it back!" Jack peered worriedly at her above the triangle of red fabric tied over his nose and mouth. Sunny was dancing in tight, nervous circles. Kate was having trouble reining her in.

"Whoa there, girl." He spoke firmly to the sorrel, grabbing its reins and hauling it, side by side, with his mount.

Swinging up and out of his own saddle, he maneuvered in front of Kate and onto her horse. Kate wrapped her arms around his waist.

"Won't Sunny tire too fast carrying both of us?" she shouted in his ear, squeezing her eyes shut against another assault of sand and water.

"We'll go slow. I can't chance losing you in this storm. If Sunny spooks, it would be easy enough. Visibility's all of two feet right about now!"

Kate burrowed her head into Jack's shoulder blades, while he urged the mare on and led Apache by his reins. The wind roared. The rain slashed at them. By inches, they moved across the trailless prairie. Sage and mesquite tumbled past them with each violent gust, a gray wall hemming them in and cutting them off from all but their little patch of Texas hell.

Above, the sky turned an evil reddish green. Thunder crashed all around them, and with each strike the horses gathered their legs beneath them in preparation to bolt. But they only got a few steps, each time, before Jack fought them back under control. He kept both on a short rein, monitoring their every step and talking to them in soothing, low tones that Kate doubted they could hear. Still, his voice seemed to have a calming effect on them.

"How do you know we're going the right way?" Kate shouted.

"Call it a good guess," he answered.

"How reassuring." Kate closed her eyes, held on to Jack for all she was worth and prayed for both of them.

Then suddenly it was over.

The storm passed as quickly as it had started, or maybe they simply rode out from under it. There was no wind, no rain. A setting sun blazed low on the horizon. A patchy blue sky stretched overhead. The earth beneath the horses' hooves appeared bone-dry, as if it had never rained at all.

"The weather sure changes fast around here," Kate gasped, releasing Jack's soggy waist long enough to reach up and wring out her hair.

"It's the one thing you can count on in these parts," Jack commented. He twisted around in his saddle and looked at her.

"Guess we'd better stop and—um, dry you off before we hit town."

Kate stared at him. "Dry *me* off? You're just as wet."

"I'm not the one who'll get all the attention, riding into town in a see-through dress." He grinned at her wickedly, his glance centering on her chest.

Kate looked down.

The homespun had soaked through and showed a crisp outline of both her bra and her nipples.

"I told you, you weren't wearing the right underclothes," Jack teased.

"Shut up," she snapped. "I don't need you to tell me how to dress."

"Well, if you'd worn proper—"

"One more word, Ranger, and I'll take myself straight back to Vermont," she threatened.

He closed his mouth meekly. "All right," he said after another minute. "Do you want to go back to town like that? Or should we get you out of that dress long enough to let it dry?"

"How long will that take?" she asked, wondering what she was supposed to wear in the meantime.

He looked at the potent orange orb creeping slowly toward the western horizon. "Even this late in the afternoon, if you spread that dress on the hot sand, she'll bake out in fifteen minutes."

"Good."

She slid down from the saddle to the sand and started unbuttoning. To her way of thinking, bikini panties and a bra covered as much as most two-piece swimsuits. There was no one around for miles, except Jack. And Jack, by his own admission, had his heart set on another woman.

She looked up to find him watching her, a smile of anticipation tickling his lips, his eyes twinkling.

"Turn around," she ordered.

"What?"

"You don't have to stand there gawking as if you've never seen a woman in her underwear."

"I've never seen a woman in underwear *like that*," he said.

"I'm not doing this to put on a private show for you, Jack Ramsey," she snapped. "So you just turn yourself around and pretend you're a gentleman."

With a regretful sigh, Jack dramatically marched himself around in a circle and glared off into the distance.

"Do I have to stay like this the whole time the dress is drying?"

"Yes."

"Fine," he snorted.

"Fine," she said, stepping out of the dripping garment. She folded it in thirds then twisted it until no more water dripped on fine, dark grains of sand. Shaking it out, she laid it flat on the ground. Almost immediately, a thin curtain of steam began to rise.

Kate found a patch of shade created by the horses. She stretched out, leaning back on her elbows and turning her face up to the sun. She hadn't realized how unused she was to riding distances. The muscles in her legs and bottom complained. The warm sand felt good against the dull ache.

Kate felt as if she were being watched. She twisted around, sure she'd catch Jack peeking, but he still had his back to her. He was casually rolling a cigarette.

"I didn't know you smoked," she said.

"I don't, anymore."

"You did, back then . . . I mean, back now?" Funny, she thought, talking about the present as if it were the past. Or was it the other way around?

"Yup. I sort of got out of the habit, living in your attic for those hundred-plus years. Besides, back in my day, the advertisements claimed tobacco was good for you. Relaxed the system, cleared the mind. Your modern newspapers say different. A man doesn't know what to think."

"I don't think any scientist has proven there are benefits to smoking." She smiled softly, liking the line of his wide shoulders against the sky. "Where did you get the tobacco?"

"Found it in my pocket when we got here. Like my gun, it was just on me this time." He patted the Colt at his hip.

She nodded. A lot of things didn't make sense to her, but they seemed not worth questioning. Maybe it was simple. Maybe they'd returned on a day when Jack happened to have been carrying both his gun and smokes.

"Where are we staying tonight?" she asked. "You talked about a fort before."

"Naw, that's a good two days' ride at least. We'll stay at the Sweetwater Inn in town."

"I didn't see any signs for rooms. It looked more like a saloon."

"There are four rooms out back. The owner has plans for buildin' a second floor on top someday. Meanwhile, things are pretty makeshift, but it'll do."

Kate laughed, shaking her head.

"What's that for?" he asked.

"It's hard to believe that in just a few decades Texas will boast some of the most prosperous cities in the whole country."

Jack smiled thoughtfully and lit up, taking a long, smooth draw off of his cigarette. "I spent a lot of time reading those old newspapers stored in your attic. You even used some to wrap around china and glasses. A lot has changed all over this country." His profile darkened. "And a lot hasn't changed."

Kate could almost read his mind. "You mean, violence . . . wars."

He nodded.

"The Civil War—your war—was the only one fought on our soil, though. Maybe it was the worst of any of them for Americans," she said sadly, "the hardest because we were fighting our own countrymen."

"No," Jack said, his voice hollow, "no, I expect one is as bad as another. Your World Wars, one and two, Korea, Vietnam, Desert Storm. American soldiers died just the same."

"Desert Storm," Kate murmured. Two boys from Chester had gone over. Only one came back.

"We never learn . . . never learn," Jack whispered hoarsely.

Kate felt an overwhelming surge of sympathy for Jack. She pushed up from the ground and rushed to him.

In a way, he'd experienced the passing of time in the most depressing way possible—locked away in her attic with only a tiny square of window to reveal the passing of time. All he knew of life came from batches of yellowing newspapers and magazines that revealed the bitter progress of politics and world affairs. The world must have seemed always in turmoil. Floods, famine, earthquakes, wars—they were the events that made the headlines.

Jack had been robbed of the chance to experience the simple joys of life, the love and loyalty of a good woman, seeing his children born.

"It's not all bad, Jack," she whispered.

He didn't move, didn't turn to face her.

She came up behind him and touched his shoulders through his still-damp shirt. "There is an awful lot of good in the world. I wish you'd been able to see that, too."

"I know it exists," he said tightly, still not looking at her. "It's just not enough sometimes."

"It can be. People like—" She'd been about to say *like us,* and quickly changed her wording, because they weren't the couple it implied. "People like me, we learn to make a bright spot for ourselves in the world, and share it with our children, friends and community. If there are enough bright spots, the world can grow to be a happier place. I truly believe that, Jack. Start small, but think big."

He turned then and stared down at her, his face taut with grief. What horrors had he seen on the battlefield that had eaten at his soul for over a century? She longed to soothe them from his mind.

"I've seen your bright spot—the farm, your children. But you've grieved, too."

"Max." She nodded.

"Yes, you lost your husband."

"It was pretty awful, for both of us, knowing he was dying." She made herself unknit her fingers. "But Max planned ahead for me and the children. He knew we'd be all right."

"And are you? What about *you,* Kate? For once, don't think of yourself as an extension of your children. Are *you* going to be all right on your own? Or will you let another man into your life someday?" He gazed at her so intently, she felt compelled to look away.

"I—I don't know. Maybe. I hope so."

Jack's hand settled on her bare shoulder. When she looked from his hand to his eyes, she became aware of how hard he was studying her, waiting for her answer. She straightened, not wanting to flinch as his eyes crested the soft mounds of her breasts above her bra. His searching gaze lowered, possessively taking in all of her.

"You know, if I could . . . I'd be that man for you, Kate."

A lump swelled in her throat. "You would?"

"Yes. If I could. If I had no rendezvous with the future—"

"If there were no Kathleen," she whispered. She bit down on her lip to keep from crying.

He swallowed and nodded. His hand dropped away. With noticeable effort he turned away from her.

"Your dress is probably dry enough," he said abruptly. "Put it on, and let's get moving. It gets dark fast on the desert."

Ramsey, if you were another man thinking these same thoughts, I'd run you out of town, Jack thought.

He rode steadily, keeping Apache at a trot, poignantly aware of Kate riding at his side. Every now and then she glanced at him with a puzzled expression. He refused to look back at her or explain his teeming emotions. Now that they were back in his world, in his time, and his body and mind functioned as those of a living man, he seemed to be having far more trouble controlling his feelings for Kate, and his lust.

How could he love two women? How was that possible?

Yet he did—Kathleen in her way, Kate in hers.

The problem was, Kate was here with him now, and he'd already weakened once, already touched her in unspeakably intimate ways. To make love to her again, to whatever extent his body, in its present state, allowed him, would truly be unfaithful to his fiancée.

But there was something mystically appealing about Kate . . . something he simply couldn't turn his back on. In the attic, after he'd watched her scale the heights of ultimate passion, well, he'd tried to tell himself he was just being kind to her, just giving her what she so desperately needed. He knew there'd been no other man in her life, knew she'd let no one sleep in her bed since Max. Yes, he was simply thanking her for helping him out.

But that was clearly his male ego talking. What she'd needed was also what he'd wanted, perhaps even more urgently than she. And it wasn't just the act, the sexual jolt and thunder. There was more to their intimacy than that. *Much more, damn it!*

Certainly, he'd been with other women since he'd come to Texas. At first, for many months, he'd only let Kathleen's sweet face fill his dreams. Then that was no longer enough. He'd sought comfort, for a price, with a girl in San Antonio. Later, a woman in Ciudad, just across the Mexican border, had helped him spend his month's wages in three days. They'd been women of spirit with a gift for satisfying lonely men. But he'd never thought of himself as being disloyal to Kathleen, and they'd never wiped her sweet image from his dreams.

He wondered fleetingly if Kate would wait for him forever, as Kathleen had promised she would, and had done. He had to smile at the thought. Something told him Kate would not. She wasn't a woman to pine away eternally or feel sorry for herself.

At last Jack allowed himself to glance over at Kate as she rode beside him, her back proudly rigid, chin tilted up, as if to prove to him it mattered to her not in the least, whether or not he talked to her. Her soft brown eyes fixed on the twin buttes that rose up ahead of them.

"We're almost back to town, aren't we?" she asked, her voice sounding rough. The desert dryness, he thought. She wasn't used to it.

"Yes, almost there."

Slowly she turned her head to study him. "Are you all right, Jack? You've been quiet."

"I'm fine," he said gruffly. "Just thinking about . . . you know . . . who to interview next, where to go. If someone's gunning for me, he may be braggin' about it, working up his courage. But I can't let on that I know what's going to happen to me."

"Maybe if I ask—"

"No."

"Jack, why not? It would make more sense that your cousin from the East, who's worried about you, would ask about dangers. People will be more likely to talk to me about something like that."

"I don't want you talking to folks in town."

"Why in heavens not? You didn't mind my visiting with Pamela."

"She's different. She's a refined, law-abiding woman. Almost everyone in town is a male. Half of them are crooked bushwhackers, the other half may be honest and hardworking, but they're as starved for a woman's affection as the first half. And any of 'em would likely kill for a kiss."

She grinned prettily. "You're jealous."

"Am not."

"You are, you definitely are!"

She giggled like a schoolgirl, and it tugged at his heart to hear and see her so carefree and alive, only days before his demise.

Kate reached across the space between the horses, rested her hand on his arm and said lightly, "Don't fret, Ranger. I'm yours alone till the bitter end."

The expression on his face must have reminded her that his end might not be far off.

"I'm sorry," she murmured quickly. "I wasn't thinking. We'll find out who he is. We'll find out before it happens again." She looked thoughtful for a moment. "How many chances do you get?"

"One . . . just one."

She sighed. "Then I guess we'd better not make any mistakes."

"I guess," he said grimly.

Jack led Sunny and Apache to the watering trough where he'd muddied Kate's face on their last trip, and left the horses to drink. "You'd better stay with them," he told her. "I'll go over to the Sweetwater—see about rooms and ask around."

"The horses will be all right. I'll go with you," she said quickly.

"No, you stay."

"Jack."

"I mean it. A drinkin' establishment is no place for a respectable woman. I'll bring you out something to eat and drink."

A defiant look flashed across her eyes, and it surprised him. She was usually so cautious anyway, remaining outside a saloon didn't seem like something she'd challenge.

"Water will be just fine," she stated haughtily. "And I'll make do for food with what's in the saddlebags."

"If that's what you want." He cast her a final *stay put* look and strode off across the street toward the Sweetwater Inn.

Kate glared at Jack's departing back. She didn't know what had gotten into him since they'd left Pamela Kennard's spread, but she found herself itching to break through the wall he was building between them.

He was probably regretting bringing her along, for more reasons than one. Pamela was a very beautiful woman. Kate had sensed some underlying tension between the two of them. Had it been sexual, or something else? And she was definitely slowing him down at a time when he needed to move quickly and gather as much information as possible to save himself from dying of a fatal gunshot wound.

She watched his elegant, long-legged and purposeful stride as he approached the Sweetwater. Jack's lean, muscled body moved with a natural masculine grace, his boots sending up puffs of dust, his body parting the heat waves that rippled across the plaza.

An open wagon rumbled noisily past, cutting him off from her for an instant; then she saw him step through the timber-framed opening in the stucco facade. He disappeared inside the shadows of the saloon.

Kate looked around, feeling suddenly alone. Fears she'd temporarily forced to the back of her mind snapped into focus again. What if something happened to Jack while he was in there? What if fate worked faster than Jack anticipated, and he was gunned down tonight in the Sweetwater?

Kate thought fleetingly of Jesse's and Anna's sweet faces, of well-meaning Barbara . . . who might end up with two orphaned children on her hands.

The sooner Jack found out who was going to shoot him, the sooner she could return to Chester and resume her normal life.

Kate shot a glance up, then down the street. She spotted two men in leather chaps, intricately tooled boots and ten-gallon hats. One was a big man with a mustache. The other was small and wiry, and looked two sizes too small in his clothes. Grit and dust clung so thickly to them, she wondered if they, too, had been caught in the storm.

Combing her almost-dry hair back from her face with her fingers, she wished she had some makeup to highlight her features just a little. She felt naked without a bit of lipstick and eyeliner. Although she had no mirror, she was sure that every speck of her last application had been washed away in the storm.

"Well, Sunny, there's no use worrying about what we can't have, is there?" She patted the mare's rump. Was she talking about cosmetics, or Jack? she wondered.

Sunny flicked her tail in docile agreement, just happy to be at rest.

"Wish me luck, girl," Kate murmured and started across the street.

Kate felt rather proud of herself as she marched toward the two strangers. Maybe Texas and a harder way of life was changing her in subtle ways she wasn't even aware of. Back in Vermont she rarely approached strangers. Here it seemed necessary, if she was to help Jack at all.

"Hello," she called out when she was halfway across the plaza.

The men looked up, eyes widening, then narrowing suspiciously. The taller one, she noticed, wore a star, somewhat different from Jack's, on his shirt.

"Are you the sheriff?" she asked.

"Yes, ma'am—Stony Phelps at your service—and you be?"

"I'm Kate Fenwick, Ranger Jack Ramsey's cousin."

The sheriff touched the brim of his hat. "Reckon I'm pleased to meet you, ma'am."

The other man removed his hat and crushed it between his hands in front of his chest. "You sure are better lookin' than any Ranger, if you don't mind my sayin'. I'm Clint Dewey, mining expert."

"He means he's a prospector," Phelps explained. "Worked the gold rush up along the Oklahoma border in '49, then gave up and started tryin' his luck farther south. Mean old cuss, ain't smart enough to give up when everyone else has." Phelps chuckled, grinning at his friend.

"There's a vein in these parts," Dewey whispered to her, moving closer.

His breath was thick with whiskey, his body pungent with unwashed male odors she'd rather not try to distinguish. Kate stepped back.

"I hope you find it," she said, trying not to breathe in.

"Oh, I will, miss...I will." Dewey wet his lips with the tip of a purplish tongue. His swollen hands were scarred with breaking rocks and they never stopped kneading his hat. "And when I do, I'll have plenty for buyin' purty trinkets for purty ladies."

"Is that so?" Kate turned back toward the sheriff, who smelled a little less disagreeable than Dewey. "I need to speak with you in private, about Jack Ramsey."

"What about him?"

She glanced meaningfully at the prospector.

"Clint's harmless. Go on. What about Ramsey?" Phelps asked.

Kate hesitated for only a second. "Do you know of anyone who'd want to kill Jack?"

"Kill a Ranger?" Sheriff Phelps laughed. "Why, half of Texas, I expect."

Kate stared at him in disbelief. "But the Rangers protect the settlers and guard the borders and—"

"Ma'am, no offense to your cousin, but half o' the population of this county is wanted by the law for one thing or another. Everyone knows, Rangers shoot first and ask questions later, when they ask at all. They ain't liked much by a lot of folk."

She studied Phelps's hard eyes and the sharp lines around his mouth. "Who would hate Jack enough to shoot him in the back?"

"Anyone smart enough to sneak up on him." Dewey wheezed on a laugh, and coyly edged toward her again. The perfect lounge lizard, she thought dryly.

"There ain't no code of honor between men that hate one another—no matter what you might read in those Eastern papers of yours," Phelps added.

She squinted at him. "You're saying almost anyone might be gunning for Jack."

Phelps let out a long breath and gazed solemnly the length of the town's main street. He didn't answer.

Four riders passed them on horseback and dismounted in front of the Sweetwater. She glanced quickly. Like every other man she'd seen in town, they were wearing guns. Two had rifles strapped to their saddles, as well.

Kate looked back at the sheriff, and something suddenly felt as if it were curdling in her stomach. "What about *you?*" she asked when he didn't respond. "What do you think of Rangers?"

He shrugged. "Long as they do their jobs outside of my town, fine with me. But San Antonio is *my* territory, and no Yankee range rider's gonna interfere with me or my folks."

Kate couldn't tell if it was pride talking, or malice. "Thank you for your help," she murmured. "It was nice meeting you, gentlemen."

She spun on her heel and started toward the Sweetwater. Following the four cowboys as far as the doorway, she peered inside.

Jack stood at a short bar fashioned of planks laid across wooden barrels. A half-dozen tables, with four spindle-back chairs at each, were occupied by men. Some were playing cards, others concentrated stoically on their drinking. No flashy saloon girls flicking feather boas flirted with the customers.

The riders looked around and, seeing no seats, approached the man behind the makeshift bar. The tallest of them pointed out one of the bottles on a shelf, and the bartender started pouring.

Kate swallowed, moving into the room and feeling less sure of herself now that she was here. She'd hoped to circulate through a crowded room of gamblers and cardplayers, listen in on conversations, pick up valuable information for Jack. This grim drinking room wasn't at all what she'd expected.

She felt male gazes swerve laconically toward her, then away, as if their owners weren't sure what to make of her and had to think about it a bit.

Pressing herself against the cool stucco wall, she waited and watched, her pulse thrumming in her ears. She really hoped Jack wouldn't see her.

Maybe, she thought, she could quietly kibitz with the cardplayers at the table nearest to her. She'd started to edge toward them when a figure stepped in off the street.

"There you be, girl!" Dewey announced triumphantly.

Kate winced.

Jack spun around and glared at her, his face rigid with fury. He motioned with his eyes for her to get out. Kate blinked at him stubbornly. *I have as much right to be here as you do, Jack Ramsey,* she thought.

Besides, the sheriff was right outside. What could possibly happen?

Dewey oiled his way across the floor toward her, kneading his hat brim in grimy hands. "Buy you a drink, miss?"

"No, thank you," she said politely. "I just wanted to get in out of the sun."

Dewey's eyes shot across the room to Jack, and a wily expression crept across his eyes. "Man should be 'shamed of his self, leaving a purty lady like you outside, alone in that sun." He leaned toward her so close, she could smell his acrid breath over his body odor. "Bet you'd be wantin' a nice cool bath to soothe your delicate tissues," he purred, reaching for her arm.

She pulled away from his cloying fingers. "Please, leave me alone. I just need to rest a little. I don't want to make a scene."

He chuckled. "Now, now. Old Clint knows what will make you happy. Old Clint can sure please a woman if she lets him...."

With unexpected fervor, his arms flung wide open, and he lurched forward, not totally in control of his movements but with enough weight behind him to pin her to the wall if she failed to act quickly.

Out of the corner of her eye, Kate saw a flash of motion on the other side of the room. But before Jack could reach them, Kate's knee reflexively shot up between Dewey's thighs, catching him squarely amidships. The prospector doubled over with a groan, and Kate stepped neatly aside as he toppled helplessly to the floor.

Jack arrived with his gun drawn. Men jumped up from tables and dove for the door or ducked behind barrels.

"What the hell are you doing in here?" he shouted at her.

"I came to help," Kate informed him in a reasonable voice. She looked down at Dewey who was still writhing on the floor. "I thought I'd just talk to some of the—"

Jack grabbed her by the arm and steered her forcibly toward the door. "You *thought?* I told you to wait with the horses."

"And I decided it made more sense for me to question people," she shot back at him. So what if it hadn't worked out quite as she'd hoped. At least she'd gotten a little information from the sheriff. "Jack, you're hurting my arm. Let me go."

"Not until I get you out of here," he ground out, dragging her along with him.

She noticed how his eyes kept moving, scanning the dim corners of the room for the slightest motion, for signs of anyone trying to stop them.

They were almost to the door when Phelps stepped into the rectangle of sunlight, blocking their exit.

Jack stopped, holding Kate firmly by the arm. "Howdy, Stony."

"Oh, good—you know each other," Kate said, trying to sound conversational. Neither man gave any sign of hearing her.

"Hey, there, Jack. I see you found your cuz."

"Yup."

"She causin' trouble?"

"No more she ain't."

Phelps nodded, chewing contemplatively on a wad of tobacco.

Kate looked from man to man. There seemed to be some wordless message being passed between them, and she was pretty sure it had nothing to do with her.

Phelps's miss-nothing glare settled on a slowly recovering Dewey. "I expect there won't be any more trouble from the lady, or from you, Ranger," he added darkly. "You leave any law upholdin' to me in this town."

"Your friend was out of line," Jack said. "The lady made her wishes known."

"You were just protectin' her virtue?"

"Right."

Kate felt a little miffed that no one seemed to be acknowledging she was the one who'd decked the prospector.

Jack's eyes absorbed the whole of the man, from his fixed glare to the fingers that were inching down to the level of his holstered gun. Kate wondered what might have passed between the two men before she'd known Jack.

"We won't be causing any more trouble," Jack said. "We'll just arrange for rooms for a couple of nights—" He turned toward the bar, but the bartender, who doubled as room clerk, had wisely disappeared from his station.

"I don't believe there are any vacancies," Phelps stated.

"There are *always* vacancies," Jack countered.

"Not tonight. Not for quite a few nights. Maybe not for a week or more."

"We'll try somewhere else in town."

"Every roomin' house in San Antonio is full up," Phelps said, spitting a globule of tobacco juice across the room with evident satisfaction. "I'd say you best move on."

Chapter 10

Kate started breathing again only when the sheriff turned away and slowly walked out of the Sweetwater, his spurs grating on the splintery wood floor. By fractions of an inch, Jack's grip on her arm loosened, and she felt the circulation flow back with annoying prickles.

"I don't think he likes you," she commented.

"Feelin's mutual."

She sighed. "So where do we stay tonight? We could go back to Chester, then return in an hour or two, my time. That would be about the right time difference to make it morning here."

"We can't leave now," Jack bit off.

Kate looked up, and his eyes were dark and deeply troubled. "Why?"

"It's not something I know for sure...more like, something I feel."

She flexed and straightened her arm several times, hoping to bring it back to life. "I'm beginning to think you just say that whenever you want your own way."

Jack shot her a dangerous look, but his expression lightened when he saw her teasing smile.

"You're accusing me of being spoiled?"

"Most men are."

He laughed a deep, resonant laugh that rumbled delightfully through her. "Come on, we'd better get movin' before old Dewey regains his strength. Where'd you learn to do a man like that? He went down like a felled oak!"

She grinned at him. "YMCA—I took an aikido martial-arts class. Got as far as yellow belt. Max's idea, bless him."

He shook his head, chuckling, although he had no idea what she was talking about. "Come on. Mount up, darlin'. We'd best move out. Phelps isn't a patient man." Jack couldn't seem to stop laughing. "Aikido," he grunted. "Modern women."

They rode out of town the way they'd come in, heading south and a little west.

"Are we heading for Galveston?" she asked after a while.

Jack pulled the black Stetson down over his forehead and squinted into the distance. "Nope."

She followed his gaze. "There's nothing out this way as far as the Rancho del Sol."

"I wasn't thinkin' of going that far tonight."

"But we have to sleep somewhere."

"There will be fine." He pointed.

The evenly rounded buttes, patched over with scrub grass, mesquite and cacti stared back at Kate.

"Out here? In the middle of nowhere?"

"You never camped out in Vermont?"

"Well, sure, in a tent, with a Coleman stove and lantern and sleeping bags with inflatable mattresses and—"

He gaped at her in amazement. "How'd you ever carry all that junk?"

"A car."

"Figures," he grumbled as they continued to ride at a relaxed pace. "I don't know what you people would do without your automobiles."

Kate dismissed his fussing over modern conveniences and looked around the desolate, heat-baked landscape. "Is there shelter of some sort behind the buttes?"

"We'll build a fire in the hollow between them. Keep the critters away."

She arched a questioning brow. "Critters?"

"Mostly bats and coyotes. Snakes aren't a problem at night."

"Oh." She wasn't sure a night on the desert would turn out as romantic as she'd imagined. Sleeping on the parched ground and wondering if she'd wake up to stare into wild yellow eyes wasn't her idea of a relaxing evening.

"You're not afraid, are you?" he asked.

Kate leveled her chin upward as proof. "Of course not. I just prefer a normal bed."

"Me, too. Maybe we can make some kind of *accommodations* to compensate for inadequate sleeping conditions," he said, winking at her roguishly.

"Like what?" she demanded suspiciously.

"We'll see." He kicked Apache into a gallop.

Kate let Sunny feel her heels, and together they raced after Jack. "If that means what I think it means," she shouted at his back, "forget it, Jack Ramsey. I'm not interested!"

"You're not?" His blue eyes met her brown ones, and latched on to them as he eased Apache back down into a trot. He's much too perceptive, she thought, feeling vaguely rattled.

"No, I'm not," she insisted. Kate took a moment to settle Sunny Girl into a moderate gate, bouncing gently in her saddle. "What happened the other day in the attic, just happened. It doesn't mean anything because you're not real, you're dead. And I'm not here, I'm from another time. Scientifically, philosophically and logically—we're an impossible match. It wasn't real, Jack."

"Sure felt real to me."

She felt herself blushing and had to look away from him. "You know damn well what I mean."

"But that was *there*. This is *now*. We're on my turf. I'm not a ghost here in Texas."

"True," she admitted, the nuances of what he was saying sinking in. "So maybe here, in this time . . ." She tried to keep her eyes from drifting up his muscled body astride the mustang. It didn't work. She couldn't pull her eyes away.

"Maybe," he echoed cheerfully. "Care to give it a try?"

Kate glared at him. "Jack, how could you? What about your fiancée?"

"You're not real, remember? Isn't that what you just said? If you're not real, then I might as well be fantasizing—albeit in a very graphic way—about a beautiful brunette, with eyes that shine like a colt's and long, lovely limbs bared in the sunlight." He shot a look at her legs.

Kate brushed ineffectually at the hems, but she was sitting on the bulk of the skirt and her hurried attempts to smooth it over her legs did little good.

"One can't account for dreams, can one?" Jack continued. "Especially if the dreamer is a man who's been without a woman for nearly a hundred and thirty years."

"That's not my fault," Kate countered.

"Are you saying getting shot in the back was *my* fault?"

She bit down on her lip. "Forget it, Ranger. You'll have to satisfy your base urges without me. I'm not about to get into an emotional hammerlock with an almost-married man, who lives two thousand miles away from me...and happens to have died before I was born."

Kate slapped Sunny on the flank and galloped off ahead of Jack, annoyed at the laughter she heard echoing behind her. He'd damn well see that she was serious when they bedded down for the night. She'd keep a couple of cacti between them for good measure.

It didn't take them long to make camp. Kate unsaddled the sorrel, stroked her long mahogany neck and white mane as she removed the bridle and bit. After giving her water from the canteen, she set her to graze on sprigs of tender mesquite grass that poked up through the crusty soil.

She found hunks of dried bread wrapped in a cloth napkin in one of the saddlebags, and some brown, dried stringy substance that smelled vaguely of old meat.

"Is this dinner?" she asked, hoping she was wrong. It hadn't occurred to her until now that she'd eaten nothing since breakfast. Suddenly she was ravenously hungry.

"Reckon so." Jack didn't turn around but continued gathering dried tumbleweed and sagebrush for a fire. Squatting in the lowest point of the hollow, he arranged the twigs in a pile. "Unless I can rustle up some game. Might be able to shoot us a jackrabbit or lizard."

Kate rolled her eyes. "Never mind. You must be tired, too. Does this jerky or whatever it is need to be cooked?"

"It's good as it is."

"Delightful," she muttered.

"What?"

"Nothing." Kate sighed and carried the food over to the fire that Jack had finally succeeded in lighting.

He went to fetch the saddles, laid them down nearby, then spread out his saddle blanket. Kate took Sunny's blanket, shook it out energetically and arranged it on the ground ten feet away from his.

He watched her with an amused expression. "Making your point again, I see."

"Someone has to be sensible about this situation. If everything works out, you'll live through a shootout and go home to your Kathleen in 1867. I'll return to my own life, in Chester, thirteen decades later." She drew a deep breath, forcing back annoying emotions she felt bubbling up inside of her at the thought of their parting. "I don't intend to carry a torch for another woman's man or spend my life wishing things were different," she added crisply.

"You don't?" he said, visibly struggling to keep a straight face.

"No, I don't!" Kate spun on him angrily. "Look, this may all be jolly fun for you, hopping around through time on this quest to put your past right. Very romantic. Very macho, too, no doubt. Maybe you know how it will all turn out, but you've decided you'll make out better if you don't tell me. Maybe you figure, what the hell, I'll just jump into bed with any woman I want while I have the chance, because I'm going to be married to Kathleen next month. Just one long bachelor's party! Well, that's just great for you, but it's not what I want."

Jack stood up from the fire. It crackled loudly, burning too bright, too hot and too fast, just like—Kate imagined—any love they might share. No, not for me, she thought. Not for me...

"What *do* you want, Kate?" Jack asked, his voice suddenly calm and solemn. "Do you know?"

"Of course *I know*. I know I want—" She broke off, flustered. What was it Barbara had said, time and again, about looking for a man who was too perfect? "I want a relationship that's strong, one that won't burn itself out in a few years. A love that will last—"

"Forever?" he finished for her, moving closer.

"Nothing's forever," she said. "I know that. But Max and I, we were all right for a long time, and I think we would have made it."

"You would have been bored to death of each other. At least with him you would have been," he said.

"No."

"Yes." Jack reached out and gripped her arms high up, near her shoulders. "You and Max might as well have been matched up by an accountant. You were fiscally sound and capable of producing healthy, attractive children. He didn't excite you. He never excited you."

She turned her head away.

"He didn't, did he?" Jack demanded.

"Max was a kind man, and he had many virtues."

"No doubt." Jack released her, looking torn. Disappointment swirled with regret in his eyes. "I'm sorry, Kate. I didn't mean to speak ill of the dead—God knows, I should sympathize with Max on that count at least. And I have no right to interfere with your memory of him or your personal life." He raked a hand through his hair and picked up his hat from where he'd laid it beside the fire. "No right," he muttered, stooping to stir the glowing embers with a stick. "Not after what I've asked of you."

She watched him, the fire's heat reflected in his face as he balanced on the balls of his feet in the stance of a baseball catcher, his forearms propped on his knees. He stared into the flames.

She thought about all he'd been through—the Battle of Petersburg and possibly other skirmishes just as bloody. They'd left him haunted, unable to return to a normal life with his Kathleen. Then there was the long journey to Texas and enlisting in the Rangers. There must have been agonizing weeks of dusty rides, futile attempts to bring peace to a wild frontier.

He had flirted with her, perhaps not even expecting her to flirt back, maybe only wanting to get a reaction out of her or hoping to shorten their ride by taking their minds off of what lay ahead. But he'd made her aware of her own deeply felt needs. She couldn't deny that she yearned for the touch of his hands again. She needed to hold him within her and return to him some of the pleasure he'd given her.

Maybe he was right. Maybe she *wasn't* real as long as she traveled in the past. When they each went their separate ways, he might not remember her, and she might not remember him. Because none of this, this melding of two eras, had ever really happened.

Perhaps, she thought, we're being given the comfort of each other's companionship to get us through a time too painful to handle any other way. Even Jack didn't understand all of The Rules, as he'd called them. He'd admitted that much.

Kate turned to him, as the sun rode low and red on the horizon, striking purple and pink streaks across the desert sky, like the striations in a fine Italian marble.

"Jack."

"What?" He eased back onto his heels and looked across the fire's flames at her.

"I was wrong," she whispered. "I was lying. I want to make love with you."

Jack gazed at Kate, transfixed by the way the firelight flickered in her eyes. In some ways she was poignantly vulnerable, but she had the strongest spirit of any woman he'd known. "I badgered you. I've frightened you, I'm sorry," he blurted out.

"No. Maybe you were a little pushy, but frightened me? No way." She smiled at him.

"I can't give you what you want, Kate. I can't give you forever. There's only here and now for us...." He nearly choked on the words. "It's out of my hands, darlin'."

"I know," she said softly. "Life's short, though, isn't that true? It's so terribly short, and I can't let you leave me without showing you how much I—"

"No!" he shouted, leaping up from the ground. In two long strides, he'd skirted the fire and was beside her, pulling her into his arms. "Don't say another word." He lost himself in her eyes, her mouth, the luscious curve of her throat, then began to tenderly kiss her. "You don't have to prove anything to me. I knew you loved me the moment you agreed to risk your own life and come with me."

With sudden, glaring insight, he understood. "Kate," he blurted out, "you'll be happy."

"You'll make me happy for the time we have together," she murmured, her eyes misting over as she drew back from his lips for a moment.

"That's not what I mean."

Somewhere in the deepest recesses of his mind, he knew all the answers, understood every twist of fate he and Kate would encounter. Yet he couldn't explain to her the whys or hows of their destinies, because his own grip on the truth was far too fragile to verbalize. It was like waking from a dream and grasping at the quickly dissipating images. Minutes from now, he might remember nothing. But he had to make her understand that she was not marked for the life of loneliness Kathleen had led after his demise.

Jack held Kate close, breathing in the scent of her. "What I mean is, I know that you'll find happiness. You won't be alone the rest of your life. *He* will find you and—"

"I want no one but you, Jack Ramsey. No one but you—"

Tears trickled down her cheeks.

Kate pressed her damp face against his shirtfront, melting into him as naturally as a gentle spring rain seeps into the half-thawed earth, bringing it nourishment and hope for new growth. He held her to him, moved beyond words, beyond thoughts. No teasing jabs came to mind. No lighthearted taunts to set her on edge so that he could enjoy the fireworks of her hard-to-provoke anger.

Jack felt her fingertips moving restlessly across his chest, unfastening the buttons of his shirt, slipping her silky hand inside to caress him. Damn it all, it felt good—too good to tell her to stop.

Worst of all, he didn't feel the guilty twinge that had floored him after he'd been with her in the attic. He didn't feel the least remorseful as she lightly brushed her warm lips over the hairs on his chest, kissing him softly, beautifully. The scent of her crazed his mind, weakened his will. More than ever, he felt their being together was right, was what had been meant to be all along.

Yet, wasn't that impossible? he thought wildly. Absolutely impossible because they were born in disparate times, no parts of their lives slated to cross. Ever.

Her lips edged lower across his chest, brushing erotically over his nipples, pressing softly over the muscled ridges of his abdomen.

He looked down into her face and gloried in the rapt smile on her lips, the reflection of flames bright in her dark eyes. An excited flush pinked her cheeks.

"You are beautiful," he murmured, barely able to breathe for the remarkable way she made him feel.

She smiled, releasing the buttons of his pants, one at a time, slowly reaching in. He'd no doubt he was ready for her this time. He'd been full with his need for her since her fingertips first started working their magic on his body. But it amazed him to think, after all this time, he was still capable. The realization only added fuel to his already blazing passion.

Heat surged through him as she brought him out, stroked him, her eyes wide, watching him respond to the slightest movement of her hands over him.

"You're—" She shook her head, looking embarrassed to say the words.

"Yup," he whispered hoarsely. "Ready, willing...and able, ma'am. And you?"

In answer, she knelt on the ground, coaxing him down with her. Grasping his hand she lifted her skirt and guided him beneath its folds. As soon as his rough fingertips grazed her thigh, he lost the fine thread of control with which he'd held himself in check.

Jack found her hot liquid center as welcoming as before. This time, though, he knew there were other ways to satisfy her. Best of all, he'd be satisfying himself, too.

Hungrily, he pressed her back into the sand, missing the saddle blanket completely but not caring. He left her only long enough to wrench off his boots and struggle out of his pants while Kate wriggled from her dress, then fought with the corset.

"I knew wearing this thing was a rotten idea!" she cried impatiently.

He flipped her over, fumbled briefly with the laces, and somehow loosened them enough to draw the contraption over her head. His eyes fell to the pale span of skin on her back between her bra and her panties. Impulsively he pulled down the lacy bottoms and cupped the full mounds for a moment, savoring their softness before rolling her back over so that he could see her face, for with every second he feared she might change her mind.

Then he'd have to kill himself.

Short of raping her, there'd be no other way of dealing with his runaway hormones. And he'd have given his life willingly to keep her from harm.

Yes, he'd definitely have to kill himself—or at least shoot himself in the foot to quell his lust.

But Kate's eyes were full of him, brimming with passion and the desire to please. "Thank God," he muttered deep down in his throat. "Didn't fancy losing a foot."

"What?" She laughed breathlessly. "Jack, what?"

"Nothing. I love you. Oh, Kate, believe me now and forever...I swear by all I hold dear, *I love you* and I always will!"

Tears filled her eyes, and she moved herself under him, grasping his hips and pulling him down so that the unbuttoned sides of his shirt tented over her naked body, cocooning them in warmth and the heated scent of each other and their shared hunger.

"Show me," she whispered, low and lusty, in a voice he'd never heard her use before. "Show me how much you love me, Jack."

Holding back no longer, he took her. He wanted to fill her again and again, ached to reach so far into her that not an inch of her flesh remained virgin to his touch. His driving impact slid her across the sand, and he reached up under her arms and over her shoulders, pulling her down to him even as he entered her, again and again.

To his amazement, she encouraged him, lifting her legs to wrap around his hips, opening herself to him, moving with his wild rhythm until he was racked by hot spasms of his release.

Jack heard himself roaring out her name, again and again— as the coyote calls to its mate, as the male species has howled its possessive claim since time immemorial.

At last his body settled into a sated hum and he felt Kate shuddering beneath him, her own orgasms rippling through her as she gasped and dug her fingernails into his knotted shoulder muscles. He eased his body's weight slightly off of her but pressed his hips forward and up, knowing he could intensify her pleasure by staying with her this one last mile.

At last she clutched him and, trembling, cried out as she crested a final wave. He remained within her, watching her features register a mesmerizing series of feminine emotions, kissing her tightly closed eyelids, letting her find her own time to come down from her ecstasy before resting in his arms.

They slept naked in each other's arms, between the two blankets. Frequently during the night, Kate heard a brief scuffle or animal call from the brush and woke Jack. Each time, he drew her closer, pulling her hips toward him for the pure pleasure of nestling his most sensitive part into the double swell of her flesh. He kissed the nape of her neck, whispered soft words of love into her ear and soothed her back to sleep, his arms encasing her, his palm tenderly cradling one of her breasts.

Very late in the night, when a thin layer of clouds drifted from across the face of the moon, the cacti around them became silhouetted in its silvery light, and Jack roused her gently.

"Look."

Kate peered sleepily into the night, following his pointing finger.

"They've bloomed!" she gasped. "The cactus flowers—they're beautiful!"

The air had grown chill, plummeting nearly fifty degrees between noon and early morning, as only a desert environment can. Jack threw the blanket around her bare shoulders and stood with her, marveling at the lush orange and red blossoms that would close into tight, protective buds at dawn.

"The bats come to drink their nectar and pollinate them at night," he whispered. "But they'll stay away as long as the fire burns."

"Then put out the fire," she said. "There must be new life."

They lay in the absolute dark, then, her body spooned within his, with only the moon and stars to break through the solid black.

"I want you," Jack murmured in her ear, kissing its tender rim.

"You've had me," she said, laughing.

"Again," he growled, "and again, and again."

She rolled over to face him and, holding her hands on either side of his lightly beard-stubbled face, brought him down to kiss his mouth. Opening her lips to his, she invited him to taste her, to drink of her. He did, letting his lips travel onward to the most delicate parts of her body—savoring her breasts, the lovely hollow between her hip and stomach, the matched dimples low down on her back and the sweet nectar of her center, tinged with the flavor of his own release.

Never had there been a more exotic drink for man.

Chapter 11

Kate slowly rose through layers of sweet morphia, feeling the coolness of the night slake off her skin like water flowing over a smooth, shale riverbank. She stretched and turned over, sensing the coarse horse blanket beneath her. Replacing the smell of horse was another—the pungent, intoxicating scent of Jack erupted from its fibers, reminding her of the countless times they'd awakened and held each other, warming to gentle caresses that grew impassioned and, inevitably, wild.

She felt limp with satisfaction, warmed from within, and smiled with delight at the slight soreness still tingling between her thighs.

"Might find riding a little awkward this morning," she mumbled to herself.

"Hmm?"

Kate opened one eye, surprised that Jack's voice hadn't come from her side. He was crouching in the morning light beside the fire, which he'd rekindled. His black hair, as dark and sleek as the night sky, was wet and smoothed back from his face. The deepening stubble of beard gave him a faintly roguish look that seemed appropriate after last night. His blue eyes turned lazily to take her in, curled up in the blanket, bare limbs poking out at odd angles. He smiled.

"You look delicious, darlin'," he rumbled in his sexiest Texas drawl.

Shivers ran up her spine and she extended an arm. "Come here, Ranger, and kiss me."

He did, thoroughly, and she collapsed back into her nest of rumpled wool. An intriguing odor drifted over to her. Kate twitched her nose. "What's that?" she asked, sniffing.

"Coffee boilin'. Want some?"

"Mmm-hmm."

"I've got a little bit of the jerky left."

"Please, not the first thing in the morning."

"There's bread," he offered, "but it's pretty stale."

"It'll do fine dunked in hot coffee." Kate sat up and reached for her clothes. Jack had piled them within reach of where she'd been lying.

She was aware of him watching her put on her bra. She scooted her panties up over her hips while she was still half under the blanket. "A hot shower would feel wonderful right now. A bath would be even better," she commented.

"Sorry."

Kate finished dressing, with some assistance from Jack in lacing the detestable corset. After finger-combing her hair, she accepted a tin mug from him, full to the brim with steaming black coffee.

"If you take cream and sugar, we're out of luck," he said apologetically.

"I do, but don't worry about it." This morning, he could have handed her mud in a cup and it would have seemed ambrosia.

She sat, sipping her coffee, dunking the crusty bread into it, watching Jack do the same as he sat across the fire from her with his long, blue-jeaned legs hinged up in front of him.

His eyes drifted away from her toward the dusty trail that led into town, and she knew he was thinking about the day ahead. With the passing of every hour, they came closer to the time of Jack's death, which would happen all over again if they didn't find his killer first and do something to stop him. Only, this time, she would be there to *see* it happen. Kate didn't know, in her heart of hearts, if she was capable of surviving that horrible moment.

Not now . . . not after last night.

She finished her bread and stared into the depths of her mug, swirling the dregs of her drink thoughtfully. Kate considered the men they'd come across already—the ranch hands at del Sol, Sheriff Stony Phelps and that lascivious drunken prospector, Clint Dewey. Any one of them might have cheerfully shot Jack.

Then there was Yancy, of course. He was the most obvious suspect. But Jack didn't seem at all worried about him. He claimed he saw Yancy die. That should eliminate Yancy from suspicion, but Kate was beginning to wonder how much faith they should put in Jack's memory or his hunches. Maybe everything wouldn't happen the same way as it had before. Maybe, as Jack himself had said, her presence was acting as a catalyst to change the balance of events and people's reactions.

Kate shook her head to clear her mind. If her being here changed everything, there might be too many factors to investigate in the time they had left. She'd try returning to more straightforward theories.

Yancy's friend Hornsby was a strong possibility. He was older than Yancy, probably pictured himself as the boy's protector. Hornsby seemed to always be there, willing to do the younger man's bidding. Jack implied the cowboy might have taken part in the colonel's murder, although he had no proof.

How would Hornsby react if someone killed Yancy? Wouldn't he go gunning for the man who'd done it? What if he thought that man was Jack? What if it *was* Jack?

She sipped her coffee, now nearly cold. Her mind shifted gears again—thoughts drifting freely through her still-awakening mind in the crisp desert morning air—and returned to other suspects.

Stony Phelps. Maybe he was a good man, just trying to do his job and keep peace in San Antonio—a town plagued by violence, only beginning to recover from a bitter war and severely challenged by its multiethnic makeup.

One thing was clear about Phelps: he hated Rangers, made no secret of it. He seemed to especially dislike Jack's interference in his town. But would one man of the law shoot another in the back? Wasn't that totally against his sworn duty, if not against his character?

Clint Dewey. Slimebucket that he was, he must have left the Sweetwater with a shattered pride as well as a mighty sore groin after his run-in with Kate's knee. In her experience, a man might forgive many things—being cheated by a car dealer, losing at cards, even an unfaithful woman—but he rarely forgot the person who humiliated him in front of his friends. Dewey had been reduced to a bawling lump when she'd nailed him with her knee. And Jack had been there to rub it in. A snake like Dewey might well plot to sneak up on his nemesis and gun him down from behind.

Then, of course, there must have been dozens of others—the border raiders, Comanche or Kiowa taking a desperate stand to regain their lands, Confederate renegades—all men Jack and his fellow Rangers had tried to run off or capture. Who among them might have ambushed Jack on some lonely stretch of trail or lain in wait for him in a San Antonio alley and fired a bullet into him?

The mere thought of Jack's violent end brought hot tears to Kate's eyes. She wiped them away before he could see. She had to be strong for him.

"Ready?" he asked.

She blinked up at him, took a last swallow of cold coffee mixed with acidy grounds and pasted on a smile.

"As I'll ever be." Standing, she handed him the mug, which he packed away in his saddlebags.

They kicked sand on the fire, folded the blankets and saddled the horses.

"Where are we headed now?" she asked.

"North," he said.

"Not south, toward the border? The sheriff seemed to think that's where Yancy was headed."

"He may be, or my boys may be chasing a shadow. Yancy's not as stupid as he acts sometimes. He might figure the Rangers expect him to leave the country. Might even send a few of his friends as decoys down toward the border."

"But why? Why not just get the hell out of here?" she asked.

They rounded the buttes and pointed the horses toward town.

"Because Yancy's got plans back this way," Jack said darkly.

A shiver curled up Kate's spine. She sensed Jack had reached one of those bends in the road of his memory that afforded him a limited view of what lay ahead.

"What's going to happen, Jack?"

He shook his head. "It's not all that clear to me yet. But I do know that kid's askin' for dyin'. And I know it won't happen down in Mexico. I wish I could remember it all, wish there was some way..." He shook his head in frustration.

Kate felt herself tighten up all over, sharing Jack's dread of the days to come. But another part of her, in a way she couldn't explain, was excited by the prospect of being a part of this untamed world and a life that never stood still. One day never mirrored the day before it, or the one to follow.

Back home in Chester, five days a week, she walked Jesse and Anna to their bus, walked back up the driveway to the farm house, drank a second cup of coffee, dressed for work and drove herself to the bank. She chatted with Annette until the doors opened, then set up accounts for customers and answered questions over the phone about bank services. She ate her fruit and yogurt for lunch. She chatted politely with her boss. She went home, set out the kids' snack, then watched them step off the bus and run to her as she waited on the porch for them.

Every day—the same.

Every day with no surprises—just dealing with life. A case of the flu, a forgotten homework assignment, Barbara's perpetual nudges to date her relatives...

The same.

And now, here she was riding across the Texas desert beside the most handsome, sexiest man she could ever imagine. Jack was hers, for the brief time they had together. She could envision no greater thrill than sharing his adventure and helping him find his destiny...even if finding it took him away from her.

A twinge of sadness bit into her heart, and she winced involuntarily.

How hard it would be to go back to her old way of life. Maybe impossible. She wondered if, after knowing Jack and his world, she could ever really be the same woman.

Maybe she'd take Barbara up on her offer to go out with her New Jersey cousin. He'd never shine a light to Jack, she was sure of that. But he might be fun, or interesting or even somewhat good-looking. He might be a fair and decent man, like Max. A man who deserved a good woman.

"How far will we ride today?" she asked, over the lump in her throat.

Jack didn't seem to notice the change in her tone.

"Depends. There's some settlers out to the northwest of town, trying to range cattle on a few hundred acres. Families. Good people facing hard lives. I know one of the men. He goes into town for supplies and seems good at picking up on the gossip and reading into it. He might give us a couple more leads."

She nodded. "Why don't we cut due north then? It's not like this is a superhighway we're following."

Jack pulled a face at her. "Very funny. You may have noticed, we need supplies. That was the end of the bread and jerky. I thought you might appreciate a regular meal and some decent food in the saddlebags."

Kate's stomach responded immediately to the mention of food with a persistent rumble. She laughed. "Sounds wonderful. What's the specialty of the house around here?"

He looked down his nose at her as if she must be joking. "Beef."

Because they were still banned from town, it seemed unwise to venture into the middle of San Antonio to the Sweetwater, where Phelps often hung out. Jack had explained that only rudimentary eating establishments and one general store were located just off the trail at the town's edge. They were expensive and not very good, but their location was better for a quick escape, if it came to that.

Their meal wasn't fancy or at an ideal time for fine dining. Kate could never have imagined eating a two-inch thick, platter-size sirloin at 9:00 a.m., but the juicy, panfried cut of meat, done just to her liking—charred outside, lightly pink inside—accompanied by a mountain of potatoes, filled her stomach happily.

She would have been in heaven if the bartender at the No-Name Saloon had brought out a Caesar salad and a bottle of good red wine.

"I've been thinking," she said, as she popped the last morsel of meat into her mouth, long after Jack had swabbed the final traces of juice from his plate with a hearty slab of fresh bread.

He leaned back in his chair and observed her with a contented smile. "What, darlin'?"

"I know I'm supposed to be a schoolteacher, but riding in a corset and dress is the pits."

"You said you don't want to wear men's clothes."

"Yes, but—"

"Around these parts you won't find any of those fancy department stores I saw advertised in your newspapers."

Kate sighed. "Maybe when we go back to Rancho del Sol, Pamela will have a suggestion."

Jack nodded. "Good idea. I hope you won't be too uncomfortable in the meantime. We don't have time for you to consult a seamstress." He stood up from the table, anxious to leave now that their hungers were satisfied.

They stopped next door at Peterson's General Emporium and Feed Store. There they laid in a supply of cornmeal, flour, coffee, bacon, dried beans and, for the horses, oats to supplement their grazing. After loading everything into the saddlebags, they filled their canteens. An hour after they'd ridden into town, they were off again.

It was three hours later before the first house came into view, although it wasn't really much of one. The structure was more of an elaborate lean-to, rough-hewn timbers and boards, some of which looked as if they'd been salvaged from a junk wagon. Beside the lean-to was a large pen constructed of sticks and rusting, coiled wire—just strong enough to barricade a half-dozen sorrowful-looking sheep and two lambs.

A man with graying hair and a weathered face came out into the sun to greet them, a rifle balanced in the crook of his folded arms.

"Howdy," he said warily.

"Afternoon," Jack said, smiling. "It's been a while since I've been out this way. You're new."

"Yup," the man answered, eyeing Kate with interest. "This your wife?"

"No, my cousin."

"Oh." He looked more interested. "Name's Josiah. Josiah Johnson."

"I'm joining my husband in Galveston," Kate inserted quickly. "I'm to open a school for young ladies there."

The sparkle in Josiah's eyes dimmed. "That a fact." His attention returned to Jack. "Yer headin' the wrong way, son."

Jack smiled. "I know the way to Galveston. I wanted to show my cousin a little of the hill country before I took her down to the gulf."

Josiah looked around. "Nothin' much t' see."

"I'm interested in the early settlers," Kate said, then realized she sounded as if she were a twentieth-century historian. "I mean, I'd like to talk to some of the families. One day, after the area's population has grown, I might open another school here."

"Are there many families with young girls hereabouts?" Jack asked, taking up her lead.

The old man squinted toward the west. "There's the Mc-Carys. Got themselves two purty girls nigh on twelve or thirteen, fixin' to be marryin' age." He spat on the ground and eyed Jack curiously. "I've see'd you before somewhars."

"Have you?" Jack asked.

"Shure have." Josiah lowered his rifle butt to the ground and used his free hand to swipe across his cracked lips. "I know, you was with that company of Rangers come and run off the those murderin' renegades up Austin way."

"Yes, I was," Jack said slowly. "But that must have been almost a year ago. I was assigned there when I first came to Texas," he explained to Kate before turning back to Josiah. "You were living up there then?"

"Shure was. Went up north to look for a wife. Didn't find none, though." He scratched his head thoughtfully. "There was a lot of hard feelin's after the Rangers left—you probably know that, son." This was the second time they'd heard this complaint, and it made Kate uneasy.

"Why?" Kate asked. "The Rangers were there to protect people."

"Oh, not from the settlers, from the raiders," Josiah explained. "Them rebel raiders had a durn good business fer themselves up there. Find a house, wait for the menfolk to leave, then ransack it for money and valuables. They'd run off the horses to sell before torchin' the place."

"That's terrible," Kate said.

"Shure is. Those boys got no heart. Never give a mind for the women and younguns. Kill 'em all, after they done with—" He looked sideways at Kate and coughed. "Just ain't right, but they don't cotton to being run off."

"Or hanged, when we catch them," Jack inserted.

Josiah chuckled. "That, neither. The ones that got away from you Rangers, they shure was steamed. Swore they'd get back at the lot of you."

Kate looked at Jack. "You really were involved in this?"

He nodded slowly, his eyes solemn and dark. "Yup. We chased a bunch of those bastards into a canyon outside of Austin. Half got away. The rest ambushed us, but we managed to turn the tables on them. One other man and I scaled the canyon walls and circled down behind them."

Kate swallowed. "You shot them?"

"Not before warning them to drop their guns and give it up." Jack's eyes locked grimly with hers. "They turned round and fired on us . . . one shot apiece. That's all they got off."

Josiah squinted up at the sun and scratched his grizzly beard. "Like as not, them boys have pardners lookin' for you, son."

"Reckon you're right," Jack agreed. "We'd better get moving."

Josiah nodded and held Sunny's bridle while Kate climbed onto the mare's saddle. "You two take care, hear? Don't go turnin' yer back on strangers."

Kate shivered, feeling as if someone had walked over her grave. She turned and stared at Josiah before looking at Jack. Was it a coincidence Josiah had warned Jack in the way he had? Watch your back.

Jack's eyes locked with hers. He nodded his understanding, and tugged the brim of his Stetson over his eyes. "We'll be careful, friend."

"Thank you," Kate said.

Josiah looked up at her wistfully, as if he wished they would stay so he'd have someone to talk to a little while longer.

Kate smiled at him. "Those young girls that live not far from here . . . ?"

"Yes, miss?"

"You said they were close to marrying age. Why not take their father one of your lambs—as a neighborly gesture." She raised one brow, knowingly.

Josiah's face brightened. "A lamb? Like a present."

"Right."

"Them girls is a little young for me."

"How old are you?" Kate asked.

"Not as old as I look." He winked at her. "And in a year or two, why I might have got me a few score of longhorn. Hate sheep. Meanin' to get rid of 'em. Smell horrid, they do."

Kate laughed. "I'll bet if you had a nice little cabin to offer your bride, that would make a difference, too. A woman wants a home to furnish and make nice for her husband and children."

"Children." Josiah beamed at her. "Shure yer set on Galveston, miss?"

"I am, Josiah. I've found my man. Now you go after your woman."

They left him, scurrying around between the pen and lean-to, picking up scattered sticks and yanking knee-high weeds, standing back to view his property from a different angle, then busying himself again. Kate could imagine Josiah planning his cozy cabin to lure a young wife to his side. She could think of no happier prospect. And who knew? In time, Josiah and his wife might have a dozen children and thousands of acres to their names.

"How old do you suppose Josiah is?" she asked Jack as they moved Apache and Sunny farther along the trail into hill country.

"Maybe forty. Maybe less."

She stared at him. "Is that *all?*"

"Life is hard out here—back in my time," he said. "People live and age fast."

"Do you think he'll find a wife?" she asked, feeling a flush of excitement at the prospect of having sent Josiah off on a mission of romance.

"Oh, I'd guess he will, soon enough. Now that he's had a look at you." Jack laughed. "I suspect you set his pulse racing, darlin'. You did indeed!"

They rode for almost an hour, following a riverbed that sometimes ran with cool, green water and sometimes went dry when the stream disappeared beneath the rocky ground. The bank was bordered by live oaks, overhung with graceful billows of gray Spanish moss.

More houses had been built along the crest of the hill above the river's banks. Many were of stone, and some sported pretty bay windows with planters of bright flowers beneath them.

"A German settlement," Jack explained. "They've been growing corn and cotton, doing quite well."

"They're snug-looking little houses," Kate remarked.

Jack nodded, but didn't seem inclined to talk anymore. As they rode higher into the hills, Kate knew his mind was elsewhere.

Her own thrill with having lit a fire under a prairie romance had waned as the reality of their situation returned full force. They'd found another set of enemies for Jack. Instead of eliminating suspects, they'd doubled them. Whether the renegade soldiers killed out of misplaced patriotic fervor, anger or—as Josiah had suggested—purely for profit, they'd certainly murder for revenge.

Jack rode in silence, the muscles in his face taut. He must have been thinking about the renegades, too, she decided.

Kate reached across the space between them and touched Jack on the arm. "We'll make it. We'll find him before it's too late."

He shook his head solemnly. "I was just thinking—in a way, how this all turns out won't make much difference one way or another to you."

Kate stared at him, shocked. "What are you talking about? You think I'm looking forward to standing by and watching some gunfighter blast you to kingdom come?"

"Not at all," he said softly, and leaned out of the saddle to kiss her on the cheek. "It's only that, either way, I'll be out of your life in just a few more days."

Kate had been trying very hard not to think about that. But it was true. Jack would either die as he had in his first life, or he'd live through the day and continue living in the nineteenth century, while she returned to Chester and her own time. Either way, she'd be without him. Either way, her days of adventure and happiness would abruptly end.

She swallowed and looked up to blink at the sun, now past its meridian. "Let's not talk about that," she whispered. "Let's just enjoy what time we have now. This is beautiful country."

She concentrated on the thick, fragrant screen of live oak and cedar lining their trail. Birds flitted through the upper branches and chirped as if they, at least, hadn't a worry in the world. Patches of sunlight dappled Sunny's lustrous neck, and she stroked the sorrel's mane thoughtfully, regathering her emotions.

Jack brought Apache to a stop and took Sunny's reins in his hand. In the next moment, he'd slid from his own saddle and was pulling Kate down from hers. He held her tightly, kissing her so deeply, she gasped for breath.

"You are the most exciting and bravest woman I've ever known," he rasped. "Why fate didn't deal us the right cards to spend eternity together, I'll never understand. *Never!*"

She buried her face in the collar of his shirt and wrapped her arms around his ribs tightly. "Just hold me," she whispered. "Hold me, Jack."

And for the moments they were lost in each other's embrace, nothing else in the world or in all of time mattered.

Chapter 12

A sound from the valley below broke through Kate's sleep-drugged mind, and she rolled over on the bed of pine needles where she and Jack lay. A hot wind had followed them into the hills from the desert. It blew around them, rustling the leaves of the stunted oaks and slender fir trees overhead. The air was fragrant with spicy pine, moss and wildflowers.

"We'd better get moving before someone sees us and decides we're acting suspiciously. Folks out here can't afford to trust strangers," Jack said, tenderly easing Kate away from him. "I expect the McCary spread isn't too far from here, maybe just beneath us in the valley."

Kate brushed the telltale forest floor from her dress and plucked twigs from her hair. A few minutes later, she felt reasonably tidy and mounted Sunny. They rode slowly down the graceful, green slope to the cabin below.

This ranch had a more established look than Josiah's lean-to, but was far less glamorous than del Sol. There was a log house—big enough for at least two good-size rooms—a shed and two sturdy corrals. Several men were working in the larger of the two fenced compounds, where twenty head or more of longhorn cattle jostled each other nervously.

"Looks like they may be brandin' today," Jack commented. "Ranchers free-range the cattle around here, but at the rate the land's bein' stripped bare, cattlemen will probably throw up fences to keep the sheepherders out."

Kate had read about terrible range wars between cattlemen and sheep men in the West. "Why can't they share the land?"

"Sheep totally strip grazing land. They leave it barren, useless for anything," Jack explained. "Cattle will starve if set out to graze after sheep have had a go at it."

As they approached the house, one of the men motioned to a young boy, who left the corral and headed toward them. The boy observed them shyly from beneath a sandy lock of hair. He reminded Kate of Jesse, a little older perhaps, but just as bashful around strangers.

He walked stiffly across the yard and halted in front of Apache, looking up at Jack. "Pa says if you come to help with the brandin', go on into the house first. Ma has coffee and biscuits."

Jack smiled at the boy, and Kate's heart melted at the warmth in his eyes. *He'd be good with children. He likes them,* she thought. Good with the children he'd have with Kathleen. Good with Jesse and Anna, if he'd ever had the chance to meet them, she thought sadly.

"We're not here to help, son. Sorry. Came to ask your pa some questions." Jack lifted a hand casually to the star on his vest.

The boy's eyes grew wide. "You a Ranger?"

"Yup." Jack's eyes twinkled.

"For honest gosh real? Yer not joshin' me?"

"Nope."

Kate couldn't help cracking a smile behind her hand.

The boy spun around and ran, hell-bent for leather, toward the corral, shouting for his father.

"Come on," Jack said. "We'd better ride on up. No telling what that youngster is telling his pa."

Kate looked around her. Even in the middle of the wilderness, all around the property there were signs of a real home, of beginnings of what might someday become an important and lovely ranch. Someone had brought in enough rich loam to cultivate a small flower garden near the front porch. A red-painted rocking chair sat near a small table with a basket of knitting on it. The outbuildings looked new and sturdy, and there were signs of a new wing being erected off one end of the house.

Neighbors helping neighbors, she thought as she looked at the men in the corral. Times in the country hadn't changed that much.

The big man who'd sent the boy to them looked up and frowned, said something to the other men, then strode across the yard toward them. Jack dismounted and helped Kate down from Sunny.

"Howdy," the man boomed. "I'm Daniel McCary. Sorry I didn't come over myself, Ranger. Thought you were more neighbors come to lend a hand. The county's growin' so fast, sometimes you can't keep track of everyone." He turned to Kate with a warm smile. "And who is this? The governor hasn't started recruitin' ladies, has he?"

"I'm Kate Fenwick, Jack's cousin from Vermont. I'm starting a school for young ladies."

"You are, are you?" He looked at her as if this were a novel idea. "I heard of 'em out East, but here... Guess somethin' like that wouldn't hurt my girls. Or my boy, either. Someday they'll need to know more'n runnin' cattle."

Kate liked him. He was a smart man, thinking about his children's future. "Unfortunately, I won't be setting up the school here. It will be in Galveston."

Daniel nodded. "Can't say I blame you. Hear they got about everything in Galveston—library, fancy concert hall, hotels near as fine as in Europe. Hard on a woman out in these parts—dang hard." He glanced toward the house. "My wife, Amy Jo, she's done real good by me and the younguns. She's a strong woman, but I knowed there's times she'd like the company of another woman close to hand. We been here since before the war, and it ain't been easy for her."

Kate smiled at him. "You're a lucky man." She hesitated. "Some men around here would count themselves very lucky to have a wife like Amy Jo for company."

"Yes, ma'am. That's the truth."

Kate tipped her head to one side, as if considering examples. "Take that gentleman down the road from you—Josiah Johnson. He seems like a good man, and so lonesome."

"He is a good fella, all right. Comes on by to lend a hand whenever he can."

Kate looked at Daniel meaningfully. "I'll bet he comes by for more reasons than pure neighborliness."

The rancher's expression was a blank. "I knowed he likes Amy Jo's biscuits." Then his eyes widened. "You mean my girls?"

Jack grinned. "I expect he fancies one of them. He's a good man, ready to build himself a home, if he can find a woman to share it with him."

"Well, I'll be," Daniel shook his head, smiling. "I been thinkin' those two girls were goin' to have a hard time findin' a husband without leavin' here. Their mother wants to keep 'em close by—you know how women are about their families."

Kate found a stray pine needle stuck between the threads of her skirt, and quickly pulled it out. "It would be nice for your wife to keep at least one of the girls on a bordering spread."

Daniel looked thoughtful. "'Course, there's some age difference there. Amy Jo isn't too happy when the older fellas eye the girls."

"Age is relative." Just like time, Kate mused. "Besides, a more mature gentleman, ready to settle down...wouldn't he be better than some young buck with wanderlust?"

"You got that right. Wouldn't want either of my girls left in the dust by some young cowboy." Daniel winked at Kate and put an arm around her shoulders. "I'm gonna work on Amy Jo, and see if either of the girls got a secret spark for old Josiah. Who knows?"

Kate giggled, thrilled with her matchmaking. Something told her a McCary-Johnson match might be a good one.

"Why don't you go on into the house," Daniel suggested. "Amy Jo will have something cool for ya'll to drink. The Ranger and I'll have a talk."

"Thank you," Kate said.

Jack followed Daniel McCary up onto the porch of the log house and leaned against the timber supporting the low roof. He watched Kate disappear inside the door, heard the voice of another woman greeting her, and knew she'd be well taken care of. Strangely, that made him feel more melancholy than reassured.

Soon there would be someone else to take care of Kate, maybe even to make love to her. A morning would break...and he'd never see her again. She'd go on to live out her own life, in her own time, in her own way.

Without him.

Infinite sadness dragged at his heart, to know he wouldn't share those years with her, to know he'd never lie in her bed, touch her silky skin, burrow himself within her, in her own world and time. That could only happen here, in the past. Here, he reminded himself for the hundredth agonizing time, she didn't truly exist and he was living on borrowed hours.

When he thought he couldn't bear the thought another second, a faint, subtle refrain of hope filtered through the back of his mind, soothing his anguish. Jack couldn't have articulated its message to Kate, or even repeated it out loud to himself, but it promised him that Kate would survive, somehow. She was strong, stronger than she realized. She was smart, and a good woman and mother. Passionate and true and loving, she would find a mate with whom she could share the future.

Jack just regretted it couldn't be him.

Setting aside the ache in his heart, he turned to Daniel McCary, who had lighted a cigar. The rancher blew out a long, white puff of smoke as he propped one boot on his porch rail.

"So, what's this visit really about, Ranger?" he asked in a voice too low for anyone else to hear. "I don't for a minute believe that lady in there, cousin or not, and you are sightseein'."

Jack smiled wryly. McCary was no fool. "I'm trailin' a man name of Yancy... Yancy Kennard."

Daniel nodded. "Heard of the fella."

"He's got himself into a load of trouble."

"So they say." Daniel studied Jack, then the glowing tip of his cigar. "I get into town when I can, as much to keep up on the news as put by supplies. Pays to know what your neighbors are up to. Pays even more to know when the drifters and troublemakers are fixin' to raise a ruckus."

Jack nodded. He had no doubt that was how McCary and his family had lasted as long as they had out here in the middle of nowhere. Daniel counted on his neighbors and took any trouble seriously.

"So," Jack said, "what have you been hearin' about Yancy?"

"That he's out of control. I guess his sister just isn't tough enough to rein him in when he needs it."

Jack thought about that. "Strikes me, Pamela Kennard could lock horns with any man, Yancy included, and come out the winner."

"Well, now," Daniel drawled, "you never know. He's her kin, her kid brother. Probably got a soft spot for him, and he knows he can get what he wants from her. Seems he's never short of gamblin' or womanin' money. And I can't say as the boy's ever done a lick of work, leastwise not from what I heard."

Jack sucked in a long breath, and the air tasted of sweet cigar smoke and something good baking inside the house. "You're probably right. Hard as it is to believe, that boy's got Pamela twisted around his little finger."

Daniel straightened up, his glance drifting over to the corral. "Reckon I can't help you find Yancy, though. He ain't been up this way in months, near as I can tell. No talk of him anyway."

"What about renegade soldiers? We had trouble with them up north a while back."

"Run off a couple of 'em myself, back in the fall. Wished I'd shot 'em dead instead. Ornery types, they are. Heard later they'd killed a man and raped his wife before doing her, too. All for the few dollars they kept in their cabin."

Jack nodded. "Keep an eye out. And watch those girls of yours."

Daniel touched the brim of his hat, his eyes like flint. "You can bet I will, Ranger."

Kate had a wonderful visit with Amy Jo McCary and her daughters. The girls wanted to know everything about where she'd come from in Vermont, and what she planned to do in Galveston. It was clear they entertained few female visitors, and they were starving for social news from the more civilized world.

The best Kate could do was to dredge up information from her college history courses, trying to remember what the northeastern U.S. after the Civil War possessed or lacked in the way of architecture, means of travel and culture. They discussed the luxury of train travel, and of streetcars in the cities. Boston, Kate told them, was a grand city, with magnificent stores full of bonnets, lace gloves and ready-made dresses of the latest styles. Whatever she said, Amy and her girls clung to every word.

When Kate ran out of information, she took advantage of their rapt attention and brought up Josiah's name. The older of the two girls suddenly seemed to glow, and Kate wondered if she already nursed a crush on Josiah.

Amused, Kate wished she could have been at the ranch when the would-be suitor showed up with his beard trimmed, body scrubbed and dressed in a clean pair of jeans.

Amy showed her around her home with obvious pride. The main room of the cottage served as living room, kitchen and dining area. It was quite spacious by standards of the day and area. The walls had been plastered and tinted a pale peach, with stenciled panels along the tops of the walls and around the doorway and windows. The design was delicate and carefully drawn, full-blown roses and entwining green vines. Set into the window openings were panes of glazed, ripply glass that let in plenty of light. Crisp white eyelet curtains shaped themselves around the wood sills, and Victorian lithograph prints had been hung on two walls.

The furniture—a long, heavy table with rolled ends, benches and cupboard—were all of a dark-stained oak. On the cupboard's shelves were a blue glass pitcher, a milky-hued glass creamer and sugar bowl, and assorted pottery pieces of Mexican design. The back room was where the family slept, sharing two brass beds, plump with feather mattresses and lovely, hand-pieced quilts.

It was a beautiful home that seemed remote from the troubles of the times—a haven for a family at the cutting edge of the last frontier. Kate loved everything about it.

Kate and Jack left after eating a meal of ham, early-spring peas, buttery biscuits drowned in thick milk gravy, fresh peach compote and cups of dark coffee.

"Any word about Yancy or anyone else looking for you?" she asked as they rode away.

"Daniel's worried about renegades in general, but he couldn't give me any names. You find out anything?"

"Nothing that will help you, I'm sure, although I had a lovely visit. I have a feeling, if I did live here and now, Amy Jo McCary would be a good friend. And her girls are lovely. They can do anything a boy is capable of, but their mother has made sure they know how to act like ladies, too. She's a very modern woman."

Jack smiled and reached out to touch her arm.

"What's that for?" she asked.

"I love you, Kate Fenwick. I always will."

She stared at him, overwhelmed by the simple honesty she heard behind his words. *Always,* she thought. *Yes, and I will love you, too, Jack Ramsey, through eternity. Time and again.*

Tears welled in her eyes, and the ache in her heart, which seemed never more than a shadow away since she'd met Jack, intensified.

Jack reined in both horses. Apache and Sunny stood, stomping their hooves restlessly in the dry loam, snorting their displeasure with the delay.

"This is all too much for you," he said, leaning out of his saddle to cradle her head against his shoulder. "I didn't know...couldn't have guessed when I asked you to help me that things between us would turn out this way."

"I know you didn't, Jack. It's all right. I'll be fine."

"If I had believed we'd..." He let out a low groan of frustration and pain. "I can't change how I feel for you, Kate. If I had a choice, a way of bringing you into my life or joining you in yours, I would do it. I'd do it in a minute. You must believe me."

"I do." She sighed. "Let's just finish what we set out to do."

He sat back in his saddle and gazed at her. "I'm amazed," he whispered. "Absolutely amazed."

She thought to herself, *How many women, at any time in the their lives, have a man like this? How many ever experience an ecstasy so vast, a peace so deep as I have with Jack?*

It was this realization, that she was one of the fortunate few, that at last balanced her emotions.

Reaching up around his thick neck, Kate pulled Jack toward her and found his lips with hers. Their kiss was long and sweet, and spanned both time and space.

"I love you, too, Jack Ramsey," she whispered as her mouth parted from his. "I wouldn't have passed up this chance to be with you, even if I had known how hard it would be letting go when the time came."

He gazed at her, speechless, as if she were the only woman he'd ever loved, could ever love. And she felt stronger for the devotion and respect she saw mirrored in his enigmatic blue eyes.

"We'd better get moving," she murmured at last. "Time's running short, and—" Kate swallowed the rest of her words, and blinked in shock. An image flashed across her subconscious. Her heart suddenly raced, as if her entire body were reacting to imminent danger.

"What's wrong?" Jack asked, watching with concern as her hand fluttered to her breast. "Are you in pain?"

"No...yes!" Kate shook her head, trying to snap the image into sharper focus, but it faded and then was gone. "It's one of the children...maybe both! Jesse and Anna are in trouble. They need me." She looked at him pleadingly. "I don't understand how I know, *but I do,* Jack."

Leaving San Antonio now, she knew, would mean losing precious, irreplaceable time Jack couldn't afford to give her.

"We'll go back," he said without missing a beat.

"What about Yancy? About the others?" she cried.

"To hell with them for now. Your children need you. I can't ask you to sacrifice them for me."

Barbara turned away from Anna for just a moment, but it was long enough for the little girl to slip under the fence rail and dash across the meadow toward the spirited coal-black colt.

"Come back!" Jesse yelled.

Swinging around to the fence, Barbara followed the little boy's terrified stare, and a sick sensation filled her stomach. "Anna! No, stay away from him!"

Like all young creatures, the thoroughbred quarter horse was bursting with energy. Because he hadn't been around long enough to learn the ways of human beings, he was as wild as the wind.

"Come here, Licorice," Anna coaxed, holding out a handful of sweet green spring grass. "You're so pretty," she cooed. "Come here, boy."

The colt rolled a glassy eye, observing her warily, then darted away—mane and tail flying. Not in the least discouraged, Anna took off after him with a peal of giggles.

"Anna!" Barbara shouted, her eyes on the tiny, sharp hooves that kicked at the air. It was impossible to predict the animal's behavior. He might walk up to Anna, as gentle as lamb, then take it into his head to turn and race off, hooves flying. Anything in their way would be slashed. "Leave him alone, sweetheart! He might hurt you!"

"Licorice won't hurt *me*," the little girl warbled. "We're friends."

"Mom will *kill* us if anything happens to her," Jesse moaned.

"You've got that right," Barbara tossed over her shoulder. She vaulted the fence and tore across the field toward Anna.

Barbara thought for a moment she was going to make it.

The colt had settled down to munch a few stalks of grass that had poked up through the remains of the last Vermont snow. He seemed to be either unaware of or ignoring Anna as she stole up on him from behind. Barbara was only ten feet behind the little girl when the child let out a squeal of triumph and rushed forward as if to hug the little horse around its elegant neck.

A dark eye rolled in alarm, and the creature wheeled, bucking and lashing out with its hind legs. One hoof caught Anna just above her eye. She let out a little whimper, tottered for an instant, then collapsed on the ground.

Barbara scooped her up, running with her for the fence, not bothering to check on the severity of the wound until she'd gotten her inside the house.

"Is she okay? Is she dead?" Jesse shouted, bursting through the door to the den, only a few strides behind her.

Barbara laid Anna on the couch.

"No, she's not dead," she said.

She touched the soft flesh of her forehead. Miraculously, the hoof hadn't broken the skin, but an ugly lump was quickly rising beneath the skin. In the two minutes it had taken her to get from the field to the house, the purpling flesh had stretched and filled with fluid like a tiny balloon.

"We'd better take her to Urgent Care. Grab my keys there on the table, Jesse, that a boy."

Barbara lifted Anna's limp, almost weightless body. The little girl let out a soft moan and blinked up at her.

"Mommy?"

"No, honey—"

"Mommy's right here," a voice said from the stairway leading to the second floor.

Barbara nearly dropped the poor child.

"Wh-what are you doing home, Kate?" she gasped.

"We got home earlier than I'd planned," Kate said, rushing over to her daughter, who was sobbing softly. "It's okay, sweetheart. I'm here now. You're going to be just fine. Has your auntie Barb been beating you again?"

Barbara's mouth dropped open in dismay. "Kate, I swear, it was an accident—the new colt—"

Kate took Anna from her arms. "I'm teasing, silly. I saw everything from the upstairs window."

Barbara frowned at her. "I didn't hear you come in."

"You were already around in the back," Kate said briskly. "You drive the Explorer, I'll hold her in my lap. I think she's just a little woozy. I was afraid this would happen. She's been ogling that little fellow all week, waiting for her chance to touch him. I warned her to stay outside the fence."

"It's my fault. I wasn't watching her closely enough."

Kate shook her head at her friend. "You haven't been around kids enough. No amount of watching will keep some of them from trying the worst stunts."

Barbara drove, casting sideways glances at Kate as she negotiated the narrow back roads to the main highway. From there they would be only ten minutes from the hospital.

She felt somewhat better now that Kate was here, making so little of the incident. But she expected Kate's calm posture was for her benefit, so she wouldn't feel so badly.

Jesse sat in the back seat, unusually quiet. Barbara took this as a sign that he, at least, recognized the possible seriousness of his sister's injury.

Glancing back at Kate, Barbara felt sure there was something different about her friend. She knew Kate was good with kids, pretty levelheaded in the face of the usual catastrophes. But a doctor hadn't even examined the child yet, and Kate seemed implausibly secure in her expectation that Anna wasn't seriously injured. There was something else, too, an inexplicable serenity in her features, and emotions that had been lacking since Max's death—or, maybe, had never been there.

Barbara pulled the car up in front of the ambulance entrance, and Kate jumped out, carrying Anna. She was met at the door by a medic who hastily ushered her and the little girl inside.

"Do we have to stay in the car?" Jesse asked. "I always have to stay in the car when something important happens, except Dad's funeral . . . then I wished I could have stayed outside."

Barbara looked over the back of the seat at him, his blond hair mussed, a swatch falling over one eye. He was trying to be tough, not quite making it.

"We'll go inside. Let's find a parking space first."

Anna's injury turned out to be, in the technical jargon of the urgent-care physician, "A whopper of a goose egg."

He advised Kate to keep her daughter awake for the next eight hours, and watch for any signs of concussion. But he didn't expect she'd have more to deal with than a headache. He gave her a list of instructions, handed Anna and Jesse root-beer lollipops and warned the little girl about playing with animals bigger and stronger than she was.

After they were back at the house and the kids were settled in front of the TV with tuna sandwiches and potato chips for supper, Kate asked Barbara to stay for something to eat.

"I'm not very hungry," she said, her normally ruddy complexion pallid after their experience. "Let's just sit down and talk for a while. I could use a good cup of coffee."

"Good idea," Kate said.

Ten minutes later, they were seated at her kitchen table over steaming cups.

"So, tell me why you're back so soon," Barbara demanded. "You were only gone for seven or eight hours."

Kate shrugged. "We changed our plans, just took a day trip, driving around the countryside. . . ."

"And your friend—what's he like?"

"Jack? He's—" Kate's mind drifted away. How could she describe the wonderful things she felt when she was with him? Days in the hot sun, riding across the desert and up into the lonely, beautiful hills. A night lost in his arms. How very black the Texas sky became, and how many more stars glimmered in that ebony firmament than she'd ever seen in the heavens over Vermont. How could she make anyone understand how vastly the world had changed for her, after she'd been away for such a short time? Nothing in her life would ever be the same.

"Yes? Jack is what?" Barbara prompted, sipping her coffee and eyeing Kate.

Kate looked up over the pottery rim of her own mug. "Jack is marvelous. Perfect."

Barbara let out a whoop. "You're in love! Katie, I can see it in your eyes! That's great! When do I get to meet him?"

"You don't."

"What?"

"I said you don't. Don't ask me why, don't expect me to explain anything about him, or us, or the trip. Just be happy that I'm happy."

Barbara scowled at her. "I don't understand. You love the man, had the time of your life. You came back too early, and you're acting as if you'll never see him again. This doesn't compute!"

"I'll see him again. In fact, now that I know the kids are all right, I'd like to join him for the rest of the weekend, if you can still manage Jesse and Anna."

Barbara studied her face. "Good. Go." She took a swallow of coffee and stood up from the table.

"Where are you going?"

"To get some aspirin. My head hurts like hell."

Kate laughed. "In the cupboard above the sink. I'm sorry if this is hard on you. But I really appreciate all you're doing. The kids love being with you."

"Even if I do botch the job and nearly let them kill themselves." Barbara pried the cap off the plastic bottle and popped two tablets into her mouth. She swallowed them dry.

"Even then." Kate smiled at her. "Knock it off. I trust you with my children."

"Don't know why you should," Barbara grumbled, sitting down to finish her coffee. "Well, you run along and change. I can listen for Loverboy and answer the door when he gets here," she offered.

Kate stared at her across the table. As soon as she and Jack had arrived in the attic, she'd torn off her traveling dress and pulled on old jeans and a sweatshirt she'd found in a bag of mending. Now, to satisfy Barbara, she'd have to dress in something that looked like she was going out on a date, and then, somehow, sneak up into the attic to change yet again into her traveling dress. But then what? She couldn't simply disappear from there with Jack. Barbara would expect to see her walk out the front door, like any normal person.

"Yes, um, change," she stammered. "Listen, so I don't get the kids all stirred up, I'll just slip out quietly while you're with them. Jack said he'd meet me out by the road."

"By the road," Barbara repeated, quirking a brow at her. "Does this guy...have something to hide, or does he have some sort of ghastly scar? Like he might scare the kids?"

"No." Kate glared at her.

Barbara looked thoughtful. "You're not in any trouble or anything, are you, honey?"

"Of course not."

"Because if you were...if this guy has some kind of hold on you or is bad news, and you don't know how to handle him—"

"It's nothing like that. Really, I'm fine. I *will* be fine anyway..." Kate forced her chin up and managed to look her friend in the eye.

Barbara sighed. "All right. See you tomorrow night when you get back. Have fun."

Barbara waited until she heard Kate's footsteps moving along the second floor hall overhead. Then she followed her.

At the top of the stairs, she peeked around the corner. She saw Kate step through the door that led to the attic. A moment later, the stairs creaked.

"Why go up there?" Barbara muttered. It was, of course, none of her business who Kate met, where she went with him or why. *I should,* she told herself, *just be happy she's getting out of this house and seeing someone—anyone.* It was far better than the way she'd shut herself up in the old farmhouse and let the world go by for the past year.

But Barbara couldn't shake her curiosity, or the feeling that Kate might be getting herself into hot water. Something about this guy wasn't right, and Kate was as vulnerable as they came. Here she was, a financially independent woman, with a heart as big as all outdoors. She'd be an easy mark for any smooth-talking creep with even an ounce of charm.

Then there was the matter of the answering machine.

When Kate had called her the other day to ask if she'd baby-sit the kids, Barbara had walked in on the end of her message. There had been a long silence, and she'd thought no one was there. She reached out to shut off the machine, then Kate's voice came to her as if from the other side of the world.

"I refuse to let him do that to me," she'd said. "I won't confuse love with what can only be lust..."

Confuse love with... lust.

It seemed a conversation a woman might have after getting in pretty deep with a guy. And now, here was Kate with some story about going off on a weekend trip with some guy named Jack—but she'd miraculously popped up right when Anna needed her. Now she was disappearing again.

Something was definitely fishy, and she was bound to find out what it was.

Moving cautiously, Barbara sidled along the hallway wall. At the attic door, she paused and, pressing her ear to it, listened.

"She's fine... just a bump on the head."

Kate was talking to someone. Barbara was sure she didn't have a phone in the attic. Either Kate was hallucinating and dreaming up phantom dates, or someone was up there with her.

Barbara held her breath, listened again.

"I know what you said, but I'm honestly not jeopardizing their safety. Barb is great with the kids. Anna would have been fine even if I hadn't come back, but I'm glad I did because now I know it's nothing serious."

He's in the attic with her! Barbara thought wildly. *She's hiding some guy in her attic!*

Normally it wouldn't have crossed her mind to spy on anyone, especially her best friend. But she was convinced there was a question of a higher good involved. This Jack person had reduced Kate to lying and sneaking around as if she were a criminal.

Criminal.

The word burned like acid in Barbara's gut. That was it—maybe Kate had fallen for a prison inmate she'd somehow sprung, or some other kind of fugitive from justice. She was hiding him from the police right here in her house!

Barbara clenched and unclenched her fists, trying to calm herself. She didn't normally engage in flights of fancy, which was what this sounded like. But, as insane as the idea of Kate harboring a fugitive sounded on the surface, it was the only explanation Barbara could come up with.

Knowing what she had to do, she marched out to her truck and retrieved the shotgun bolted into the storage area behind the bench seat. As she passed the living room on her return trip, she noted that the children were still engrossed in their TV show.

She climbed to the second floor and stood in the hallway, breathing and listening, breathing and listening, while she loaded the gun. Unless things were even worse than she suspected, all she'd have to do was show the gun, and the guy would clear out. She hoped. In any case, it wouldn't be the first time she'd bluffed a man . . . or the first time she'd fired one of these things because she'd had to.

Slowly Barbara opened the attic door and eyed the long, straight run of wooden steps. The bare bulb above was on, but she could see nothing beyond the waxy yellow circle of light. With a strong push against the railing, Barbara launched herself up the flight in a mad dash and spun to face the length of the attic and confront Kate with her mysterious lover.

All she confronted was a pile of unmarked boxes and assorted junk. The room appeared empty.

Pivoting around, breathing hard, she stared into dark corners, taking a shaky step forward, still believing she'd surprise Kate in the arms of a stranger. But five minutes later she had searched every corner and finally admitted to herself that no one was there.

Chapter 13

The white stucco walls of Rancho del Sol glistened distantly in the desert sun. Kate had never seen such a beautiful sight. Even the green hills of Vermont, which she loved dearly, couldn't compete with the drama of the Spanish-style enclave rising out of the middle of the prairie like a mirage.

"It's stunning," she breathed. "Pamela is so fortunate to have such a beautiful home."

"I expect she works hard to make it that way," Jack commented. "They say, even before her father died, she had a hand in running the ranch. He must have been disappointed, Yancy growing up the weak troublemaker, his daughter becoming the strong one."

"I've always believed," Kate said, "that strength is more a matter of individual character than sex. Women can be just as tough and effective as men when it comes to building a successful business."

Jack slanted her a look. "Between you and Pamela, I'm beginning to realize that not all of you gals are delicate flowers."

She grinned at him. "That isn't to say there's anything wrong with your Kathleen. She probably never was encouraged to take risks, go out on her own."

Jack nodded. "There you're right. Her father expected his girls to keep a clean house, provide meals for him and the farmhands, and marry local boys. Her sisters did just that and nothing more."

"No doubt that's what he thought you'd be—a hometown boy forever," Kate commented, understanding a little better the emotional strain Jack must have suffered when he'd made his decision to leave Vermont for Texas.

"Right. It just wasn't that easy to pick up where I'd left off before the war."

They rode on, the sun climbing higher in the sky. By staying in Chester for a couple of hours, they'd missed the night in 1867. It was now early morning, the day after their trip into the hill country. Kate figured they were right on time for their luncheon date with Pamela Kennard.

As she and Jack rode, Kate enjoyed their easy companionship, following the now-familiar trail across the desert. Distances were deceptive. One moment, Rancho del Sol seemed to loom just out of reach. Twenty minutes later, it seemed no closer.

"Why did you choose Texas?" she asked. "I mean, why not somewhere else, like in the south? The war damaged vast stretches of plantation lands, and Reconstruction was a painful period everywhere."

Jack's smile was bittersweet. "It wasn't anything I'd planned. I just knew I wasn't happy at home. I felt terribly restless. Then an old friend from my days at Dartmouth, Edward Cushing, came to Chester for a visit."

"He talked you into going to Texas?"

"No, not at first. He just talked." Jack grimaced. "Ed was always a talker. But he was an even better writer, and he was a dreamer, too."

"A dangerous combination." Kate absently stroked Sunny's coarse, white mane.

"It can be, sometimes. But Ed had done all right for himself. He graduated from Dartmouth a couple of years ahead of me, and took off for Texas. Said he wanted to teach down there and see the last frontier before it was too late. That was just before the war broke out."

She nodded, guiding Sunny closer to Apache. Jack's voice lowered, as if he were drifting off with his memories. She didn't want to miss a word.

"And did he teach?"

"No, couldn't find a position. Ed finally took a job editing for a fledgling newspaper, the *Houston Telegraph*. He became editor in chief, then part owner, too, and finally bought out the original owner entirely. In the summer of 1865, after the war ended, he came North looking for a more modern press to take back with him. I think he was also trying to feel out the political whims of Federal policymakers in Washington."

"Those must have been uneasy times for the former Confederate states," she mused.

"Very. Reconstruction weighed heavily on his adopted state. Many of the most powerful men in the South suddenly found themselves with nothing." He shook his head. "Ed told me about the particular problems of Texas. The war had removed all protection from the Mexican border and the frontier. Well, I explained all of that to you before. Settlers were in terrible peril, with no one to protect them."

"But the Rangers—"

"Yes, the Rangers . . ." Jack's wide shoulders settled down and back in a determined gesture. His gaze steadied on the red tile roofs of del Sol. "Ed told me about the Texas Rangers, and how the governor had drawn up a mandate, making them the first line of defense on the borders. Later, he used them to track down Confederate raiders."

"So you thought enlisting would give you the opportunity to help."

"Right. As long as I was doing somebody some good, as long as the trails were long enough and the days' rides hard enough, I didn't think so much about men dyin' senselessly on a blood-soaked field. Petersburg was pure hell, Kate. Chester just didn't get me far enough away from it."

Kate gazed at him, moved deeply by his story. He had a strong profile. His blue eyes were softened by remembered grief. The black Stetson shadowed them and might have masked his emotion if she hadn't learned to read him so well. "You're a good man, Jack Ramsey."

With a half smile, he reached out one hand and chucked her affectionately under the chin. "Reckon that's why someone decided I deserved one last chance."

* * *

The sun was high overhead when they rode into the yard at Rancho del Sol. A familiar lanky figure was leaving the main house as they handed their horses over to a young boy with golden skin and handsome Spanish features.

"Howdy, Sheriff," Jack said, touching the brim of his hat.

Stony Phelps peered at him from under thick brows as he tipped his own hat back on his head. "Hullo there, Ranger. What are you doing out here? Thought you'd be long gone for the border by now."

"Not much sense in my following on the heels of Company F. They either got Yancy or they didn't. I took a coupla days' informal leave. Better I keep an eye out around these parts for the boy, in case he decides to double back."

Phelps eyed him long and hard. "I still don't want to see you anywhere near my town. And if you find Yancy, I want a talk with him before you take him anywheres."

"Why? You know the governor issued an order for the Rangers to bring in the colonel's murderer."

"I know that well enough, but no one's sure it was Yancy who done it."

Kate coughed softly. "I understand there were witnesses, Sheriff."

Phelps turned his cold gaze on her. "Witnesses sometimes tell the truth, and sometimes don't, miss. Sometimes they're not even where they say they were." He took a step closer to Jack and jabbed a finger at him. "I told you, this is *my* territory, and I mean to see justice is done here. Your sidekicks come ridin' in here a few years back, with fancy papers sayin' they'll make everything peaceable-like. Well, I ain't seen it happen. Until it does, Ranger, you stay out of my way and let me do my job."

"Is your job protectin' killers?" Jack asked, his eyes darker than she'd ever seen them.

Phelps spat on the ground. "My job's protectin' the citizens of San Antonio and her territory. *My* territory. I ain't seen no proof young Yancy was in on that killin'. Until I do, you won't get any cooperation out of me. And if you rile up my people hereabouts, I can tell you sure as there's twin buttes in that there desert, I'll come lookin' for you—lady cousin or no. If you don't want her to be short one relation, you best be leavin' my territory real soon. Understood?"

"Understood, Sheriff." Jack looked at him evenly.

The two men stood, glaring, looking as if they were each waiting for the other to leave.

Kate took a deep breath and blew it out in disgust. "You two are ridiculous. You're on the same side of the law, for crying out loud! You both want to find out who killed the colonel, and you want peace for Texas."

"This isn't any of your affair," Jack ground out.

Phelps didn't so much as blink, but his left hand gravitated slowly toward his holster. "You don't understand, miss. Better be steppin' out of the way."

Kate shuffled back a few feet, a lump of fear clogging her throat. "Wait. Please don't do anything you'll be sorry for. Either of you. Stop."

The hate in Phelps's eyes was unmistakable. Jack seemed just as unwilling to back down or leave.

"Jack, no—"

"Shut up, I said!" he barked, cautiously moving one side of his vest to clear a path to his gun.

"That's no way to talk to a lady," a cool voice pronounced from the veranda.

Both men swiveled around, and Kate looked up to see Pamela Kennard standing in a slim, black riding suit with a rifle balanced skillfully in her hands. She cocked the hammer and leveled the barrel at the two men.

"He don't belong here!" Phelps bellowed.

"Ranger Ramsey and his cousin are my dinner guests," Pamela said, her voice as unruffled as a nighthawk's feathers. "This isn't a very hospitable way to treat company, Stony."

"But he's gunning for *your own brother!*" he objected. "How can you take him into del Sol? Your daddy would roll over in his grave, Pamela Sue."

"The Rangers have little chance of running into Yancy. I suspect the foolish boy has taken himself off into the hills or struck out for California by now." She sighed wearily, but her eyes were still sharp, alert to any move either man might make. "This here gun is getting mighty heavy, Sheriff. I'd just as soon put it down, but if you don't move yourself off my property, I'll have to figure out another way of lightening it."

Her finger eased the trigger back.

Phelps's eyes widened. "Now, Pamela—"

"I mean it, Stony. You leave my guests alone while they're on my land. Now move."

He moved. Striding quickly across the dusty yard, Phelps made for his horse, mounted and wheeled it around and out of the gate. He rode off without looking back.

Kate felt her knotted fists relax at her sides. The tension in her stomach slaked away.

"I don't like that man," she murmured.

Pamela leaned her rifle against a porch rail and came down the veranda steps to take Kate's arm. "The country's crawling with them, my dear. Don't let a little male ego fluster you. I've found a little gunpowder works wonders. Come on inside where it's cool."

Kate allowed herself to be led through the ornately carved wooden doors, into the dim interior of the foyer. "The sheriff doesn't fluster me," she said, at last finding her voice. "He's dangerous. I don't trust him."

She glanced over her shoulder at Jack, who'd followed them inside. He was shaking his head, warning her not to give away the source of her fear.

She knew she couldn't confide in Pamela that she was afraid Phelps might be the one who would fatally wound Jack. But the suspicion haunted her. This was the second time she'd witnessed the man's pride edging him toward the breaking point.

Pamela led them into the parlor and rang a silver filigree bell. A servant girl immediately appeared in another doorway with a tray of crystal, and ice for drinks.

Kate stared at the sparkling cold chips. There were, of course, no electric freezers. "That looks refreshing. How on earth do you have ice in the desert?"

Pamela looked pleased. "A luxury, I admit. I send a boy into the mountains once every week. There are a few places, very high up, that hold the snow and ice almost year-round. He brings a wagon load back, enough for special occasions." She smiled.

"Well, I think it's wonderful," Kate said. "And if that's lemonade, I could drink a gallon."

"It is, and you shall if that's your choice of beverage. Jack?"

"Whiskey," he grumbled, still emanating angry vibrations from his confrontation with the sheriff.

Pamela winked at Kate. "Men," she whispered.

The two women chatted over their lemonades for a few minutes, then Pamela glanced across the room to where Jack sat, pensively nursing his drink. "I don't know what's wrong with you, dragging this poor girl all over the prairie in her teaching garb."

Kate laughed. "I really didn't have much choice. What do you wear when you ride?"

Pamela stood up. "Something like this, only a bit more practical. Come with me. I'll show you."

Kate followed her from the room, across the foyer and along a white corridor lined with brilliant oil paintings.

They arrived at a string of rooms, doors closed, and Pamela opened one. Inside, dark Spanish wood furniture, heavy and ornate, pressed against the walls. The white stucco offset the weighty furnishings, making the room look still larger than it was. A thick brocade tapestry of red and black covered the bed, and the long spikes of an enormous yucca plant rose nearly to the ceiling.

It was a very masculine room, Kate thought, not at all delicate or flowery. It suited the woman who slept there.

Pamela strode over to a huge armoire and pulled wide the doors. "Now, let's see. . . . There is this, and this, and this."

As she spoke, she pulled out one outfit after another.

Leather and cloth chaps, split skirts and Spanish-style riding britches. She flung all on the bed.

"You see how much more practical apparel of this sort is?" Pamela said. "Not very pretty or ladylike—but better suited to the desert and trail. They protect your legs from chafing."

"I see," Kate said, holding up one of the split skirts. It was beautifully tailored, a suede so fine, it looked as if it could breathe, so light it felt almost like silk between her fingertips. "This is lovely. I've never seen anything like it."

"I had it made for me in Ciudad. A woman there, she sews like a dream. I will give you her name. On your way to Galveston, you may stop and see her."

Kate smiled, trying to look enthusiastic even though she knew she'd never be able to follow up on Pamela's suggestion. Somewhere around San Antonio was where Jack met his end. She'd vowed to stay with him until his fate was decided, one way or another.

"Thank you. I'll look her up." Reluctantly she folded up the skirt.

"Try it on," Pamela said, waving a hand heavy with silver rings.

"No, I couldn't."

"Do it. No fussing."

It seemed that arguing with Pamela would do little good. With the other woman's help, Kate slipped out of Kathleen's dress and into the split skirt. She worried about her modern undergarments, but Pamela simply glanced at them and muttered something about Parisian fashions and let it go at that.

The skirt fit as if it had been made for her. Each hand-sewn seam gently hugged her hips and waist, and the soft folds of leather caressed her abraded legs.

"This is beautiful." She sighed.

"Keep it," Pamela said. "I have others."

"No, I couldn't."

"Why the hell not? It's perfect for you."

Kate shook her head.

Pamela glared at her in irritation. "How much longer before you leave for Galveston?"

"Just a few days."

"Well, then keep it at least that long. Or send it back to me by stage from wherever you are when you're done with it."

Kate doubted stage delivery could be arranged from modern-day Chester but decided it would be impolite to refuse. "Thank you. The skirt will make traveling a lot more pleasant."

That much decided, Pamela insisted upon selecting a blouse, proper hat and boots for her, as well. Although the size of boot Pamela now wore was too large for Kate, she'd kept one pair that she'd had made while she was a teenager, and they fit Kate well enough. They went downstairs to show everything to Jack.

He'd picked a book off of one of the shelves that lined a long wall of the room and was reading when they walked in. As she held up the clothing for his inspection, Kate sensed a tension about him that somehow didn't fit his relaxed pose. She wondered if he'd used their absence to search rooms at that end of the house, for signs of Yancy, and she felt a little irritated with him for doubting Pamela's word.

Still, it was possible her brother might have sneaked back to the house without her knowing it. His friends were still here. They'd undoubtedly hide him.

An older woman with a proud tilt to her gray head stepped into the room and spoke in Spanish to Pamela, who nodded to her.

"Good, the meal is ready." She seized Jack's arm, then took Kate by the hand. "Come. Maria is a marvelous cook. You'll never taste better."

Solid silver place settings had been arranged on a massive table. The china was fine bone porcelain, a thin gold rim running around each plate and platter. Kate had once admired a similar set in an antique store, and nearly choked on discovering the price.

Pamela was right about Maria's cooking, Kate thought as she accepted a second helping of the delicious rice-and-chicken dish. There were fresh vegetables, cooked crisp-tender and seasoned with a delectable mélange of spices. The wine was served just below room temperature. Kate guessed it must have come directly from the wine cellar.

"Jack tells me you've had a hand in the ranch for a long time."

"Yes," Pamela said, glancing across the table at him quickly, "although I'm surprised he knows. You are a newcomer to San Antonio, relative to the rest of us."

"Word gets around," he said pleasantly. "Especially about unusual things. A girl running a ranch."

Pamela arched an eyebrow and looked at Kate. "You must educate *him* before educating the young ladies in Galveston. A *girl*, indeed. If allowed, we women would run the world on our own, and do it much more efficiently."

Kate laughed. "I think men realize that. They just don't like to admit it."

Jack rolled his eyes dramatically. "This is unfair. Two against one—although both of my opponents are truly lovely."

Kate raised her wine goblet to him. "Shall we forgive him, Pamela?"

"For the time being." She turned back to Kate. "You see, the people around here don't understand how it was for me, so they think of Pamela Kennard as rather an oddity. My mother died when I was eight years old. There was no other woman in the household, only servants. My father—he would have let the house go to ruins. All he cared about were his cattle, his land—buying more, protecting what he had. The house..." She waved an elegant hand. "This was nothing to him. A bed in which to sleep, a place to come to for food, then out again to where his heart lived, with the cattle and horses."

"So the outdoors remained his, and you took over the indoors, the house."

"Yes, I did. At eight years of age, I took over my mother's job. I made him tell all the servants that I was to be in charge—at first only when he was away on a long drive. Then all the time."

Kate looked around her. "You've built a beautiful home. The art, the furniture and—" her fingertips ran down the crystal stem " —just everything. It's so lovely."

"Thank you," Pamela said. "I cherish it all." She sighed. "But since my father's death four years ago, I have less time to deal with the house. It cannot stand without the ranch to support it. And I dare not leave running del Sol to foremen, who are all crooked and would cheat me at the drop of a Mexican peso."

"There are some good men about who would do well for you," Jack said.

"I've yet to see them," she snapped, her eyes suddenly afire. "Don't think I haven't tried to hire the right man. At first I thought I might train Yancy, that he might at last grow up and learn responsibility . . . but that's a dream. He's twenty-three, you know, and still impossible. He was a wild, untamable child, and he will always be so."

Jack leaned over the table. "He loves you, Pamela. The boy may have gotten himself into a hellhole of troubles, but he does love his sister."

She looked away and frowned. "How would you know?"

"Something was said one day. Yancy interpreted it as a slight to you. He would have killed the man."

"You?" she asked, glancing back at him with a curious smile.

"Yup. It wasn't an insult. He just thought it was."

"I was there," Kate put in. "He nearly exploded at the thought of anyone saying something nasty about you."

"Well," Pamela said brusquely, lifting her damask napkin to her lips, "I suppose he can't be all bad. There must be some loyalty there. We are, after all, of one blood—the only heirs to Rancho del Sol."

Kate smiled at her and laid her hand over Pamela's. "If he'd just give himself up, perhaps there's some way that he could prove himself innocent of killing the colonel. Maybe he's telling the truth."

Pamela sighed. "I wouldn't bet that Sheffield plate you've just finished eating off. I know my brother. I know what he's capable of. Killing, I'm afraid, comes too easily for him."

Kate looked at her sadly. What must it be like to be alone in the world, your only relation a disturbed young man with an itchy trigger finger and an explosive temper?

They finished the meal with a delicious rum-soaked cake. Kate asked Pamela for the recipe.

"I'll ask Maria to tell me, but I'll have to write it down for you. She neither reads nor writes."

They retired to the parlor for brandy and a relaxed discussion of news from the East. After another hour, Jack stood up, stretched and looked out the window. "We'd best head back to town now, before darkfall catches us."

"You do have a place to stay, don't you?" Pamela asked. She turned to Kate. "Your accommodations are comfortable?"

"Very," Kate said quickly, knowing that Jack wouldn't want to remain the night when he had so much more ground to cover and so little time.

"You know, you could leave your charming cousin with me, Jack. I think she might enjoy a break from being dragged across the desert, scouting for criminals." Pamela fixed him with a stern look.

"I want to go," Kate insisted. "I asked if I could, actually. How often does a woman from the East get to see the real frontier? I'll be able to teach my girls so much better, knowing more of the real world myself."

"I suppose," Pamela said, sounding unconvinced. "Still, if you decide you've had one too many days in the saddle, tell Jack to drop you off here. We can spend a day together, just the two of us in this big, cool house. I could have Maria make us her specialty—her version of a German torte, with so much chocolate and coffee mixed in, you can barely force yourself to swallow, each bite is so delightful."

Kate laughed, standing to give Pamela an affectionate hug. "I'll remember that and threaten him with it if he refuses to stop often enough along the way."

Chapter 14

As Jack and Kate rode away from Rancho del Sol, Kate turned in her saddle and waved. Pamela was leaning against the veranda pilaster, watching them. She raised a hand in farewell.

"She's such an elegant woman—charming and beautiful," Kate mused. "Her mother must have been Spanish. That glistening black hair is a dead giveaway."

"She was, I believe," Jack said absently.

Kate looked back again over her shoulder at the cluster of low, white adobe buildings. She'd never felt a strong tie to the land like Max had felt for his family's farm. That was why it had been relatively painless for her to sell off most of it to Barbara, keeping the house and garage, with an open-ended agreement to sell those, too, when and if she chose to leave Chester or move into a smaller place.

A heartfelt connection with the land, Kate thought, must be something in the blood. Having lived in apartments when she was growing up, she didn't have it, but Pamela obviously did.

"If raiders ever hit Rancho del Sol, I believe Pamela would go down fighting for her property," Kate remarked.

"Reckon you're right," Jack said.

They rode in silence for over an hour, as the light shifted from midafternoon brilliance to softer, reddish-gold tones that spread like honey across the western skies. Kate marveled at the changes she began to note as they rode. Whereas in hill country, the plants seemed to remain basically the same, dawn to dusk, in the desert, the flower buds on the cacti swelled as night approached, in preparation for opening. She found herself looking forward to the spectacle of their rebirth. The bats, that mysteriously appeared out of nowhere with darkness, fascinated her. As they sipped away the bright blossoms' nectar and unwittingly pollinated the blossoms, they were doing essentially the same job as the bees in her own garden.

"Will we be sleeping in the desert again tonight?" she asked.

"I'm afraid so," Jack said. "I doubt if Phelps has lifted his ban on the Sweetwater."

"I'd rather sleep outside anyway," she murmured contentedly.

Jack turned and looked at her. "That's a change of heart."

She shrugged. "It's a lot nicer than I'd thought it might be . . . and more private than some places." She felt her cheeks growing pink, but managed to hold eye contact with Jack.

"If you mean there's an advantage in not having to worry about thin walls and nosy neighbors—"

Kate laughed. "I don't suppose the bats mind."

Guiding the horses closer together so that they ambled shoulder to shoulder, Jack took her hand as they continued riding. "I don't suppose they do." He kissed her fingertips. "In a way I'm glad we're *personae non gratae* in town. I love lying with you under the stars, knowing there is no one within miles of us. It helps to—"

He shrugged, unable or unwilling to finish the sentence. Kate knew what he meant anyway. Losing herself in the intimacy of Jack's body helped her forget how little time remained for them to be together. She supposed Jack felt much the same way.

Kate swallowed with difficulty over the raw lump in her throat. She felt as if half the desert were lodged there. When they stopped a few minutes later to drink from their canteens and discuss the next leg of their search, the trickle of tepid water did little to soothe her anticipation of losing the one man in the world she could ever truly love.

*   *   *

As Jack unsaddled Apache, he watched Kate make up their campsite as if she'd done it a hundred nights before and would continue going through the mundane but somehow comforting routine for the rest of her life. She adapted so easily to new situations, new people. It never ceased to amaze him how she simply did whatever needed doing. No complaints, no squabbling over details. Just do it. She faced life head-on.

Kate hummed as she spread out Sunny's saddle blanket, then shook Apache's blanket out over it. She took the makings of their evening meal from the saddlebags while Jack brushed the horses and saw to their dinner. As she passed behind him, she playfully brushed her fingertips across the back of his neck, and he made a grab for her, intentionally missing because they both had jobs to do.

It was as if she'd determined not to brood about the days ahead—how few they had left, how unlikely it seemed that they'd discover the truth in time. Jack admitted to himself they were no closer now than when they'd begun their search. Kate put on a brave face and refused to let him see her unhappiness, although he knew he'd brought her a terrible burden to bear.

Slapping Sunny companionably on the flank, he sprinkled a portion of oats on the ground for the horse. "Eat up, old girl. Life is short. Better make it sweet while you can."

Jack glanced across the fire that Kate had already started. She was tearing hunks of bread off the loaf they'd picked up in town earlier that day. Pouring dried beans into a small pan, she mixed them with water and a chunk of salty bacon.

"You know how to cook beans from dry?" he asked, coming over and squatting beside her. Reaching out, he twisted a lock of her brown hair around his finger, fascinated by the way it spiraled around his finger as if it were made to do so.

"Ever heard of Boston baked beans?"

"Yup."

"Well, these will be Boston boiled beans…minus the brown sugar and spices."

"I thought everything you people ate came from boxes and cans," he teased.

"Hey, now, I can cook. Besides, baked beans are the staple of every New England church supper. For Saturday socials, families bring casseroles by the dozens. Half of the covered dishes will be baked beans. Most recipes include cut-up hot dogs and ketchup.''

"Hot dogs?'' He looked confused.

She giggled. ''You'd love them.''

Jack looked doubtful.

The beans took a long time to cook, and used more of their valuable water than she'd expected. But Jack reassured her they'd ride to the outskirts of town to fill their canteens first thing in the morning.

''Then where do we go?'' she asked. ''After Yancy, or after more clues?''

''Yancy,'' he said without hesitation this time.

''Why?''

''He and I have a meeting with destiny,'' he said darkly.

Kate put down her plate and moved onto her knees to face Jack. Her hands settled over his forearms, stopping him from lifting the spoon to his mouth.

''What are you talking about, Jack? Is it him? Did he ambush you that day, sneak up behind you and—''

''I don't know, Kate.'' He blinked, as if trying to concentrate. ''It comes and goes. Sometimes, like while I was talking to Phelps and, later, to Daniel McCary, I can almost hear the words I'm going to say before they come out of my mouth. It's all happened before, and I know it.''

''Déjà vu,'' she murmured.

''Exactly.'' He shook his head. ''Most of the time, though, there's almost no warning—I know seconds before something happens, then in a flash I can see events playing themselves out, but there's not enough time for me to react differently and change things.''

Kate thought for a moment. Something told her there was a way for Jack to save himself, but what it was she couldn't put her finger on just yet.

''You told me you know that Yancy dies young. You said you know because you were . . . will be there when it happens.''

He nodded. ''Yes. I'm sure of it, but I can't tell you *how* it happens or any details at all.''

She leaned toward him urgently. *''Do you kill each other? Is that it?''*

Jack's blue gaze shifted to a distant spot beyond her. When she turned to see what he was looking at, his eyes were focused far beyond the horizon.

He let out a low groan of exasperation. "I—I don't know, Kate. It's as if the past and the future are one. But I can't quite see how it all works. I only know Yancy doesn't live a long life. But maybe I'm wrong about being there when he dies. Maybe he outlives me, and I only know about him in the same way I know some things about Kathleen and you, because I was already dead, and when you're dead you can sense things about people who are important to you."

A strange sensation rippled through her Kate's veins, and she sat back on her heels and stared at Jack in horror. "You mean, like someone a person was once married to?"

The faraway look cleared from Jack's eyes. "Like you and Max. Yes."

She swallowed and tried to breathe without hyperventilating.

Jack's eyes sparkled with sudden amusement. "I expect he knows you're with me."

"Oh, God."

Jack laughed, putting down his nearly empty plate on the blanket beside him. He reached out and pulled her into his arms, brushing his lips softly across her brow. "Max was a very practical man, even more practical than his charming wife. He'd have expected you to someday welcome another man into your life."

"You make it sound as if you knew him," she murmured, feeling a little queasy at the idea of Max watching her with Jack.

"I did know Max, quite well." He traced a finger up the sleeve of her blouse. "You're forgetting, I lived in that farm house long before either of you showed up. And I was there all of Max's life from the time he was born and through all of your married life until he died."

Kate flinched. "I'm not sure I like that idea, either."

Jack laughed. "I learned a lot about you, before we actually met. I learned what a wonderful wife you were, and how good a mother you became from the moment Jesse was born. You continue to be a wonderful, loving mother for Max's children. But you deserve your own happiness, darlin'." He turned her face up to his and kissed her sweetly on the lips. "You deserve a man who—"

Kate couldn't bear to let him finish; she pushed him away.

"Shut up, Jack. Just shut up."

Jumping to her feet, she marched away from him, across the sandy dunes sprinkled with mesquite grass, where the horses munched between clumps of Spanish bayonet. She marched off in no particular direction, desperately needing to put space between herself and Jack.

She needed to breathe, to feel whole... by herself... without thinking of him as a necessary part of her.

It didn't take him long to catch up. Kate felt his hands come down hard on her shoulders and whip her around.

"What's gotten into you? What did I say?" he growled.

She exploded at him. "I deserve *a man*... that's what you said. Damn it, I don't want a man... I want *you*, Jack! Have you got that? I don't want a banker who cheats on his wife, or one of Barbara's endless string of cousins, or another farmer like Max. I want a Ranger with blue eyes and coal-black hair, who left Vermont to help people he didn't even know, clear across the country. I want to ride with you *forever*, not just for a few days. *I want to be a part of your life, not your death!*" She seized the front of his shirt and shook him hard. "Can you understand that?"

Jack held on to her as she fought each successive wave of her grief. He weathered the storm of her frustration and the impossibility of their love. He said nothing, steeling himself against the assault of her fists against his chest and her furious words on his ears.

And at last, when she'd spent herself and there was nothing more she could rail against, no unstruck target for her words or blows, she leaned limply against him and sucked down huge gulps of desert air.

He stroked her hair, held her and rocked gently, pressing his lips soothingly to her forehead.

"You have every right to feel used."

"I'm not feeling *used*," she rasped. "I agreed to come with you, knowing the rules and the consequences."

"Then you have every right to feel cheated by fate."

"Why did I have to fall in love with you, Jack? Why *you*— a ghost? Why couldn't we have met in my time, two human beings with the rest of their lives to live?"

"I don't know," Jack whispered as darkness closed in around them. "I don't know, darlin'." A little chuckle escaped from his lips.

"What is it?"

"Do you suppose you'd recognize me on the street, if you bumped into me?"

"Of course," she said quickly.

"No, think about it. A modern Jack Ramsey might be a teacher or a doctor in a hospital . . . or a farmer."

She gazed up at him, memorizing every line of his face, wanting never to forget the man who made her feel more alive than she'd ever felt. His nose crested his face, slightly arrogant, but infinitely masculine. The corners of his eyes crinkled pleasantly. His lips drew together in a warm line that parted on white teeth when he spoke. She remembered his mouth opening to welcome her lips as they'd kissed.

"I can't imagine you as anyone but a bullheaded lawman on a mustang," she murmured affectionately.

"You see, you'd pass me by, not even recognize me as your predestined lover."

"No." She shook her head, sure of herself. "I'd know you, Jack."

"How can you be so sure? Before I showed myself, you'd shut yourself up in that farmhouse with your children, involved only with them and your job. You never gave yourself the opportunity to meet new people."

Kate cuddled in his arms, content to let him talk. It seemed so strange to her, though, this conversation. She could see what Jack was trying to do. He was preparing her for when he'd no longer be around. As remarkable as it seemed, he was paving the way for another man to enter her life! Jack wanted her to be happy, and if it couldn't be with him, he would encourage her to open up her heart to another man who might be a strong and kind companion.

Kate gazed up at Jack in sheer amazement as he continued to speak.

"See, you have to realize, I might have red hair, or a beard . . . or be short and happily plump."

Tears of thankfulness brimmed in her eyes.

"Shut up, Jack Ramsey," she choked out, laughing at him. "I know what you're doing."

"You do?"

"Yes, and it's appreciated. But there will never be a man capable of replacing you."

"I didn't expect there would be," he retorted smugly. "But there's bound to be someone who will do in a pinch." He winked at her, and she belted him good.

"Or as egotistical—don't forget your other traits."

Then his expression grew serious again. "I mean it, Kate. If you refuse to open your eyes to possibilities and your heart to strangers, they can never become friends or lovers."

She nodded. Yes, of course, he was right. She had shut herself off. It had become her nature to keep a closed circle of acquaintances, discouraging new relationships. That had seemed so much easier than risking disappointment. She must try harder to allow for change in her life. At the very least, she didn't want Jesse and Anna to pick up on her isolationist nature and be afraid of newness and adventure. She wanted them to learn to accept challenges.

"I'll try," she promised. "That's all I can do."

She reached up and brushed her hand along the line of Jack's jaw. Turning his head, he caught her fingertips between his teeth and nibbled them as his eyes brightened with ardor.

"You know that I can't pass up a night without making love to you," he said, his voice husky. "No more worries. No more tears. Just us and this night."

"Just us . . . now," she agreed.

Kate wondered fleetingly if he was asking too much of her. She'd decided she wouldn't dwell on their parting. And she'd have been fine if only he hadn't started talking about leaving her. It was hard, so very hard to think of life without Jack.

Hearing him tell her to let other men into her life made her feel cherished and shattered at the same time. Even as he followed the steps that would inevitably take him away from her, he was being completely selfless. He thought of her future.

Kate felt Jack's rough hands manipulating the buttons on the front of her blouse. A sudden intoxicating warmth coursed through her, like brandy running through her veins. She lifted her head to gaze into Jack's eyes, as dark as midnight and seductive with arousal.

"Let's make this night count," he murmured in her ear, then kissed its rim and followed the line of her throat to the top of her breasts, which he now revealed as he unbuttoned.

She couldn't answer him, couldn't even *think* words, let alone form them on her lips. Every mechanism within her responded to his touch, to the moist, heated kisses he was trailing across her breasts, her sensitive nipples. Nothing mattered except Jack and the love they shared.

With infinite care, he laid her back on the saddle blanket beside the fire and lowered himself over her, propping his body on his elbows, kissing her deeply as his hands worked their magical, maddening way down the opening of her blouse to her waist. Feeling his way, he found the buttons on the suede skirt and released them. Jack moved the supple fabric low enough to smooth his hand over her tingling hips and thighs.

"I love to watch the pleasure in your eyes," he whispered. "Please don't close them."

She forced herself to look up at him. It was almost impossible not to let her lids drift closed as the first delicious waves of ecstasy parted over her.

His hand slid lower, seeking the intimate folds between her thighs, then, still not satisfied, the hot liquid center of her womanhood.

Kate arched her back and let out a cry of approval.

His fingertips stopped their hypnotic caresses.

"Oh, Jack, don't—"

"Don't?" his voice teased.

"Don't stop, you cruel man! Oh, please, *don't stop now!*"

A low, satisfied chuckle issued from deep down inside of him, and he reached farther within her, releasing spasms of heat, joy, euphoria bordering on agony. Kate curled her fingers into his back, feeling the muscles harden through his shirt.

As she reached the height of her pleasure and the sensations slowly began to thin, she pulled him down and kissed him deeply. "Take off your clothes," she begged throatily. "I want to see all of you . . . in the firelight."

He released her and sat back on his heels, slowly undoing his shirtfront, then the cuffs. He wore nothing under his shirt. In the orange light of the fire, the contours of his chest, deepened by the fine, dark brush of hair, looked sharp and taut. She stretched out her hand and touched him, swirling her fingertips down the rough terrain over each brown nipple, across the ridged, tight surface of his stomach to his belt.

Rolling over onto her stomach, she worked at unbuckling his belt, her fingers shaking with anticipation, her body flushed with passion. He was like a drug, soothing pain, yet inducing a need for more of the opiate. Kate gave no further thought to the future. All practical concerns and cares were gone, flying away like the hushed-wing bats on the desert air.

As she released Jack from the confines of his denim jeans, he worked her hips free of the split skirt and shifted it off of her legs. She lay naked, inviting him with her eyes. Within the time-honored ritual of man mating with woman, words were no longer necessary. Eternities passed between breaths.

Jack took his time, letting his eyes range over Kate. He lay on his side next to her, his palm warmly covering her breast. Slowly he smoothed it over her stomach and down onto the dense, erotic triangle, darker than the hair on her head. Still holding him, she arched up against his strong hand and felt his pulse race as he hardened, broadened, lengthened within her curved fingers.

Her eyes never left his as she guided him into her, rolled onto her back and drew him along with her. Kate felt his first thrust penetrate the very depths of her soul. She spun off into other worlds, other realms—mystical, unknown, beautiful. Whether or not anything in her life made sense no longer mattered.

Not until they'd satisfied each other completely did they lie, blissfully exhausted, a fine sweat beading their bodies, the moon high in an obsidian sky. The gentle whoosh of dark wings above them, intent on nature's perpetuation of life, was the only sound. The lingering warmth of the desert sand seeped up through the blanket and into Kate's tingling flesh.

Curling up within Jack's arms, she distantly felt him pull the second blanket over them, and she slept a tranquil and perfect sleep.

Chapter 15

When Kate awoke, Jack was already up and dressed. She had a feeling he'd been moving silently around her for some time, letting her sleep as the sun started its steady, blazing trek up into the Texas sky. She stretched, lazily, feeling each part of her body come slowly alive in the warming air.

"What's cooking?" she murmured, her tongue reacting sluggishly within her mouth. "It smells delicious."

"Coffee, bacon and corn bread, of sorts."

"Should that *of sorts* worry me?"

"Not if you don't ask what it means." Jack crouched over the fire, his wide back to her, tapering to the slim waist of his jeans. He flipped yellow cakes on a griddle with expert ease.

Kate couldn't help herself. "What does *of sorts* mean?"

"I know how diet conscious you are. But the only way I could figure out to bind the cornmeal together was by rendering some of the bacon fat and mixing it into the meal and flour."

"Somehow I don't think it'll kill me. I've lost at least five pounds, riding all these hours and eating so little."

"Sorry 'bout that, darlin'."

"Oh, that's not a complaint," Kate said, stretching beneath

the blanket as she observed Jack with a clearer head. "I feel wonderful."

Jack wore a blue-gray flannel shirt and rough-textured pants with leather chaps buckled over them. As striking as he was when he was dressed, she ached to see him naked again.

"Are you expecting to be served breakfast in bed?" he asked, casting her a smile over one shoulder as he poured coffee the color of dark chocolate into a tin mug.

"No, but I might be able to work up more of an appetite, with a little help." She smirked at him.

Without comment, Jack laid the griddle to one side of the fire and turned to her. His eyes roamed over the hills and hollows of wool covering her, as if he were seeing straight through it to her bare flesh.

She demurely allowed the blanket to drop from beneath her chin, then gave it an extra tug to reveal her breasts.

Jack straightened up and stood over her, his boots braced wide apart, knuckles propped on his narrow hips, hat pulled low over stormy eyes that studied her bare shoulders and peaking nipples. "You shouldn't a done that, darlin'."

"Why not?" she asked, innocently fluttering her eyelashes.

"We have to get movin'... not much time."

"All the more reason to take advantage of the time we have." She lifted her long arms to him. "Jack—"

He needed no further encouragement. Stripping off the blanket, he threw himself onto her with abandon. They'd made love only a few hours before, but now, in the bright light of day, they discovered new delights in each other.

Seizing Kate's hand, Jack guided her tingling fingers to his waist, then farther down.

"Can you feel what you do to me? Just the sound of your voice, and I'm hungry for you. Seeing you like this...it's plain old overkill. What sweet weapons you possess, Kate."

This time, they made love in a frenzy, each taking from the other what he or she needed. Never asking, never apologizing. Forbidden whims, unspoken impulses...neither held back. Kate welcomed and provoked the storm of Jack's passion as he rained burning kisses and harsh caresses over her. In a distant place in her mind, she recognized his need to brand her as his and his alone.

For now...for tomorrow...for eternity.

She raked her fingers through his hair and clenched her fists around the short, black shafts, pulling his head back. She feasted on his bearded throat and chin, pressed her sandpapered lips to his and ran her tongue inside his mouth, tasting and reveling in every vibrating nerve in her body. She had her own needs. She intended to fix this moment so thoroughly in her heart and mind that nothing . . . nothing could ever take it from her. She'd never forget Jack Ramsey. And she'd make damn sure he'd never forget her.

At last Kate lay in the sand, gulping down huge lungfuls of hot, dry air, tangled in sated repose with Jack. One muscled, hairy leg draped across her thighs. His dark head rested peacefully on her breasts, where moments earlier his lips had drawn the tender flesh between razor-sharp teeth.

She breathed in and out, concentrating on the subtle melding of their pulses, and stroked the short hairs around his ear. "You're right," she breathed. "We should eat then leave right away."

"I wish it weren't so," he murmured. "I wish to the heavens that—"

"Hush," she said. "I know . . . I know."

The corn cakes, though somewhat overcooked, turned out to be delicious, which only reinforced her belief that high-fat content in almost any food guaranteed palatability. Try replacing good old chocolate and French fries with diet anything. It couldn't be done.

They ate, poured the leftover coffee in the brush, scoured out the griddle with sand, packed up and mounted.

As Kate rode, Sunny fell into an easy gait beneath her, matching Apache's lazy amble. The two horses seemed to have become accustomed to the routine of traveling together with their pair of humans. Kate found she was pleasantly sore, and the saddle felt harder than before under her bottom. She smiled, but said nothing, enjoying her secret. The gentle undulating rhythm of her mount beneath her made her feel slightly drowsy; they hadn't slept more than four hours altogether that night.

"Into town first for water?" she asked, stifling a yawn.

"Right."

"Then where?"

"We'll head east, I think. It's the only direction we haven't looked, with the exception of a lot farther south, toward the border. Company F will have covered that pretty thoroughly by now."

At the outskirts of San Antonio, they came to a stretch of the river by the same name and filled their canteens from its crystal blue water. Kate doubted any river in all of America in her time ran as clear or sweet, and it made her a little sad. They were about to move out again when an idea that had been brewing at the bottom of Kate's mind during the morning's ride began to percolate itself up to her conscious level.

"I think I know where Yancy might be hiding," she ventured hesitantly. "If I'm right, he could be a lot closer than we'd expected."

Jack looked at her. "In town? I doubt it. Phelps may be a pigheaded, blustering tin star, but he's no dummy. He doesn't like me chasing after Yancy, but he'd sure pluck that boy off the street himself, if he got the chance."

"No. Not in town." Kate grew more excited with each passing second. "Remember the bats?"

"The bats?" Jack grinned at her. "That's it! Clever girl, you are. Yancy's turned himself into one of 'em? Hey, I think I read about that in a novel someone stuck up in your attic—*Dracula!*"

"Don't be silly. There are no such things as vampires."

"Just as there are no such things as ghosts?"

She shot him a withering look. "Let me finish." Kate drew up on Sunny's reins, and Jack's mustang ambled to a halt beside her. "The bats that pollinate the cactus flowers, they fly only at night—right?"

"Sure."

"Then they fly off to roost somewhere during the day. Wherever it is, it has to be pretty close. Probably somewhere closer to the buttes than town is."

Jack's eyes brightened. "There are no barns or any other kind of buildings between the buttes and town, or as far west as del Sol."

"Right," she said. "So there has to be a natural cave of some kind or—"

"Or a mine shaft," Jack added, poking his Stetson back off of his forehead. He stared along the trail the way they'd come, his brow furrowed in concentration.

"Are there such things out there?"

"Yup. An old prospector once told me that about the time of the California gold rush in '49, there were rumors of nuggets being picked up off the ground not far from here. I'm not sure of the exact location, though."

Kate immediately thought of Clint Dewey, who'd tried up north and failed. "Did they find a lot of gold?"

"Nothing more than a few flecks, after the initial nuggets. It was enough to start a brief local rush, though." Jack shook his head. "Still, I doubt any mines were dug deep enough to interest bats."

Kate nodded. "So we're back to natural caverns. Do you know of any?"

Jack scratched his head. "Now that you mention it, yes. Almost due south of here, closer to the salt deposits Yancy and the colonel were scrapping over. Underground springs washed the salt out and onto the flats, leaving caves. Some of them are quite extensive. At least, that's what I've heard."

Kate observed him solemnly. "Then Yancy would know about them. Maybe even be familiar with their passageways." Kate climbed up onto Sunny. "Come on, then . . . let's go!"

Jack vaulted onto Apache and deftly maneuvered his horse in front of hers, blocking the way. "I know of no reason why you have to be there, Kate."

"You mean, aside from the fact that I promised I'd stand by you all the way through this? I need to be there when you take on Yancy."

"You make it sound like a marble-shootin' exhibition. This is life or death, darlin'—it won't be pretty." His tone was grim and his eyes dark with sadness.

Kate sighed. "I've enjoyed some of the very best times with you, Jack. It seems a little selfish of me to run off when the going gets rough."

"Not selfish. Smart."

Kate shook her head firmly. "You can tell me to stay in town, Jack, but I won't do it. You need me. You keep talking about your feelings, that things will somehow work out for me. Well, I have feelings too—call them a woman's intuition." She leaned forward over her saddle horn. "I have to be there with you because you *need* me, and I can't tell you why. All I know is I have a purpose on this trip. None of this makes sense if I'm just an excursion ticket through time."

Jack rested his hand over hers, resting on Sunny's shining neck. "You're strong, Kate. But are you strong enough to stand by and watch a man die?" His voice was harsh, but his eyes were molten honey, reaching out to her, begging her to reconsider.

"Maybe I'm strong enough *to keep a man from dying*," she said, meeting his gaze and holding it.

After a minute, Jack settled back into his saddle with a solemn but resigned twist to his lips. "All right. Let's go, then."

They rode at a gallop, passing the buttes then cutting due south across the desert. The horses seemed to tire less quickly than they had the day before, and they made good time, although it was the hottest part of the day.

"We're almost there," Jack said when they stopped the third time for water and to let their mounts rest.

Kate looked around. "Where? I don't see anything unusual."

"See those low rills across there? Down the middle of them is a crevasse that used to be filled with salt. It was mostly all carted away before the colonel took over the land. No doubt Yancy had a hand in that. This area's a lot farther north than most of the colonel's other holdings, but it borders on the Kennard spread to the west."

Kate watched in awe as they moved toward the desolate rills and their scruffy, sunbaked plant growth. They approached at a slower pace than they'd ridden across the open land, and she could feel Jack's tension rippling across the space between them. His eyes constantly scanned the ridges above them as they passed into the salt flats.

At first, only a small, black hole appeared, low down at the base of a distant rise. As they rode closer, the opening seemed to widen.

"I should have brought my flashlight," Kate muttered when they stopped in front of the entrance to a sizable cave a few minutes later.

"I'm not sure bringing luggage is allowed," Jack said, grinning wryly.

"Clothes work," she argued.

"Yup, but what about bringing an invention that didn't exist back here?"

She had to admit, that made sense. The Rules.

"What will we do for light, then?" she asked.

"I'm hoping you're right and Yancy has moved in. If he's using the cave as his hideout, he'll have stored torches and a flint near the entrance."

Sure enough, when they looked just inside the mouth of the cave, they found fresh, oil-soaked rags wrapped around a heavy stick. Someone had definitely been there lately and seemed to be planning on returning.

Kate's mouth tasted suddenly dry, but it wasn't due to the desert heat. She sensed something frightening in the air, a hint of danger that she'd felt only once before in all of her life.

It had happened one Saturday when she took Jesse and Anna to the carnival sponsored by the Chester Volunteer Fire Department as a fund-raiser. There were the usual rides—a merry-go-round, bumper cars, Ferris wheel and roller coaster—and a fun house, along with various games of chance in the arcade. Jesse had begged all day to ride the roller coaster, but he was too little to go on alone.

"I'll watch Anna if you want to take him," Barbara had offered.

Although Kate disliked rides that made her feel as if she'd be lucky to walk away in one piece, she didn't want to disappoint Jesse. She took Barbara up on her offer.

While she was standing in line with her son, waiting to board, an oppressive chill bore down on her. It was as if the air pressure had suddenly increased tenfold and a cold front blew in at the same time. Suddenly she felt she couldn't breathe, and goose bumps jumped up on her bare arms. Yet the sun continued to shine placidly from an azure sky, and all around her people laughed and played.

Feeling suddenly off-balance, Kate reached out to grab hold of a nearby steel leg. She felt a strong vibration. Looking up, she noticed a support brace shimmying against a girder above her head, just as the coaster cars rumbled over that section of track.

Kate pulled Jesse out of line and immediately reported the loose connection to the ride operator, who told her there was nothing wrong with his equipment and dismissed her concerns as if she were only one of many hysterical mothers he had to deal with every day.

Not giving up, Kate located the carnival manager in his trailer and physically dragged the man by the arm to the base of the roller coaster, where she pointed up at two grating metal struts.

He stopped the ride in the middle of its circuit and summoned the fire department to pull passengers out of the cars and get them safely to the ground. The police cleared the area, then the manager sent the empty cars the rest of the way around the track.

On the final turn and dip, a section of track gapped just enough to derail the lead car. All five cars behind it followed, plummeting into the pasture over a hundred feet below.

It was that same terrible, knee-buckling pressure, that same inexplicable chill that passed through her veins now, in the middle of the desert.

Kate reached out and grabbed Jack's arm. "Wait! Some-one's in there, or—" She looked around them, confused now. "Or they're nearby."

"What did you see?"

Kate couldn't stop trembling. "Nothing. I just think... Oh, Jack, it's going to happen. It's going to happen here. I'm sure Yancy's going to shoot you."

Jack stared at her. "You can't know that, Kate. You're just frightened. Wait here."

"No, please—listen to me! If you go in there and he's waiting for you, he'll have won. He knows the caverns—you don't. He's at a tremendous advantage."

Jack studied the mouth of the cave. "You're right. If he's in there, he'll see me before I see him. Besides, he's got to come out sometime. And if you're wrong and he's not in there now, he'll come back before long."

Kate looked around. "We can hide over there, behind that pile of rubble. It's sheltered from the top of the ridge, too. No one will be able to spot us."

Jack pushed his hat down low over his eyes. "All right. Come on, let's get the horses out of sight."

They moved Apache and Sunny behind a thick screen of gnarled live oak. Untying the canteens from the saddle horns, Jack motioned to a shaded spot on the other side of the trees, where a few tufts of mesquite grass sprouted.

"Might as well relax. It could be a while."

Kate sat down, her back to the rough bark of the nearest tree. Jack came over and sat down beside her, then eased her down gently so that her head and shoulders were in his lap.

"If you're still sleepy, you can nap now," he said. "I'll keep an eye out. We could be here for hours."

"Only if you let me take second watch."

"Agreed."

Kate didn't think she could possibly fall asleep. But the day's ride and the blazing sun had sapped the energy her few hours of rest had given her. Her eyes grew heavy, and the heady, open-air scent of Jack, leather and sun baking down on the nearby vegetation soothed her.

Why don't men in Vermont smell like you, Jack? she wondered drowsily.

Why didn't men anywhere smell like that anymore?

Why...?

She drifted somewhere between consciousness and sleep, feeling lighter than the desert, warmer than a child wrapped in its mother's arms, protected and secure. In the recesses of her mind she recalled that danger lurked not far away. Yet, with Jack, she felt safe.

Jack knocked his hat back on his head to better view the twisted length of the rocky canyon. It was possible that some drifting prospector had set up camp inside one of the caverns, making a final stab at the search for gold in an area that had already been raked clean by hundreds of frantic men. Someone like Clint Dewey.

But in his gut Jack knew that Yancy was close by. Details of the day were drifting back to him, piece by piece. His heart pounded erratically as he saw, in his mind's eye, the hatred and fear in Yancy's cold eyes. The scar at the corner of his lip that grew white with tension. He heard the deafening blast of gunfire, smelled burning powder.

Whose bullets had found their mark?

Jack shook his head, trying to clear the vision, but the details faded again. He had been sure for some time that it was his own gun that would kill Yancy. It had first struck him when they'd been Pamela's luncheon guests at del Sol, and the realization had sickened him.

But now...now he wasn't as sure. The future seemed just beyond his grasp, just out of sight. As if he were on a train, watching the track ahead as it curved. He could only see to the bend, no farther. Then, as the locomotive rounded each curve, the future was suddenly there, so familiar that he felt a fool for not being able to predict it.

That was exactly how he felt now. Just around the bend, something momentous was about to happen. For an instant he thought he tasted something warm and salty in his mouth. Was it blood? Was it *he* who would die this day? Was this how it happened?

Jack gazed regretfully down at Kate, and tenderly lifted a damp curl from across her closed eyes. Her skin was turning a rich, golden tan. Although the hat she wore protected her from direct sunlight, the rays reflecting off the sand were still strong.

She was beautiful. So beautiful that sometimes the sight of her took his breath away. He'd loved her, loved her in his heart, in his soul and with his body as he'd loved no other woman.

Her hair, a rich mahogany brown when he'd met her, danced with reddish highlights from the few days' exposure to the intense sun. Her eyes, when they were open, spoke constantly of her devotion to him. He couldn't believe such a woman as Kate, with her own life—her children, a world so ordered and suited to her—had risked all for him...to give him one last chance. A chance that might fail even now, after all they'd done.

Jack sucked in a deep breath and fought back the emotion that rose in a fiery lump to his throat and burned his eyes. He prayed that if he did somehow live to continue his ordained life with Kathleen, all memory of Kate would vanish from his mind. He didn't think he could bear going on without her. Better not to know. Better not to understand the vastness of his loss....

It was the softest grating of gravel that wrenched Jack's tormented mind back to the present.

He tensed, instantly alert. Again he looked down at Kate. She slept peacefully, her lips sweetly parted.

Carefully he eased her off of his lap onto the grassy mound where they sat. He drew the Colt, checked to be sure all of the six chambers were loaded with the powerful .44 caliber bullets. Crouching behind the largest of the gnarled post oaks, he searched the canyon below, straining his eyes to pick out the slightest motion from the uniform, sand-colored terrain.

Jack wasn't aware he'd been holding his breath until he saw the horse and rider, moving slowly along the floor of the canyon. The pinto pony appeared to be on its last legs. The rider jabbed his spurs impatiently into its belly and, as they drew closer, Jack could hear him cursing the animal.

It was Yancy. No doubt about it.

Jack waited until the young gunslinger passed him by and was well within the circle of hills surrounding the mouth of the cave. By repositioning himself in the gully, he'd cut Yancy off. His only possible retreat would be into the cave itself, and Jack expected this was the only entrance and exit, since Yancy had come this way, which was roundabout.

Jack counted to ten, then ten again, waiting as his pulse thundered in his ears. Yancy dismounted, flinging a final expletive of disgust at his mount, and trudged toward the cave, yanking the abused animal by its reins.

Jack reached out, brushing one finger tenderly across Kate's cheek. She didn't stir. "Wish me luck in your dreams, darlin'," he whispered. "Better you sleep through this...."

With a sorrow the size of the whole state of Texas welling up inside of him, Jack stepped clear of the grove of live oak, his gun drawn, and faced the end of the canyon.

"You're under arrest, Kennard!" he called out.

Yancy's step faltered. He swiveled around to face Jack and released the reins of his horse. Squinting into the glare of the afternoon sun, he shouted, "That you, Ranger? Well, I'll be. Thought you'd given up long ago."

"I don't give up."

Yancy snickered. "Seems to me you're not strictly following the range riders' code."

"How's that?"

"When all else fails, wait until your quarry's back is turned, then fill him full of lead."

"Ambushin' ain't my style, Kennard."

Yancy shrugged. "Too bad. Maybe you woulda got me by now if it had been."

"I have you now. That's all that matters. Keep that hand away from your gun, boy. I'm warning you. Stay clear of that holster, and let's get this done."

"Done? You gonna kill me right here?" A bud of fear blossomed in Yancy's eyes.

"No, I'm not here to kill you. I just want to take that gun away from you so neither one of us gets hurt."

Yancy choked out a bitter laugh. "Why would I let you take my gun? So you can drag me back to San Antonio, and Phelps can hang me for killin' the colonel?"

"Then you did kill him."

"'Course I killed him! He was sittin' on a gold mine . . . of salt. What a business he had goin'! Mexicans and Texans both paying top dollar for salt, and him just sittin' on the load of it, settin' whatever price he wanted." Yancy glared at him. "You know, that land shoulda been my daddy's."

"That a fact?" Jack moved forward another two steps, his eyes never leaving Yancy's.

Yancy shuffled backward, toward the opening of the cave. "That's far enough, Ranger."

It suddenly occurred to Jack that he couldn't afford to let him duck into the cave. Depending upon how much food he'd stored in there, it might take days to starve him out. Fate might not give Jack that much time.

"Stop right there!" Jack shouted when Yancy took two more steps in retreat. "I'm coming to take that gun from you, boy. You leave it alone, and we'll both live to see tomorrow's sun."

Jack took three steps forward before he saw the reckless fire leap into Yancy's eyes. Yancy's hand flashed toward his fancy tooled-leather holster. Jack pulled the Colt's trigger.

It all happened so fast, his mind didn't have time to register whether his was the only shot that boomed through the desert silence.

But he was still standing as Yancy dropped to his knees and, with a look of shock contorting his face, fell forward into the sand. Jack stood rock still, watching, waiting—for what, he didn't know.

A pool of red grew around Yancy's body, seeping into the parched earth.

"Jack!" a shrill cry went up behind him.

He turned from the man he'd just gunned into oblivion. Kate rushed at him, her eyes wide with terror.

Chapter 16

"What happened?" Kate cried.

Jack held his arms open, the hot metal of the gun still molded into the palm of his right hand. She ran, full tilt, into his chest, knocking the wind out of him, and he held her tight.

"I woke up and heard voices," she gasped. "All of a sudden, there was shooting. Oh, God, are you all right, Jack?"

"I'm fine. It's over, darlin'. Yancy didn't even get a shot off."

His calming words didn't stop her from shaking, didn't banish the dull, sick feeling that tore at her insides. How could she have allowed herself to fall asleep? How could she have left Jack's side for even a minute—when he needed her so desperately?

Kate pressed her hands over his chest, feeling his heart beat, reassuring herself that he was, in fact, all in one piece and functioning.

"Thank God...thank God...thank God..." she murmured over and over. Looking up into his eyes, she witnessed an incredible sadness. One glance over his shoulder, and she, too, felt the awful realization. "He's dead?"

Jack nodded.

Kate swallowed, then swallowed again. "You know you didn't have a choice," she said. "He would have killed you if you hadn't shot him first and—"

"I understand that, Kate," Jack ground out. "That doesn't help, though, when I think how Pamela will feel as soon as she finds out her brother is dead."

Kate closed her eyes and clung to him. "The poor woman. She knows Yancy was wild, but to find out he's actually—" She blinked up at him, sharing his pain, grasping for comfort from the least likely sources. "Who knows? In a way, maybe it will be a relief to her—that it's all over."

Jack looked doubtfully down at Kate. Then a shadow of a different emotion crossed his handsome, weathered face.

"What is it?" she asked, stepping back from him. "What have you remembered? Jack?"

Before he could answer, a subtle motion from somewhere behind him caught Kate's eye. She quickly stepped to one side to see what it was.

Yancy's hand was stretching out toward the pistol that lay in the dirt, inches from his fingertips. A thin stream of blood dribbled from one corner of his mouth onto his shirt.

He was still alive, just barely. But his eyes shone with a menacing hunger for revenge.

"Jack, behind you!" Kate screamed.

She watched in horror as Yancy gripped the gun and leaned weakly on one elbow, supporting his weapon in both hands.

Although Jack reacted immediately to her warning, he hadn't moved more than a few inches to one side before the shot rang out. His gun slipped from his fingers and tumbled to the ground. His momentum carried him two staggering steps. Kate caught him, breaking his fall, but crumbled to the stony ground under the weight of his limp body.

"Oh, no, Jack! No, please—not now . . . not yet!"

Her eyes darted to the gun in the dirt—her first impulse to seize it and fling it as far away from them as possible. But her survival instincts prevailed. Grasping the Colt, she aimed it down the canyon at Yancy. If he tried to shoot Jack again, she'd not hesitate to pull the trigger.

But it seemed the young gunslinger had used his last ounce of strength. He lost his grip on the weapon, and the gray steel killing instrument dropped from his fingers with a dull thump.

"At least I ain't goin' alone, Ranger," he gasped. His eyes glazed over, and he collapsed facedown into the sand.

Kate knew he was dead.

It was all she could do to stop herself from screaming out her fury at the unfairness of life. She sobbed into the collar of Jack's shirt as his body slumped, increasingly heavy on top of her.

It had happened...happened just as he'd said it would. He'd been shot in the back, and her being there with him hadn't changed a thing. Oh why hadn't she stayed awake? Why had she left him alone?

Hot tears flowed down her cheeks, blurring her vision in the brilliant sunlight.

Tenderly she slid Jack off of her, letting gravity pull his still-warm body to the ground as she rolled him onto his side so that she could stand up. Just as she was about to release him, she felt a subtle vibration through her fingertips, and she drew a shuddering breath.

It took her a moment to realize her senses weren't playing a cruel trick on her. The crashing of her own heart wasn't what she'd just felt. A steady but weak beat was coming from the man who lay wounded at her feet.

Terrified she might be wrong, Kate dropped to her knees in the gravel and pressed her ear to Jack's chest. There really was a heartbeat!

"You're alive! Oh, Jack! Jack, hold on and let me see if—"

She scrambled around behind him and examined the growing pattern of crimson on the back of his shirt. It didn't center in his back at all. The wound seemed to be high and well to one side of where his heart would be. It looked as if the bullet had passed straight through the fleshy part of his left shoulder.

Kate moved Jack gently, and a moan escaped from his lips. "It's all right, darling," she cried, her tears turning to glistening droplets of hope. "You moved at the last minute."

The main problem now, she thought frantically, was stopping the bleeding, and preventing infection. Then she had to somehow transport Jack back to San Antonio where he could get medical attention. At least, she assumed there would be at a physician somewhere in town.

In desperation, she looked around. The only spare clothing they carried with them was the dress she'd already worn for several days, and that wasn't clean enough for bandages. Her glance shifted to Yancy. No help there. Every inch of him was covered with dust or blood.

Yancy's horse had wandered up the side of the ravine and joined Apache and Sunny to munch mesquite grass. Maybe in his saddlebags?

Running to the animal, she unbuckled one leather pouch and rummaged through it. On the very top were two shirts that were either brand-new or recently laundered. She didn't stop to ask herself how a criminal on the run had found the opportunity to pick up fresh clothes. Kate pulled out the shirts and tripped back across the rocky ground toward Jack.

On the way, she scooped up Yancy's gun then Jack's, jamming both weapons into the waistband of her skirt. She'd figure out how to reload them later, if necessary.

Clamping her teeth onto the hem of one fresh shirt, Kate started a tear. With shaking hands she shredded the fabric into long strips.

"You're going to be all right, Ranger. I promise," she vowed, ripping away. "I knew I wasn't around just for the ride. Damn you, why'd you have to be so chivalrous and let me sleep while you—"

A choking groan interrupted her scolding. "K-Kate, you there?"

"I'm here, Jack." Kate knelt beside him. "Hold still. I'm going to bandage your shoulder before you leak all over the desert."

She tore his bloody shirt up one side seam from hem to armpit, then from cuff to armpit, and lifted away the soggy pieces. It was the only way to get the thing off of him without putting him through agony.

Jack opened his eyes and stared at her. "Yancy?"

"He's dead. *Really* dead this time."

"You shot him?" He looked shocked.

"No, you did. It just took a while to work. He got up enough strength to fire a round into your back."

Jack scowled. "That's not my back, that's my shoulder."

"So I see, and it's the only reason we're having this conversation. When I called out, you must have moved just enough. Looks like he missed your heart by inches."

Jack stared silently up at her as she wound strips of cloth up and over his shoulder then around his chest under his armpits to anchor the dressing. Every time she reached around his back, she had to ease him up off the sand a few inches. He clenched his teeth and paled.

"I'm sorry," she whispered. "I know that hurts, but there's no other way. I'll be done soon."

"I don't understand," he rasped.

"What don't you understand?" She wished he'd shut up and let her concentrate. He was bleeding too heavily for her amateurish bandaging job to hold for long. Where was the Red Cross when you needed them?

"If I didn't die, why are you still here?"

"I don't know." She sat back on her heels and looked at him, suddenly understanding what he meant. She, too, had expected their parting to be swift. As soon as fate had been satisfied, wouldn't she simply be zapped back to her own time?

"Maybe my job's not done. Maybe I have to get you back to town and a doctor."

"But if I—"

She pressed her trembling fingertips over his lips. "Hush. Save your strength for the ride. I have a feeling it won't be much fun."

Kate led Apache close to where Jack lay. Bending forward, she wedged her right arm under his good shoulder and used the muscles in her legs to lever him upward.

"You know," he grunted, as he wobbled to his feet, "you're a hell of a lot stronger than you look."

"Well, I'm not strong enough to get you onto Apache by myself. So you just concentrate on helping out a little here."

He winked at her. "I'm beholden to you, ma'am. Reckon I'll have to find a way to repay your kindness."

Kate felt her cheeks warming. "Quit flirting, Jack."

It was slowgoing, but she finally managed to maneuver him onto his saddle. Then she turned around and looked at Yancy, sprawled in the dust.

"There's nothing you can do for that boy now," Jack said.

She shook her head. "It's not that. I just can't leave him here."

"We don't have much choice, under the circumstances. You can't haul a hundred eighty pounds of deadweight onto a horse by yourself."

"I'm thinking of Pamela, not him."

Jack sighed, and she turned to him. His eyes had a glazed, smoky look from the pain, and he was sitting crooked in his saddle.

"I know," he said sadly. "I know how it will be for her. I just—"

"Do you have any rope?" she asked.

"Tied to my saddle. Under the blanket roll. Why?"

"I have an idea."

Kate took the rope, then ran over to her own mount and Yancy's pony and walked them close to his body. Trying not to think too much about what she was doing, she tugged the young man's boots off, then lashed his ankles together.

The free end of the rope she tossed over the pinto's saddle. He stood docilely, munching a mouthful of mesquite while she brought Sunny around to his other side.

"Smart girl," Jack mumbled.

She looked up, wondering how she was ever going to get two men—one dead, one half-dead—across twenty miles of desert. Would she be able to follow the almost nonexistent trail to San Antonio?

Picking up the loose end of rope, Kate tied it securely to Sunny's saddle horn, then she held the mare's bridle and walked her away in a line perpendicular from the pony. Kate looked over her shoulder. Yancy's feet lifted into the air as the rope grew taut, then his body slid backward along the ground before rising, feetfirst, up and over the pinto's saddle.

"Good girl," she told Sunny when Yancy was centered over the saddle. Untying the rope, she used it to secure the body, draped across the saddle on its stomach, so that it wouldn't fall off as they rode.

They started slowly out of the canyon. Jack couldn't take the jarring motion of a trot or gallup. At a more relaxed pace, he seemed to bleed more slowly, too.

Kate kept an eye on him, riding Sunny shoulder to shoulder with Apache, laying her hand on Jack's thigh to bring him around whenever he looked as if he were teetering and about to pass out.

Yancy's horse followed docilely, tethered to hers. The short rest, the water she'd given it and its snack of mesquite seemed to have revived the animal.

Every half hour, Kate stopped and broke out the canteens and made Jack drink, although their water was running low.

The bandages completely soaked through in the first hour. Stopping to change them in the heat of the day seemed like a bad idea. They kept moving.

Kate found landmarks she could follow—a peculiar fork-shaped cactus, a low rise covered with prairie-dog burrows... She spotted the twin knolls and moved past them to the northeast.

At last, the stucco and limestone dwellings of San Antonio rose into view. Kate cast a last worried glance at Jack. His eyes were closed. He was swaying precariously on his saddle.

"Just another mile or so," she murmured, touching his arm. "Come on, Jack. You can make it."

"Yup." He pulled the corners of his mouth up in an effort to smile, but didn't open his eyes.

Kate called to the first men she saw at the edge of town, but they took one look at the grim trio and slunk back into an alley. By now Jack had slumped forward against Apache's neck, and he looked in no better shape than Yancy. She rode through the middle of San Antonio, trailing a crowd that seemed more curious than willing to help. By the time she stopped in front of the Sweetwater, a sizable group of onlookers accompanied her.

Word of their arrival must have preceded them. Sheriff Phelps was leaning against a porch rail, observing her critically.

"Looks like you got one holy mess on your hands there, gal," he commented.

Kate glared at him. "Are you going to help me get this wounded man to a doctor or not?"

Phelps nodded. "Fetch the doc," he said laconically to the man beside him. He turned to two others who stood nearest to Jack's horse. "You boys bring him on through this way to the back."

Kate didn't trust Phelps or anyone else in this town. She jumped down from Sunny and watched warily as the men eased Jack off his horse and carried him inside.

She'd done a lot of thinking on their way back across the desert. Just because Jack hadn't died in the canyon during the gunfight didn't mean he wouldn't eventually succumb from a gunshot wound, or die as a result of some harm done him while he was recovering and unable to protect himself.

"I'm going inside with him, Sheriff," she said.

Phelps put out a hand to stop her. "Doc will take care of him."

"Maybe." She looked him levelly in the eye. "I want you to know that nothing's going to happen to that man while I'm here."

"Awful loyal talk from a *cousin,*" he commented, flicking a fly off his sleeve.

"We're a close family," she bit off, brushing past him and through the door.

She was aware of Phelps following her through the saloon as she ducked behind a burlap curtain that separated the public room from a hallway behind it. The low passage led to several small rooms. One door was open, and she followed the sound of Jack's moans through it.

The room held a narrow bed, a wood-burning stove, small table and two rickety-looking chairs.

Jack lay on the bare mattress, breathing hard, clutching his shoulder. She rushed to him, and the men who'd carried him into the room stood back but seemed inclined to stay.

Seizing his hand in hers, she fought the overwhelming impulse to cry.

"In there, Doc," a gruff voice directed from the hallway.

Kate turned to see a cliché of an old-time country physician amble into the room. He was stout, with mutton-chop whiskers and a drinker's blowzy complexion. He carried a black leather bag.

"What happened here, miss?" he asked, leaning down to peel away the blood-soaked cloth strips from Jack's shoulder.

"The Ranger was trying to bring in Yancy Kennard. The boy refused to come with him and went for his gun. Yancy's dead."

The doctor nodded, pressing his fingers around the circumference of the wound. "From the back?"

"Yes. We both thought Yancy was already dead. Jack had turned away." She felt someone step up behind her, and when she glanced over her shoulder, she wasn't surprised to see it was Phelps.

The doctor nodded. "Well, I expect your Ranger will live, but I have to clean up that shoulder and stop the bleedin'. Bullet must have passed straight on through him, back to front. That's lucky. He's lost a lot of blood, though."

"He has," Kate agreed, biting down on her lip, determined more than ever not to cry in front of these men.

"Why don't you wait with Stony in the front room?" the doctor advised. He laid his hand over hers. "I'll take care of him, my dear. And I expect the sheriff would like a word with you 'bout what happened out there."

She looked up at Phelps. His expression didn't seem as harsh now. "All right."

They sat in the saloon, near the window, at a battered wooden table. Her chair had a caned seat and back, and matched none of the others at that table or any nearby. Even now it looked well used, if not already an antique.

"What do you need to know, Sheriff?" she asked, after he'd ordered them a bottle of whiskey.

"You'd better start at the beginning," he said. The bartender set a bottle on the table along with two glasses. Phelps poured two fingers into her glass and twice as much into his own. "Where did you two catch up with Yancy? How'd you find him?"

Kate took a swallow of the dark amber liquid and waited for it to burn its way down her throat and nestle warmly in her stomach. She told him about their sleeping outside of town, due to his chasing them out. How she'd speculated about the bats retreating to a cave somewhere nearby.

He listened intently, shooing off three men who wandered close to the table, obviously hoping to be the first in on the gossip.

When she'd finished, Phelps shook his head. "I was hopin' something like this wouldn't happen. It would have been better if Yancy just lit out for California, like everyone said he'd done. Better for himself, for his sister and everyone around here."

Kate thought about the fresh shirts and squinted at Phelps suspiciously. "I'm pretty sure he came back into town earlier today and bought some clothes. Why didn't you arrest him then?"

Phelps drummed his thick fingers on the tabletop. "I know you think I don't do my job, but let me tell you, miss, I watch out for this town, for my people. I take the law very serious— I do." He took a deep breath and leaned over the table toward her, balancing the whiskey glass between his fingertips and peering through it at her, as if it were a magnifying glass and she were a rare species of moth. "There's somethin' very different about you—maybe it's just yer a Yankee, but I don't think so. Since Reconstruction started, we get enough Easterners out this way for me to get used to 'em. Whatever it is yer after, you'd best be careful what you say to folks.''

"I'll say what needs saying," she said, meeting his steely glare with her own fire.

"That's all well and good, but we got our pride like anyone else. If I'd seen Yancy in town, he'd have been behind my bars faster than that bullet cut through your Ranger.'' He leaned back in his chair and fixed her with a steady gaze. "I might not be a slick-talkin' carpetbagger, but I do my job. I know that boy was trouble, and I suspect he did what the Rangers claim he did to the colonel. If I'd taken him in, he'd a stood trial—fair and square."

Kate studied him, wondering if she'd misjudged the man. After all, there was friction between the different law-enforcement agencies in her own time. Local, state or federal officers sometimes were forced to hand over half-completed investigations to a next-higher level, and that sometimes generated hard feelings. Here, Jack had told her, the Rangers, local sheriffs and the regular army troops that manned the frontier forts were often in contention.

She drew her tongue over her cracked lips, wondering if she could mend fences. "I'm sorry, Sheriff. I may have misjudged you. It just seemed a little petty to me—you and the Rangers being on the same side of the law but making each other's jobs more difficult."

The first smile she'd seen from Phelps tugged awkwardly at his lips. "Yep, something very peculiar about you, young lady. I'm gonna have to find out what it is.'' He set down his glass with a clink and pulled a pouch of tobacco and a square of paper from his vest pocket. Methodically, he began rolling himself a smoke. He sealed it with a quick run of his tongue, then lit up, all the time watching her.

Kate turned away from his prying eyes. "How much longer will the doctor be with him?"

"Dunno. Don't matter much—expect you won't be going far tonight."

She lifted an eyebrow meaningfully. "Do we have a choice?"

Phelps looked pained. "You don't think I'd toss the two of you out of town with him in that condition, do you?"

"I don't know what to think, Sheriff."

He blew out a heavy, gray puff of smoke. "Woman, you got one acid tongue on you. Of course you don't have to take him away tonight. I'll see that you can keep the room he's in now. He can rest up for a couple of days at least, and you can stay with him." He looked at her as if expecting a particular reaction.

"That's good of you, Sheriff. Thank you." She stood up. "I'll go see how Jack's doing now."

He nodded, still waiting, a small smile spreading beneath his mustache.

"What is it?" she asked, exasperated.

He shrugged. "Thought you'd correct me about the room arrangement, ask for your own . . . Cuz."

Kate swallowed, sure she'd ruined everything. But Phelps was grinning in pure amusement. "Kissin' cousins is what we got here, heh?" He chuckled. "All right—no matter to me, young lady. I reckon that Ranger is as good a man as any around here. If I weren't hitched to this town, I'd likely be ridin' with those boys."

Kate felt the muscles in her shoulders ease up. "Sheriff, may I ask you a question?"

"Shoot."

"If it had been you out there, and Yancy went for his gun—"

"I'd a shot him just the same as your Ranger done."

"Really?"

"Yep. Only difference is, I woulda taken his gun away from him right then." He hesitated, his expression darkening as he looked up at her from his chair. "And I'd a used it to put a bullet in his head to make sure."

Kate had to admit that Phelps was a hard man—some might say ruthless. But after mulling over all he'd said, later that night as she sat over a hot meal of overcooked beans with rice and pork in Jack's room, she decided that it must have taken some hard men to settle things down for civilization to take root in the Old West.

It seemed that whoever possessed the most effective weapons, won the battle. Not long ago, Jack had told her, the rapid-fire arrows and deadly lances of Indian warriors had been more than a match for the settlers' primitive muskets, which were only useful at close range and could be fired only once before reloading. Now Colt had come up with a repeating-action pistol that held six shots and could be reloaded with one hand, even while riding. And she knew from her history books that, right about this same time, Winchester was developing an even more powerful repeating rifle than the Model 66 Jack packed on his saddle. Armed with these, the Rangers might turn the tide.

Maybe Phelps was the best man for the job at the moment. But in a few years, she mused, he'd be a relic, a forgotten historical figure.

Kate ate slowly, watching Jack sleep, letting her mind drift back to their own problems. Again, she wondered—had they really cheated fate? Or were they merely slowing her down?

She also revisited an old concern. How was she going to get back home? Until this moment, her mind had been so full of Jack, she'd blocked out all other worries. Seeing her children again, returning to the home she'd grown to cherish—these problems were no less important than they'd been from the start. Yet she was glad she'd come here with Jack.

Perhaps if he hadn't shown up when he did, she'd have become like Kathleen—afraid of new places, new experiences. Traveling to Jack's world and time had changed all that. Their experiences together in this wild country had excited her and brought out reserves of strength and grit she'd never known she had! It was a wonderful form of freedom to learn she could survive in a hostile environment, could actually find her way on horseback across unmarked terrain without benefit of highway or road map, with a wounded man in tow. She'd never have believed she had that in her. Never.

But the experience had also made Kate appreciate the quiet safety of her own home in Chester, the beauty of the verdant Vermont hills and pastures, the priceless love of Jesse and Anna. Even her friendship with Barbara seemed more precious after these days of danger, of not knowing who was her enemy and who her friend. Barbara, she knew, she could count on.

Kate sighed, and the man on the bed stirred.

Chapter 17

Kate set aside her empty plate and went to sit on the edge of Jack's bed.

"You awake, Ranger?" she whispered.

"Who the hell bound up my shoulder like this?" he grumbled. "It's so damn tight, I can't even move it!"

The orange glow from the kerosene lamp beside the bed struck sparks off of his black hair. She smoothed a dark wave off of his forehead with one hand. "You're not supposed to move it."

"Says who?"

"Says Dr. Schilling."

"That German quack?"

"Hush," she said, pushing him back down against the mattress when he tried to sit up. "Doc did an excellent job of stopping that bleeding. You should be thankful."

"I hurt like hell, and I'm starving," he growled. His blue eyes flashed accusingly up at her, as if his misery were her fault.

She gave him a stony stare.

"Oh, all right. I'm just mad as hell 'cause I suppose you're going to tell me I can't ride for a whole day."

"More like a week, Doc says." Kate sighed. "I knew you'd make a lousy patient."

Jack opened his mouth to protest, but she quickly bent forward and covered his lips with her own. He settled back against the pillow with a contented moan. His good hand came up behind her head, and she didn't resist when he kept her there for a long, satisfying kiss.

"Sorry," he muttered, when their lips at last parted. "I shouldn't take things out on you."

"I don't know what you have to take out on anyone," she said. "You're alive, and Yancy won't be gunning for you anymore."

"I know. I was thinking about that while I was lyin' here, watching you polish off that whole plateful of food by yourself, without offerin' me so much as a mouthful."

"Why didn't you say anything?" she gasped, laughing at his woeful expression.

"Wanted to see how much of a pig you could make of yourself," he teased.

"Well, I like that!"

He pulled her down for another kiss, and her heart nearly shattered with joy. He'd made it. He would live.

But now what?

"Jack," she said tentatively, looping a wisp of his hair around and around her finger, "we need to talk."

He gazed at her hungrily. She could still smell the trail on him—lusty and sunbaked. "I'd rather communicate nonverbally right now."

"You're critically injured. You shouldn't."

"Maybe I shouldn't make love to you, but my condition doesn't stop me from thinkin' about it."

She smiled at him, finding it hard to fight off the electric tingles his roaming hands summoned up. "I'm serious. Something happened, or maybe more importantly, *didn't happen* out there today." She chewed her lip thoughtfully. "Do you know what's going on?"

"About what?"

"About your future, Jack. Remember, that's why we're here, to set your life on track, so that you can return to Kathleen and fulfill your destiny by fathering children and living a full life."

He put his good arm around her, pulling her down onto his chest with a sad smile. "My life couldn't be any more full than it is right now—here with you, my darlin' woman."

She fought back burning tears that clung to her eyelashes. "I love you, Jack. And you know there's nothing I wouldn't do for you."

"You've shown me that, more times than I'd have ever asked it of you."

"But what about the rest of your life? If you lived through the day you were fated to die from a bullet in your back, you were supposed to go on with your life, and I was supposed to go back to mine. But I'm still here. Do you feel any different?"

"No," he admitted.

"What do The Rules say now?"

"I'm not sure," he said, looking away from her.

She pulled out of his arms and paced the floor. "Jack, there's something wrong." Spinning around, she stared at him, and a sudden horrible thought slashed through her brain. "Oh, Jack—"

"What?"

"Maybe you won't be instantly transported off to Kathleen, maybe you're already living out the rest of your life... and I'm... I'm stuck here, trapped in a century that's not mine!"

"Kate, I don't think—" He broke off, looking as bewildered as she felt, and reached for her.

"Don't try to make me feel better," she snapped. "It's possible. You have to admit it, Jack. We know so little about how this fate thing works. What if I *can't* go home? What if I *never* see my children again, and they grow up thinking their mother has deserted them?"

"Kate, please don't—"

"I can't let that happen. I won't let that happen!" She felt a surge of determination equal to the one that had carried her across the desert to San Antonio. "We have to go back now."

Jack looked at her, his blue eyes sorrowful. "We can try," he whispered. "But if I'm no longer a ghost reliving my old life, if this is my *real* life—"

"Then you won't be able to return to my century," she finished for him, the words tasting like burnt leather on her tongue.

Jack looked at her hopelessly. "We'll try, Kate. I honestly don't know what will happen."

She squeezed her eyes shut, but the haunting images of Jesse and Anna swam before her closed lids. She couldn't bear to think of never seeing their sweet faces again, never feeling their soft little arms wrap around her neck in an adoring hug.

"Please, Jack—now." Tears trickled down her flushed cheeks.

Jack sat up stiffly in the bed and motioned for her to come to him. Kate obeyed, perching beside him on the sagging straw mattress, letting him bring her close within the circle of his strong arms. Laying her head on his bare chest, she curled her legs beneath her.

"Kate, before we do this..." He hesitated, the words coming with difficulty to his lips. "There's the possibility that... well, we might never see each other again."

Oh, Lord, she thought, *don't do this to me, Jack. Don't make me choose.*

"I know," she managed. "I might arrive in the attic, and you might stay here."

"Right."

Now she couldn't stop the flow of tears. "You understand why I can't stay here with you, Jack, no matter how much I love you."

"I told you I'd never ask you to make that sacrifice."

"And I could never expect you to give up your destiny, your unborn children for me."

He nodded, pressing his lips to her temple. They felt cool against the throbbing heat of her emotions.

"Now, Jack," she whispered. "Try now, or I'll lose my courage."

He held her tightly, so tightly, she felt she might not be able to take another breath.

Nothing happened.

Kate breathed. In and out. In and out. She waited, desperately, and thought of Jesse and Anna. *Lost,* she grieved, *my babies are lost to me forever!*

Then a distant, whirring sound gradually filled her ears, and she felt the familiar but no-less-frightening dizziness steal over her, lifting her, whisking her through time and space as effortlessly as a modern high-speed elevator.

At last she sensed the natural heaviness of her body return, and she slowly opened her eyes, praying she'd be back home—yet, terrified she'd be there alone.

Around her ranged the shadowy rafters and recesses of her attic, just as she'd left it. But she could no longer feel the steady rhythm of Jack's heartbeat beneath her ear, or feel the reassuringly firm muscles and flesh of his chest and arms encompassing her.

"Jack, no!" she cried out, collapsing to her knees, sure she'd lost him.

"I'm here, darlin'. Right here." A low drawl came from nearby.

Kate swiveled around where she knelt on the splintery planks of the attic floor. Jack slouched in his leather chair, his head tilted back against the cushion.

She leapt to her feet and rushed at him. "Thank god you're here!"

"Yes," he said woodenly, "I am indeed *here*, not *there*."

She immediately guessed the cause of his bleak mood. "Then this means Yancy's bullet wasn't the one that killed you."

"No, it wasn't. As I look back, I can remember how it happened that day. Something caught my attention at the last minute as I walked away from him, thinking he was already dead. I moved aside. It might have been a buzzard overhead, something bothering my horse. Who knows... I was wounded that day, but managed to drag myself back into town."

"Then you're still in just as much danger, and we're no closer to knowing who really did kill you."

"Right." He dropped his head into one hand.

There was a shout and a squeal from the hallway below, and Kate automatically reeled about, an expectant smile on her face.

"Your children," Jack murmured. "Go to them, Kate."

"But you don't have much time."

"I know. But you need to see them as much, I'd guess, as they need to see you. Go to them. I'll rest. Tomorrow, if you're willing, we'll try one last time."

"If you're sure. Time is short," she reminded him.

"I know," he said tightly. "Go. I feel the need to sleep. Go."

She turned toward the stairs and started hesitantly down two steps before lifting her head to look back at Jack. He had slumped in the old chair, his eyes closed, his breathing audible and heavy with exhaustion—although he'd once told her he found sleep in her world unnecessary.

His long, denim-clad legs splayed out in front of him, ending in bare feet. His wide shoulders filled out the leather upholstery. At that moment she couldn't have loved him any more than she already did.

A fleeting thought crossed her mind. There was less chance now than ever before for them to stop Jack's killer, since he was incapacitated by a shoulder wound. Despite anything she did, he might still be gunned down.

After witnessing his brush with death in the canyon, Kate didn't know if she could endure another gun duel. How could she hold his head in her lap and watch his final breath seep from his body while those mesmerizing blue eyes glazed over?

On the other hand, Jack had said that he could only return with her as a *willing* traveling companion. *What if I refuse to go?* she thought. *What if I just tell him no? Then he can't leave, and he can't die again!*

Slowly she let her feet take her down the attic steps toward the second-floor door. She'd never felt more alive than while she'd been with Jack—here in her attic and crossing the desert near San Antonio. She couldn't imagine ever feeling so in tune with a man, so thoroughly in love with and loved by, cherished and excited by—

Kate's head throbbed horribly. She lifted one hand and pressed two fingers to the bridge of her nose, where the headache seemed to have centered.

If she refused to go back with Jack this last time, what would happen? He'd remain sequestered in her attic. For as long as she resided in the farmhouse, they'd have each other. He'd have to wait for a new owner to come along, perhaps through many more generations of occupants, before he found the right person to, again, accompany him to the last days of his mortal life.

His search might extend through eternity. Or it might end abruptly in the next day or two. The Rules. The unknown laws might state that he'd used up his second chance. He'd die and be lost to both her and his Kathleen.

Her head throbbed wickedly.

But if there were no time limit, she could, conceivably, keep him here indefinitely with her. He'd still be a ghost, and she'd still be a live human being. But they'd be together, dammit, and perhaps learn methods of working around his ghostly limitations. She'd find ways to please him, to make him as happy as he could be, under the circumstances. . . .

Kate dashed tears from her cheeks with the sleeve of her shirt, then reached out for the doorknob. "It's no use," she whispered hoarsely. "No use."

She couldn't refuse to help Jack. That would be selfish. She'd never put her own desires before the needs of someone she cared about. She couldn't very well change now.

Jack listened to Kate's halting footsteps on the stairway, aching to call her back, to hold her in his arms and forget about the voice deep down in his soul that kept reminding him of his duty. Kathleen depended upon him to come home to her, and he'd vowed he would. His children...they needed birthing, and there were his children's children—and their grandchildren. In his mind, families ranged out in ever-widening circles. Hundreds of lives were at stake, lives that would never come to be if he turned his back on his destiny.

To stay with Kate forever was all he wanted in his heart. But it was the one thing he couldn't have. He felt a sadness so intense, so overwhelming, that he wondered if he could go on at all, in either life or death. Ultimately, man can only escape the pain of life through death. How does he, then, escape death?

Suddenly a wave of warm emotion washed over him, invading his soul and chasing away the oppressive weight of his sorrow. Jack looked up from his sand-chafed palms where he'd pressed his forehead, sure that some All-Powerful entity had joined him in the attic. But there was no one.

A moment later, the strangely calming sensation was gone. But within him remained an unshakable faith that all would work out for the best, that both he and Kate would live loving, deeply passionate and satisfying lives, and know the happiness of caring families. Most importantly to him, he understood that Kate would never really leave him. Likewise, some part of him would always stay with her.

"Then that's how it will be," he murmured into the darkness.

Jack wished he could somehow convey his feelings to Kate—the worth of their love, the fulfillment and unbroken connection between their spirits, or their inner cores or whatever one chose to label the true essence of a person. But this faith in their eternal love wasn't something he could easily put into words or explain in logical terms. She'd only think he was trying to make her feel better with vague reassurances.

Jack sighed, listening contentedly to Kate greeting her children. He smiled at their squeals of delight, knowing she was where she needed to be, for the moment.

Kate hugged Jesse and Anna to her, nuzzling her face in their blond curls, smelling the fresh air in their hair and clothes. "You've been playing outside," she said.

"Not *playing*," Jesse corrected her impatiently. "Aunt Barb took us riding."

"She did, did she?" Kate asked, looking up in time to see Barbara appear on the stairs leading up from the first floor.

"Was it fun?"

"Yessiree, pardner," Jesse said, mimicking a Texas accent that tugged at Kate's heart.

"Yessirree," echoed Anna. "We rided and rided and rided a long, long ways." The lump on her head seemed already smaller.

Kate winked at Barbara, who leaned against the hallway wall, observing her with a thoughtful expression. "We just rode around the ring over at my place. Probably seemed like a lot to them."

Kate moved the children away from her, worried by her friend's uncharacteristic sullen expression. "Go play, you two. I need to talk to Barb."

The children wheeled around and dove into Jesse's room. In the next instant they were arguing over who would choose the game to be played.

"What's wrong?" Kate asked.

"How long have you been back?"

"I don't know, a couple of hours, maybe," Kate hedged.

Barbara shook her head. "That's impossible. We were only away from the house for forty-five minutes."

"Oh." Kate bit down on her lip. She'd forgotten about the time differences. "Guess it was less than I'd thought."

With a grim look in her eyes, Barbara brushed past her, heading for the stairs to the attic.

Kate panicked. "Wait! Where are you going?"

Barbara didn't answer. She marched straight up the dark steps with a determined set to her shoulders. At the top of the stairs, she pulled the string on the overhead bulb and looked around the dimly lit space. "Where is he?" she demanded.

Kate raced up the last few stairs and stopped dead. Jack was exactly where she'd left him, dozing in his chair at the shadowy end of the attic.

Her heart pounded as Barbara's narrowed eyes searched the long, raftered room piled with keepsakes and trash, trash Kate had come up here to throw out, one day that now seemed so long ago. The day she'd met Jack.

If ever two people had fit a lifetime of love into a few days, she and Jack had done it, she thought fiercely.

At first Jack didn't move; then his eyelids cracked open. He stared at Barbara, his expression deepening into a frown. Kate didn't dare breathe, didn't dare move. She anticipated the next second when Barbara's eyes would inevitably adjust to the poor lighting, as hers had become used to doing more quickly. Then she'd see a darkly handsome stranger, wearing only tight riding jeans, no shirt to cover his muscled chest, lounging in a beat-up leather chair.

"What is *that?*" Barbara demanded, pointing toward Jack.

Kate closed her eyes briefly. "He's . . . Barb, this is going to be hard to believe, but . . . Please, let me explain."

Barbara stomped the length of the attic, ducking when she came to low rafters, and stopped directly in front of Jack. His eyes swept up the sturdy-looking woman, flashed to Kate questioningly, then back to Barbara as if he were unsure what to do or say.

Barbara tapped her foot impatiently and folded her arms over her formidable chest. "There's no explanation necessary. I *know* what's been going on up here!"

"You do?" Kate asked weakly.

"I'd have to be blind not to!" she ground out. "You told me you'd come up here to clean out and organize your attic. Well, that's a lie."

Kate swallowed and shot a helpless look at Jack.

"Look at that . . . *that thing.*"

Jack scowled at her finger, looking annoyed. "Hey, who are you calling a *thing?*"

"That chair must be well over a hundred years old!" Barbara scolded. "And you've got it stashed up here, collecting dust." She reached down and swept her fingertips across the seat, her hand slicing through Jack without effort.

"I—I what?" Kate stammered.

"You're always watching your budget so carefully. You said last fall you wanted to remodel the kitchen but didn't have enough money to do it right away. Why aren't you selling off some of this antique furniture? I'll bet you'd pull in enough for new kitchen cabinets at least!"

Kate swallowed and blinked at Jack. He smiled.

Apparently, Barbara couldn't see him at all.

"That . . . well, that sounds like a great idea," she agreed.

"Of course it is, and you would have thought of it right away if you weren't messing around with some good-for-nothing escaped con." Barbara sucked in a deep breath and demanded, "What's gotten into you, Kate? I can't believe you'd jeopardize your children's welfare by—"

"Whoa! Hold it right there," Kate said, shaking her head in disbelief. "You think I'm hiding a fugitive from the law in my house?" She didn't know whether to laugh or feel insulted.

Barbara glared at her. "I overheard you talking to him. And you left a message on my answering machine, mumbling something about confusing love with lust."

Jack covered his mouth with one hand, but a roaring laugh burst out.

Barbara kept on talking as if she hadn't heard him. "So if you're not trying to hide some man from the people who care about you, what is this all about?"

Kate sighed. She felt an overwhelming need to sit down and regroup. Her emotions were spinning, and she'd completely lost the ability to think. "I wish I could say for sure," she murmured, signaling Jack with a wave of her hand to slide over on the chair.

She tucked herself between the arm and his thigh. Draping her knees over his lap, her long legs over the opposite arm, she rested against his shoulder. It would look, from Barbara's perspective, as if she were leaning against the chair's back.

"I really wish I could explain what's been going on in my life, Barb. Right now it's impossible."

"Listen, you've obviously fallen head over heels for some guy you don't see fit to introduce to your kids—"

"That's not it at all," Kate said, surreptitiously stroking Jack's bare arm with one finger. "He's a very special man. I'd never be ashamed to be seen with him. Never."

She felt his lips brush the top of her head.

"Then why all this mystery?" Barbara groaned. *"Why can't I meet him?"*

"When I'm ready and he's ready... you'll meet him."

Barbara threw up her hands. "I wanted you to start dating. But you can't afford to jump into bed with the first man who comes along, without even considering his background."

Kate felt suddenly mischievous. She tossed her head. "I haven't. There have been lots of men."

Lots? Jack mouthed, glaring at her.

"Don't give me that hogwash," Barbara said. "I know you. As soon as a man shows the slightest interest, you send out No Trespassing signals. 'My husband died, and I'm not ready for dating.' Isn't that your favorite response? You do everything you can to discourage men."

Kate shrugged. "I see no reason to encourage a man I'm not interested in."

"You don't give them *a chance!*" Barbara shouted.

"She's got a point. That sort of thing would certainly turn me off," Jack whispered in Kate's ear.

Kate elbowed him, but he just grinned back. "Shut up!"

"What?"

"Not... not you," Kate sputtered, furious with the two of them. "Forget it, Barb. I'll be okay. I just need to work out some things with Jack and—"

"Jack... that's his name. Right?"

"Yes, but—"

"So let me meet him. I promise I won't cross examine the man or do anything to scare him away. Better yet, let me check him out. I know someone in the state police. If nothing else, it might save you a heartbreak down the road."

"Under the circumstances, it's impossible for you to see him, and I forbid you to snoop into his life." Not that she'd find anything.... She'd have to go pretty far back in their records.

"It's not impossible. I can just—"

Kate shot Barbara a silencing look. "Believe me, it *is* impossible. What I'm going through is totally out of the realm of—" She sighed in frustration. There was no way to explain, so why bother trying? "Maybe someday I'll introduce the two of you."

Her throat tightened on the lie. Barbara would never meet Jack, not in this life.

"All right." She sighed. "Have it your way. We'll wait. But don't you come crying to me when that creep breaks your heart. If he's not man enough to show his face to your best friend, I doubt he's very much of a man at all."

"In one way, you're surprisingly close to the truth," Kate mumbled.

Jack rolled his eyes. "Well, I like that!"

"You're a ghost, remember? A ghost!" she hissed at him.

"I'm what? A guest?" Barbara frowned.

Kate pushed herself out of the chair, then stumbled across the planks when Jack's hand on her rump gave her an extra push. "Forget it. Let's go downstairs and have some supper with the kids."

"Then you're determined to see him again?" Barbara persisted, following her toward the stairway.

"Yes."

"And I suppose you want me to watch Jesse and Anna."

"I'd like that very much."

Barbara shook her head as Kate walked past her and down the stairs. "When?"

"Tomorrow. I may be staying the night, but I'm not sure."

"Fine."

At the bottom of the steps, Kate turned to shut the door after Barbara had stepped into the hallway. Kate smiled at her and hugged her hard. "I'm sorry I can't tell you more. I would if I could. Honest."

Barbara scowled at the carpet runner. "Just be careful, okay, honey? Don't let him hurt you."

Kate drew a deep breath and nodded, although she knew that, too, was a silent lie. Jack had already hurt her, hurt her deeply although he'd never intended to cause her pain. When they parted, whether it was because he'd lived or died in 1867, the wrenching agony of leaving him to continue her own life would, she knew, be almost unbearable.

Her eyes threatened to tear up, but she willed them dry immediately. "Come on," she said. "Time for supper."

Chapter 18

Jack waited impatiently for Kate in the attic. He knew how hard going back one more time would be for her. He wondered how long it would be before she came up the stairs.

Maybe a few hours. Maybe not until morning. Maybe never.

He wouldn't have blamed her if she'd bailed out on him. He waited.

Jack was aware of her presence before he actually heard her steps on the stairs or felt her hand settle lightly on his bowed head. Her touch had become both love potion and healing elixir to him. He didn't know how he'd make do without her.

"Jack?" she whispered.

"Yup."

"I'm ready."

He looked up at her, memorizing the soft frame of her face, her deep brown eyes, the delightful curve of her lips. No other woman would ever fill the space she'd made in his life.

"Are you sure?"

She pressed her lips together and nodded.

Slowly he stood to take her in his arms one last time, for one final trip together into the past.

* * *

Because Kate had seemed sure she'd be leaving first thing the next morning, Barbara suggested she take the kids back to Willow Creek Farms to stay the night. Jesse and Anna were thrilled with the plan, and Barbara figured it would give her more flexibility for getting some work done, in between entertaining the children.

She had chores to do early that morning, both in the stables and in her office. She was gradually transferring all of her business records onto a spreadsheet on her new computer, which was going to make keeping track of payroll, supplies and breeding lines a lot easier. And Carson had said he had something important to discuss with her—what it was she didn't know for sure. She assumed it had something to do with the new mare she'd bought on her last trip to Nashville. It was being shipped north the end of next week.

When William Carson came into her kitchen at six that morning, he took off his hat, hung it on the peg beside the door, then turned to look at her. He didn't move for a full three minutes, which seemed odd behavior to Barbara because, for as long as she'd known the man, he'd had a hollow leg. Nothing much stood between him and a tableful of food.

"Well, what's taking you so long, Car?"

"Huh?"

"Breakfast is ready. Go ahead help yourself." Barbara sat down at the red-and-white-checkered vinyl tablecloth that covered the long trestle table. On it were enough places set for all of six of her hands. The other men would break for their morning meal in another twenty minutes. She and Carson always ate early, together, to plan out the day's chores.

"Oh, that . . . yeah," he mumbled distractedly.

He crossed the kitchen in an awkward gait and helped himself to scrambled eggs from the pan on the stove where the cook had left them to stay warm.

"I don't know where Martha's got to," Barbara said. "She was here a few minutes ago, finished frying the bacon and setting out the toast and home fries, then she took off upstairs somewhere. Not like her to miss serving up breakfast and having some with us."

"Probably already ate," Carson mumbled.

"Hope she's not feeling ill." Barbara forked buttery, yellow eggs into her mouth and chased them down with a generous bite of wheat toast.

"Sure she ain't, Miss Weintraub."

"Haven't I asked you to call me Barbara?"

She felt irrationally annoyed with him. Why was Carson, the most laid-back man in all of Vermont, acting so jittery? Every other bite of food, he'd shoot a glance toward the back door, or jump at the sound of footsteps on the floor above. Maybe he was going to ask her for a raise. She decided, if he asked, she'd up his salary by five percent. If he didn't, she'd give it to him anyway, in June, when she normally adjusted her employees' pay.

"Haven't I?" she repeated.

"Yes, ma'am."

"Then do it."

"Yes, ma'am. I mean, Barbara . . . ma'am." He sat at the table, staring at his plate with considerable thought, no longer eating.

Barbara decided to ignore him.

She thought instead about Kate and her phantom lover, Jack. She wished there was something she could do to stop her from getting hurt. The woman was so dense when it came to men. Couldn't she see that any man who didn't have the fortitude to face her friends and family was hiding something? Didn't she have a brain in her head?

"Barbara," a voice said, and she looked up out of her thoughts, having forgotten Carson was in the room.

"Yes, Car?"

"I've wanted to talk to you for a long time about something . . . something that's been gnawing at me."

"I know."

"You know?" He frowned, looking a little frightened.

"Yes." She shoveled another forkful of eggs into her mouth. "About your raise."

"Raise?"

"Yes, you can have it early, if that's a concern."

"Wasn't about no raise," he said solemnly. He spread his hands flat on the tabletop, on either side of his plate, and observed her.

"Oh," she said, "you're ready to set up a stall for that new mare. Well, we need to move Inventive Fashion down to the Fenwick place anyway. She'll be getting ready to foal sometime in the next two weeks, I expect." She chewed thoughtfully, trying to focus her mind on the work at hand. "That will leave a stall ready for our new arrival."

"I already moved Fashion. Yesterday."

Barbara put down her fork and stared at him. "Good Lord, if it isn't your raise or the horses, what is it, Car?"

"I, well, I've been wanting to ask you, if you, I mean—" He gazed across the table at her with a shadow of a smile that seemed to strain his craggy features. "Maybe you'll think me forward, but I was wondering if you'd like to go into Springfield and see a movie with me some night."

It took a moment for her foreman's words to sink in. "Movie?" she repeated. He might as well have asked her to run off with him to Tahiti.

"Well, yes, there's this new one I heard you tell Mrs. Fenwick you'd like to see and..." He seemed to run out of steam. His halfway-hopeful glance dropped to his plate.

Barbara stared at the top of his grizzled head. He was somewhere in his fifties, a hardworking man who'd been with her for a dozen years. She'd given the orders, he'd followed them. He had his own room in the bunkhouse, whereas all the other full-timers shared a single large dormitory-style room. They'd never had a personal conversation. And now, because of a few cautiously worded sentences, everything between them had changed.

Barbara looked down at herself—her square, strong body swathed in stained blue jeans and a denim shirt with sleeves rolled to the elbows. Her hair was only roughly combed out of its sleep knots. She wore no makeup.

What the hell does he see in me? she wondered.

But it was clear from the quick flash of warmth behind his tan eyes when they shyly focused on her again, William Carson saw something that appealed to him.

"Car, I—I'm flattered, I really am," she murmured.

He straightened his shoulders, drew a deep breath and nailed her with a no-nonsense look. "It's all right, ma'am...Barbara.

Figured it was awful forward of me to even ask. You being my boss and all.''

"Car—"

"No, no," he interrupted with a dismissive wave of his hand, "I understand completely. A woman like yourself with land and a thriving business, she's got to be careful about men trying to cash in on her."

Barbara couldn't help noticing the irony of his warning her about the very concerns she'd had on Kate's behalf. She laughed out loud. "Carson! I didn't think that of you at all."

He stood up and wiped his mouth with his napkin, although he hadn't eaten more than two bites. "You don't have to explain. Martha said I should try, but I knew it was wrong."

Barbara realized that if she didn't do something fast, he'd be out the back door and gone, taking his embarrassment with him. She'd never get another invitation to a movie or anywhere else from him.

Without sparing her actions another thought, she rocketed to her feet and dodged around the table, just beating him to the door. Her wide, strong body blocked his escape route. He was wiry and seasoned to physical labor and at least ten years older than she, but, she realized in that instant, he was the dearest man she knew.

Why not a taste of romance?

"Don't go, Car. Please."

He shook his head and took his hat down from its peg. "You don't have to be nice to me."

"I know that. I want—" Barbara broke off and sighed. She was lousy at this sort of thing; it had been so long. As often as she'd pushed Kate to take the plunge and date, she'd only infrequently made time in her own life for men. But then again, she wasn't as naturally attractive as Kate was, and she was always too busy to fuss over her appearance.

"I want to go to the movies with you," she insisted.

"You do?" His eyes widened in shock.

"Yes." She didn't know what else to do, so she stuck out her hand. He looked at it for a moment before seizing it between his two gnarled paws and shaking it as if they'd just closed a business deal. "When?" she asked.

"H-how about to-tonight?" he stammered.

"I might not be free." His face fell. "No, really. I'll still have Kate's kids here with me. I've got an idea, though. You go rent us a couple of good videos—one for the kids, the second for you and me—I'll make popcorn."

"We'll watch it here?" he asked.

"Sure. Why not?"

He looked pleased with the idea. "If that's all right with you, it's sure all right with me."

"It's fine with me. I'll see you tonight. Come to the house about eight?"

Then she did what she'd never imagined herself doing. Barbara grabbed the man by his shirtsleeves, hauled him to her and kissed him soundly on the cheek. The strain in his face washed clear away, and Carson beamed at her like a schoolboy nurturing his first crush.

"Eight," he said, stepping around her and through the door.

"Eight," she repeated, watching him slip outside and across the yard. She was sure he wasn't feeling the ground under his boots.

Kate rode the wave of decades with Jack, as she had several times before. This time, though, she was less afraid, and she savored the experience of other women's and men's lives brushing past her. This is a gift, she decided, to know how brief yet precious life is. Perhaps a few days with Jack was worth a lifetime spent with any other man. Who could say that time spent with a person counted for more than the depth of a brief but perfect love?

When a familiar density returned to her body and she felt herself settle onto a solid surface, Kate slowly opened her eyes. She fully expected to find herself in the back room of the Sweetwater, beside Jack's bed.

They were in the gentle cleft between the twin buttes, and it appeared to be the middle of the night.

"Why are we here?" she asked, turning in Jack's arms to look up at him.

"Because I needed to be with you one last time."

"You know when it will happen? The ambush or whatever?"

"Not exactly, but I feel it will be soon." Jack brushed his lips softly across her temple, kissed her on the lips and lifted her in his arms. With exquisite tenderness, he made long, delicious love to her until the sun crept rosily over the horizon.

They peeled themselves out of each other's arms reluctantly, dressed and sat for a while in the sand, letting the desert chill drift away under the sun. Kate had a feeling of minutes drifting away, too. Minutes that would never return, never be quite the same for her. She treasured every one of them, letting her eyes roam Jack's strong, lanky body, letting herself enjoy the feeling of being close to her man after they'd given each other all they could.

"The other day, I had a—" he chuckled a little "—hate to call it a vision, because it wasn't visual. Guess you might call it a message."

"Yes?" she said.

"It was about us . . . you and me."

"Jack, please, just say it."

"I'm trying, I really am. But it's so hard to grasp, I don't know if I can put it into words."

"Try." She touched him encouragingly on the arm.

He nodded. "It was a good feeling. A feeling that you'll always be a part of me, and I'll always be with you . . . in some way I can't explain."

Kate swallowed and breathed deeply, willing her eyes to stay dry. "I understand," she said.

"I don't think you do. It's as if—" He closed his eyes suddenly and brought his hand to his forehead, as if in pain.

"Are you all right, Jack?" Kate knelt in front of him.

"Fine. I'm not hurting. It's as if there's a wall in my head, and it won't let me past it. The Rules, you know. I guess I'm not supposed to talk about certain things." He shook his head, then smiled at her, and her heart melted under the dazzling blue of his gaze. "Come on. The horses are the other side of the rise. We need to get back into town."

She noticed as he pulled on his shirt, that his shoulder was no longer taped. Only a simple gauze patch covered the wound front and back, and it seemed he was no longer hampered by motion. She expected a number of days had passed during their absence. How many she couldn't tell.

They rode into town, talking very little, sometimes touching or holding hands when they brought Apache and Sunny close to plod down the dusty trail into San Antonio. Their arrival, this time, created a much more positive reaction. Women walking along the gritty planks that were the only sidewalks, smiled shyly at them, and both Mexican and Texan men tipped their hats reverently as Jack rode by.

Apparently, word had spread of his ending Yancy's days as a troublemaker. Those who were law-abiding themselves were thankful for the peace. Those who had looked on Yancy as a model for their own lawlessness seemed to be taking his death as a lesson and a warning to mend their ways.

They rode through the plaza where the historic battle for the Alamo had been fought. The once-lovely Spanish-style church, where the legendary David Crockett and Jim Bowie heroically met their ends, had been reduced to rubble some thirty years earlier, and its remains turned into a granary. A little farther along was the general store, the source of Jack's last pair of jeans, and the Sweetwater, and across from that, a barbershop. They stopped here.

"I won't be long," he said to her.

Kate looked up and down the street nervously. "If there isn't much time, shouldn't we be asking around, trying to find—"

He boosted her down from Sunny and set her on the ground. "Won't make any difference, darlin'." Smiling, he touched her cheek. "Why don't you browse through the store while I get myself a shave," he said, tying up their horses.

She watched him turn and walk away, unsure what to do. Did he know what was about to happen and when? Was he intentionally keeping the truth from her? Or had he finally become resigned to facing whatever fate presented.

She stood beside Sunny, stroking the mare's shiny neck until Jack stooped through the barbershop's low doorway. "Men," she mumbled. "Why do they have to be so pigheaded?"

The sorrel snuffled, as if in agreement.

Kate started to turn toward the general store, thinking she could at least keep an eye on the entrance to the barbershop from across the street. Several riders and wagons passed her by, churning up dust from hooves and wooden wheels. Then, from a distance, she noticed a different sort of horse and rider.

The sleek black stallion outfitted with a bridle and saddle lavishly trimmed in silver, held its head at an arrogant angle. It lifted each hoof high and seemed to prance down the middle of the street, sometimes moving in a sideways canter. Its rider, a woman, sat elegantly in the saddle, keeping the spirited animal under tight rein.

Kate drew a slow breath as she recognized Pamela Kennard.

A chill sliced through Kate, followed by deep sorrow. Poor Pamela. Had she come into town to claim her brother's body? Kate thought about that. No, she could have as easily sent a contingent of her men from Rancho del Sol for that unhappy task. Then why? Why ride all that distance, alone, if not to—

The truth settled, cold and unwelcome, in Kate's stomach. "Oh, no—" she breathed.

Kate shot a look at the barbershop, then at Pamela, whose eyes studied each storefront as she passed, examined the horses tied up to hitching rails along the way. She was looking for someone, looking for Jack.

Without thinking about what she was doing or if it could possibly help, Kate stepped into the middle of the street and waited for Pamela to see her. A second later, the ebony stallion danced to a stop, sending a cloud of brown dust into the hot air. Pamela leaned forward in her saddle, and smiled tightly at her.

"So he *is* here. And he's alive, so they say."

"Yes," Kate said. She bit down on her lip, her mind racing, reaching for something to say that would change things. "I was there, Pamela. I saw it happen. Yancy wouldn't give up his gun. He drew on Jack, even though Jack warned him."

A sharp sound that was less a laugh than a snort of contempt came from the other woman. "Of course he wouldn't give up his weapon. My brother might have been headstrong, but he wasn't a fool. Jack would have brought him back into town, and they'd have hung him."

"Maybe not. There would be a trial, and—"

"Don't patronize me!" Pamela shot back. "I *know* he shot the colonel. Yancy told me he'd done it, and he probably admitted it before Jack gunned him down."

Kate nodded. "Yes, he did." She remembered the fresh shirts in the saddlebags. "He came back to del Sol, didn't he? He didn't return to town. He went to you."

"Of course he came to me. He was getting ready to leave for California. He needed money and supplies. All he had to do was make one last stop for a few things at the place he'd been hiding."

"Then," Kate said slowly, "you were lying when you told Jack that Yancy had already left Texas."

"I wasn't lying. I thought he had. That was the plan."

"The plan?"

Pamela's smile was almost as full and gracious as those she'd showered on them at del Sol. "Of course. Do you think Yancy would rush off and kill someone like the colonel on his own? His mind didn't work that way. He'd gun a man down for laughing at him, or taking a woman from him—but for salt? It wouldn't have occurred to him."

"The land adjoins Rancho del Sol," Kate remembered.

"Yes, it does. And now it will be mine."

Kate shuddered at Pamela's words, realizing how sadly true they rang. "You talked your brother into committing murder for you," Kate gasped. "You sacrificed him for your own greed."

"It didn't take much talking with Yancy, let me tell you." Pamela glared at her. "He loved me, loved me as much as I loved him. He was more like my son than my brother—I *raised* that boy! He'd have done anything I told him. But I had no intention of his getting killed. That was all the Rangers' doing."

"You must have known the law would come after him."

Pamela stretched her long body in the saddle, rolling the fatigue out of her shoulders. She looked away, down the street.

"Of course I knew. I told Yancy exactly what would happen, and we agreed that as soon as he'd killed the colonel, he'd set out for San Diego. He'd be safe there."

"Why did he hang around?" Kate asked.

"I don't know. I suppose because he liked being the center of attention. He enjoyed seeing the look of fear in men's eyes when he rode past, and they'd whisper, 'There goes Yancy Kennard. He killed that ornery colonel who was bilking everyone out of their salt.' He liked that a lot. So he stayed a while longer."

Kate shook her head. "I'm sorry," she said. "I know Jack feels awful about it, too, but he had no choice. He really didn't, Pamela."

A slow, sweet smile crept across Pamela's lips. "I suppose not. But then, neither do I." She drew a shiny silver pistol from her belt. "Neither do I."

Kate stared in horror as Pamela leveled the barrel of the little gun at her heart. For ten heartbeats, Kate considered her options, and found none very promising. She could run. Pamela would give chase on horseback and catch her. She could beg her not to kill her or Jack, and it would do no good. She had no way of defending herself.

With a sense of fate stepping in and taking the situation out of her control, Kate watched as Pamela's thumb cocked the hammer of the pistol. Her finger slipped inside the curve of the trigger guard. The muscles in her arms tensed, and she rested her index finger on the trigger.

"Stop!" A shout came from the side of the street.

Kate spun around to see Jack standing in front of the barbershop. He'd pulled his own gun and planted his feet. His expression was wild with fury and anguish.

Pamela smiled. "Just in time, Ranger. Say goodbye to your sweet cuz."

"I'll shoot you off that stallion, lady," he warned.

Kate glimpsed a nearly imperceptible motion from the direction of the Sweetwater. Stony Phelps stepped back into the shadows of the doorway.

Pamela shook her head at Jack, too busy to notice Phelps or any of the people scampering off the street and indoors to safety. "You won't shoot until I've pulled the trigger. By then, it will be too late."

Kate knew she was right. It wasn't in Jack to gun this woman down after killing her brother. His reaction wouldn't come in time.

She stared at the front of the Sweetwater. Why wasn't Phelps doing anything? Why wasn't he out here in the street, ordering Pamela to put down her gun? Was he just going to turn his back while the woman shot both of them in cold blood?

"You can't do this!" Kate screamed. "For God's sake, it's not worth it. You've lost your brother, but you still have del Sol. That's what's really important to you, isn't it?"

For a second, she thought she'd struck a nerve. Pamela stared at her, then her lip curled. "I *loved* my brother. The ranch is in my blood, but my brother—he *was* my blood. I would have given my life for Yancy!"

Then her finger curved round the trigger and the muscles in her gun hand twitched, and Kate understood that Pamela actually was going to shoot her. Kate tried to move to one side, but her body refused to respond until the sharp bark of a weapon made her jump.

Strangely, the sound seemed to come from the wrong direction.

It was all rather surrealistic. *You should be dead!* a voice cried out from somewhere inside of her. *She was aiming right at you. She couldn't miss!* Yet here she was, still standing in the middle of the street, her knees shaking, sweat trickling in volumes down the hollow of her back, watching Pamela's pistol fly out of her hand.

With a shriek of pain, the woman clutched her bleeding hand.

Kate jerked around in time to see Stony Phelps step out of the shadows of the Sweetwater, his gun smoking and a hard look in his eye. "That's enough, Pamela. There's been sufficient killin'. The man was only doin' his job, and the girl you should be leavin' out of this."

The look of pure hatred on Pamela Kennard's face would have turned an ordinary man to granite. "You wimp, you call yourself a lawman! He *killed* my brother! He *murdered* my flesh and blood!"

Kate staggered sideways three steps and looked at Jack. His face was white, and his hands were shaking. He lowered his gun into his holster, looking as if he'd rather be dead than face Pamela's fury.

And then, what they'd been waiting so long for…happened. Time seemed to speed up and events unraveled too rapidly for Kate, later, to recall the exact order of motions and sounds and sensations—it was over and done before she could take her next breath.

Pamela dropped her injured hand alongside her saddle and clumsily swung a rifle out of a leather scabbard. Sheltering it out of Phelps's line of sight, at her horse's side, she pumped it once in preparation for firing. Jack had turned away to walk back into the barbershop. Only Kate stood at an angle enabling her to see the weapon, aimed at Jack's back, and the deadly determination in Pamela's eyes.

Reacting instinctively, Kate rushed straight at the stallion's head, waving her arms. "No!" she screamed. "No, stop!"

The horse rolled back its eyes and reared, throwing its rider backward and off. A deafening blast cut through the air at the same time Pamela hit the ground. Rushing forward, Phelps stood over her, his gun in hand, ready should she try anything else. All she seemed capable of was beating her fists into the dust and sobbing in bitter frustration.

Kate couldn't move. Couldn't breathe. Couldn't stop shaking.

As if from a great distance, she heard Phelps's authoritative voice calling for someone to catch the stallion. Then Jack was beside her, turning her into his arms, whispering hoarsely into her ear.

"That's it, it's over, darlin'. It's all over."

"She was going to shoot you in the back with the rifle," Kate gasped. "Oh, Lord, I could just see it happening. And no one could have stopped her!"

"You did. You brave, wonderful woman. You stopped her."

Kate looked up at Jack, caught in a maelstrom of confusing emotions. "Then you're all right? You've lived through the moment of your death!"

"Yes."

"Then this is . . ." She found it impossible to say the words. Her head spun wickedly, and her knees felt numb, incapable of supporting her. Kate clung to him for support. "Jack, please, don't leave me! I love you . . . I want us to—"

"I'll never leave you." His words came to her from a sudden blur of sepia images. "I swear to it, I'll always be with you, Kate. I love you . . . always will love you . . . always will . . . always . . . always . . ."

But she was already weathering the storm of passing ages. This time, she forced her eyes to remain wide open, searching for Jack's face among those that flashed past her. For she could no longer feel his arms around her, and she suddenly, shatteringly understood that, despite his promise, he was gone. Gone to her forever.

Chapter 19

The summer passed, as summers in Vermont often do—stiflingly hot at midday and replete with the heady scents of wisteria, roses and hay baking in the fields; cool and mystically silent but for the crickets during the nights. The pungent animal smells from the stalls behind the house reminded Kate of her days in the saddle at Jack's side. The pain of his loss was nearly unbearable.

The first two weeks at the end of April, after they'd parted, she'd felt numb from head to foot, and counted herself lucky. She hadn't been able to cry, couldn't confide her agony in anyone—not even Barbara. With May she began to hurt in places she hadn't believed could hurt. June, July and August, Kate dragged herself through her daily routine, trying to keep so busy, she'd have neither the time nor the energy to think about Jack.

Inevitably, the quiet hours of night came, and she was left with her memories. She'd longed to implant the touch of his hand and body on her flesh and soul, wanted so desperately never to forget him. Yet, when it came right down to it, now that he was gone she often wished for the peace of the amnesiac.

* * *

It was September now, a week after school had started again for the children. Kate drove home from the bank, parked the Explorer in the garage and walked around to the front to collect her mail. She got no farther than the front door before collapsing on the green porch swing. She watched the darkening sky, fascinated with the rapidly changing cloud patterns.

The wind was picking up, and it was a hot, dry wind turning frigid that cruelly reminded her of a norther on the desert. Heavy, sooty thunderheads roiled and billowed over the hills surrounding little Chester.

Barbara drove up in her truck and parked beside the porch. She climbed the stairs and, looking over her shoulder said, "Can't stay long. Looks like we'll be needing to get the horses in."

Kate smiled at her. "Go along. We can get together another time. You have things to do."

Barbara shook her head. "I called you at the bank because I had something important to tell you, and I wanted to do it in person."

Kate breathed in the air, smelling electricity in it. "So, tell."

Barbara looked doubtful. "First, I have to know if you're all right."

"I'm all right," Kate said woodenly.

"I mean, really. You haven't been yourself since that guy dumped you last spring."

"He didn't dump me."

"Well, I don't know what else you'd call it. You were head over heels for that man and he left you cold. Not even a phone call now and then."

"How do you know? The phone might be ringing off its hook every night. You're not here to—"

"I *know,* Kate. Of course I know. Would you be this miserable if he was still around?"

Kate sighed. "Definitely not."

"So, don't you think it's time to try again?" She looked at Kate, waited. When she got no answer, she continued. "The thing is, he was only around for a week or so, far as I know. That's not a lot of time to get hooked on a fella. My cousin down in—"

"New Jersey, I know," Kate said, laughing despite the dull ache in her heart. "Sure, I'll go out with your cousin. Why not?"

"Really?"

"Really." It would do no good to explain to Barbara that she shouldn't get her hopes up. Kate knew in her heart that no man could ever fill Jack's boots. If she let herself, she could easily spend the rest of her life comparing every male she met to her Ranger. They'd all fall short.

It wasn't a matter of feeling sorry for herself, or being a hopeless romantic, or building Jack up to be something he wasn't. He was, pure and simply, the perfect man for her. He'd made her laugh, made her cry, made every moment with him exciting and worth doing over again. The match they'd made wasn't something that came along twice in one lifetime. She was just being realistic, she told herself.

"Then you want me to call my cousin and give him your number?" Barbara asked.

"Sure, why not?"

Barbara leaned forward and took Kate's hands in hers. "I feel a lot better now. I didn't want to talk about myself as long as you were stuck in your emotional rut."

Kate smiled up at her. "I'd forgotten. You said you had news."

"Yes." Barbara blinked, looking a little dazed, as if what she had come to say was a surprise to herself, too. "William and I are engaged."

Kate stared at her. All she could think was, *William? William who?* Then the gears started turning again and she laughed out loud with shock. "You mean Carson . . . your foreman?"

Barbara shrugged. "I never thought I'd marry. It hardly crossed my mind from the time I was in my early twenties. I knew I wasn't much to look at . . . at least not the way most men look at women. Built like a brick, stronger than most of them, and stubborn as a cat with a mouse in her jaws—I guess I just never wanted to change or give up my privacy for a man. And I like being my own boss."

"Do you think Car wants you to give up any of that?" Kate asked, curious.

"That's just it. He likes leaving decisions to me, long as he can make a suggestion now and then. And he likes doing just what he's doing, working with the horses and building up our reputation as prime quarter-horse breeders. I think he'd even be content to keep on sleeping out in the bunkhouse most of the time, except I won't have it."

Kate laughed at the wicked twinkle in her friend's eyes. "I take it he's moved into the main house at Willow Creek Farms?"

"Oh, quite some time back, he did. I told him if he once set foot in my bedroom, he'd better be ready to stay there because I was no ways letting him leave without a fight. I wasn't about to go around nursing a broken heart after all you've—"

Kate reached out and hugged Barbara before she could finish the reference to her own situation. "Good for you. You hang on to that man. He's a good one."

"Oh, I know...I know that, I do," Barbara assured her. She glanced up at the sky as a tendril of icy wind broke through the barrier of silver birch to the west of the house. "It's going to be a whopper," she muttered. "Are the kids riding the bus?"

"Yes, I thought I'd better meet them. Anna's terrified of lightning, and it looks as if we're going to have some fireworks along with the wet stuff."

Pale white flashes in the distance and an ominous rumbling reminded Kate of a spring day when just such a storm had broken over her.

She swallowed and looked at Barbara. "Go on. We'll talk more about you and Carson later."

"Right. Now, you expect a call from Nathan."

"Nathan?" Kate drew a blank.

"My cousin, Nathan Weintraub, the one you're going out with. I decided the meat packer wasn't your style. Nathan's a very intelligent man, regional sales rep for an auto parts firm. He drops in all the time when he's up this way. You two will have fun."

"I'm sure," Kate said dryly. But she had to admit she was feeling better. Just spending a few hours with someone different would be pleasant and take her mind off of...things.

Kate unlocked the front door and changed quickly into jeans and a sweatshirt. She only had time to grab the umbrella and race outside before the bus pulled up. Fat, icy drops plunked down on the nylon dome. When they smacked against the warm pavement, they evaporated almost immediately into steam.

"Hurry! Run for the house!" she shouted through the rising wind as Jesse and Anna hopped down from the bus.

They ran, squealing, for the front door. "I'll meet you inside!" she called after them. "Change your clothes!"

She'd remembered there were still baskets of geraniums hanging on her back porch. The wind would knock them off their chains if she left them out in this. She'd bring them inside, then decide which ones could stand a few more weeks of mild weather, before the heavy frosts set in. Soon, all would become house plants.

Kate tucked her head into her hunched shoulders, pointed the open umbrella into the gusts and trudged up the driveway. By the time she reached the steps, the wind was almost too strong to stand against. She let out a little cry as the umbrella snapped inside out. Muttering to herself, she dragged the useless thing up the steps after her.

Kate tossed the umbrella onto the porch and turned to lift down the first basket-planter. As she reached up, she caught sight of an indistinct figure through the shifting curtains of rain. He stood with his back to her, one black-leather boot propped on the bottom rail of Barbara's new paddock fence. Familiar wide shoulders in a blue denim shirt tapered to the narrow waist of his jeans.

For a second, Kate's heart stopped, and she held her breath. "How stupid," she murmured. "It's not him, and you know it."

The man in traditional Western garb must be one of Carson's new hire-ons, she reasoned. Regardless of what she told herself, the sight of him silhouetted against the storm quickened her pulse, and she shivered at the memory of how another man, in another time, had made her feel.

"Knock it off, Kate. Don't do this to yourself."

Jack had only been able to exist in her attic during her time. And in his real life...well, he'd have died of natural causes long before she was born.

Still she couldn't help the way her heart leapt about in her chest. It was in memory of Jack that she did something very uncharacteristic for her.

"Hey!" she shouted. "Don't you want to get in out of the rain?"

The man turned slowly, as if he hadn't even been aware that a tempest was breaking all around him. Kate drew in a sharp breath at the flash of blue eyes and easy smile. He lifted a black felt Stetson he'd been holding in front of him and tugged it down over neatly trimmed ebony hair.

Kate nearly collapsed to her knees on the porch. She set down the plant before she could drop it, and grasped the porch rail for support. Her mouth dried to parchment as she watched the stranger amble leisurely up her steps. Kate let go of the rail, but overestimated her knees' recovery rate, and they buckled on her at the storm's next blast. The man reached out and easily hauled her back onto her feet with a lazy smile.

"Pretty gusty out here, ain't it?" he rumbled in a voice that more than hinted of Texas.

"Uh-huh." She nodded like a rag doll.

"Rain never bothers me much. We get big blows like this all the time where I'm from."

"And where are you from?" she asked weakly, unable to stop herself from staring at the hauntingly familiar face. If this wasn't Jack Ramsey, it was his contemporary double—she'd swear to it. Right down to the way his lips lifted just a little higher on the right side than on the left when he smiled. She'd never noticed that when she was with Jack, but now she remembered it.

"Houston."

"Houston. Texas?" she repeated numbly, knowing she must sound terribly stupid.

"Yup, that one." He laughed at her. "Hey, you sure are lookin' mighty pale. You all right, miss?"

"I'm...I'm just fine," she murmured, desperately trying to pull herself together. She considered her next words for only a heartbeat. "Listen, this storm's going to take a while to blow over. Would you like to come inside and have a cup of tea while you wait?"

He beamed at her. "Best invitation I've had all day."

She was aware of a cautious warmth in his voice, something beyond the general friendliness that she read in the weathered lines around his eyes and mouth. And as she led the way from the dark mudroom, along the rear hallway and into her brightly lit kitchen, she felt him studying her.

If this had happened a year ago, she told herself, he'd have had to fend for himself in the rain or run for the barn. She didn't make a practice of inviting strangers into her house.

But this was different. This man was no stranger. Or did she just believe that because she wanted it to be so?

"Have a seat," she said, gesturing toward a kitchen chair. "I'll put on the water."

Kate made herself busy, only daring to sneak an occasional peek at him when she sensed he was checking out the room, not her. She arranged a plate with cookies and sliced fruit. She set out the canister of herbal and regular tea bags.

When she looked up from the table, he was peering with considerable interest into her dining room.

"Is anything wrong?" she asked.

"I might as well confess," he said. "I was sort of hoping to get myself invited inside."

A warning shiver worked its way up her spine. Maybe she'd been too hasty. She looked across the table at him through a screen of her lowered lashes.

"Why?" she asked, trying to keep her voice steady.

He coughed lightly behind his hand. "Guess I should start with an introduction. I'm John Franklin. My mother is crazy about family genealogies—she's been working on ours for years. When I told her I was traveling on business to Vermont, she made me swear I'd stop by a few addresses in Chester to check out the houses and see if I could dig up any old records."

"You're from this area?" Kate asked, noticing he didn't wear a wedding band.

"I'm not. But one of my great-great-great-grandparents was from here. In fact—" he pulled a small black notebook out of his shirt pocket "—my mother said the lady lived in this very house and it stayed in our family until around 1920 when it was bought by a family, name of Fenwick."

Kate grinned, suddenly dizzy with her discovery. This man, this gorgeous Texan sitting in her kitchen was one of Jack's descendants!

"Tell me what you do in Houston," she said, then added, "John," although the name felt funny on her lips.

"Do?" He shrugged. "I'm a police detective for the city of Houston. At the moment, I'm on loan to the Vermont State Police. Seems they're reorganizing and adding a violent crime team. That's an area I've worked in for some time. I've traveled around the country, helping other forces set up special units." He blinked at her modestly, as if this was nothing out of the ordinary.

With a sense of shock, Kate remembered Jack's parting words: *I'll always be with you.* And before that, he'd talked about his duty to fate . . . and how, in the end, she'd be happy. Was this why he'd had to return to Kathleen? Was it because John Franklin would never have been born, and if he hadn't, there would have been no chance for her to meet him in her own time?

Or, she wondered, was John more than a descendant? Could he actually be a reincarnation, of sorts, of Jack Ramsey? By making love to her and building strong emotional ties between them in his time, had Jack actually been preparing her for his own sudden reappearance, this time as a living man, in her lifetime? Hadn't he asked her if she'd recognize him? Hadn't he taken great pains to encourage her to look for a special man to come into her life?

Over the lip of her tea mug, Kate observed Detective John Franklin. She could find no feature of his face, no mannerism that didn't strike her as intimately familiar, although she wasn't absolutely sure they were all Jack's.

"I think there are some things upstairs that your mother might be interested in," she said. "Old family records, mementos, letters . . . Some go well back into the nineteenth century."

"Really? Hey, she'll be thrilled." He propped his elbows on the table, his eyes sparkling with curiosity as he studied her face. "You know, there's something very . . ." He frowned. "I almost feel as if I know you from somewhere. I . . . I don't think I got your name."

"Kate," she said softly. "My name is Kate."

"Kate," he repeated in a solemn tone, sounding as if he were testing the flavor of her name on his tongue. "It suits you."

"By the way," she asked, "your close friends don't happen to call you Jack, do they?"

"Now how did you know that?" He set down his mug and reached for a cookie, eyeing her with amusement. "They sure do. And I hope you'll call me Jack, too."

That won't be hard, she thought, shooting to her feet. "Let's get started," she said, snatching up the plate of cookies before he could reach for another. "Bring your tea along. We can start looking through things in the attic while we drink."

His hand came down on her arm, stopping her as she passed his chair. His eyes locked with hers. "What's the rush? We got all the time in the world, darlin'."

Kate stared down at him. *You were right, Jack,* she thought, *It's your soul I fell in love with... and here you are.*

The man's cheeks flushed a vivid red. "I'm sorry, Kate. I don't know why I said that. I don't normally flirt so outrageously. Please, don't be offended."

"I'm not," she assured him with a radiant smile that reached down inside her, warming her from toes to fingertips. "I was just wondering when that would slip out."

And before he could ask her what she meant, she took his hand and led him up the steps into her attic, to teach him about his past and to begin their future.

*   *   *   *   *

COMING NEXT MONTH

Take 4 bestselling love stories FREE

Plus get a FREE surprise gift!

Special Limited-time Offer

Mail to Silhouette Reader Service™

3010 Walden Avenue
P.O. Box 1867
Buffalo, N.Y. 14269-1867

YES! Please send me 4 free Silhouette Intimate Moments® novels and my free surprise gift. Then send me 6 brand-new novels every month, which I will receive months before they appear in bookstores. Bill me at the low price of $3.12 each plus 25¢ delivery and applicable sales tax, if any.* That's the complete price and a savings of over 10% off the cover prices—quite a bargain! I understand that accepting the books and gift places me under no obligation ever to buy any books. I can always return a shipment and cancel at any time. Even if I never buy another book from Silhouette, the 4 free books and the surprise gift are mine to keep forever.

245 BPA AWPM

Name	(PLEASE PRINT)
Address	Apt. No.
City	State	Zip

This offer is limited to one order per household and not valid to present Silhouette Intimate Moments® subscribers. *Terms and prices are subject to change without notice. Sales tax applicable in N.Y.

UMOM-995   ©1990 Harlequin Enterprises Limited

Are your lips succulent, impetuous, delicious or racy?

Find out in a very special Valentine's Day promotion—THAT SPECIAL KISS!

Inside four special Harlequin and Silhouette February books are details for THAT SPECIAL KISS! explaining how you can have your lip prints read by a romance expert.

Look for details in the following series books, written by four of Harlequin and Silhouette readers' favorite authors:

Silhouette Intimate Moments #691
Mackenzie's Pleasure by *New York Times* bestselling author Linda Howard

Harlequin Romance #3395
Because of the Baby by Debbie Macomber

Silhouette Desire #979
Megan's Marriage by Annette Broadrick

Harlequin Presents #1793
The One and Only by Carole Mortimer

Fun, romance, four top-selling authors, plus a FREE gift! This is a very special Valentine's Day you won't want to miss! Only from Harlequin and Silhouette.

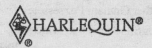

You're About to Become a

Privileged Woman

Reap the rewards of fabulous free gifts and benefits with proofs-of-purchase from Silhouette and Harlequin books

Pages & Privileges™

It's our way of thanking you for buying our books at your favorite retail stores.

PROOF OF PURCHASE

SIM-PP94

Offer expires October 31, 1996

Pages & Privileges ™

Harlequin and Silhouette— the most privileged readers in the world!

For more information about Harlequin and Silhouette's PAGES & PRIVILEGES program call the Pages & Privileges Benefits Desk: 1-503-794-2499

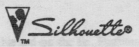
Silhouette®

SIM-PP94